Soldier, Sail North

Freedman
The Wheel of Fortune
Last in Convoy
The Mystery of the *Gregory Kotovsky*
Contact Mr Delgado
Across the Narrow Seas
Wild Justice
The Liberators
The Last Stronghold
Find the Diamonds
The Plague Makers
Whispering Death
Three Hundred Grand
Crusader's Cross
A Real Killing
Special Delivery
Ten Million Dollar Cinch
The Deadly Shore
The Murmansk Assignment
The Sinister Stars
Watching Brief
Weed
Away With Murder
A Fortune in the Sky
Search Warrant
The Marakano Formula
Cordley's Castle
The Haunted Sea
The Petronov Plan
Feast of the Scorpion
The Honeymoon Caper
A Walking Shadow
The No-Risk Operation
Final Run
Blind Date
Something of Value
Red Exit
The Courier Job
The Rashevski Icon
The Levantine Trade
The Spayde Conspiracy
Busman's Holiday
The Antwerp Appointment
Stride
The Seven Sleepers
Lethal Orders
The Kavulu Lion
A Fatal Errand
The Stalking-Horse
Flight to the Sea
A Car for Mr Bradley
Precious Cargo

The Saigon Merchant
Life-Preserver
Dead of Winter
Come Home, Toby Brown
Homecoming
The Syrian Client
Poisoned Chalice
Where the Money Is
A Dream of Madness
Paradise in the Sun
Dangerous Enchantment
The Junk Run
Legatee
Killer
Dishonour Among Thieves
Operation Zenith
Dead Men Rise Up Never
The Spoilers
With Menaces
Devil Under the Skin
The Animal Gang
Steel
The Emperor Stone
Fat Man From Colombia
Bavarian Sunset
The Telephone Murders
Lady from Argentina
The Poison Traders
Squeaky Clean
Avenger of Blood
A Wind on the Heath
One-Way Ticket
The Time of Your Life
Death of a Go-Between
Some Job
The Wild One
Skeleton Island
A Passage of Arms
On Desperate Seas
Old Pals Act
Crane
The Silent Voyage
The Angry Island
Obituary for Howard Gray
The Golden Reef
Bullion
Sea Fury
The Spanish Hawk
Ocean Prize
The Rodriguez Affair
Bavarian Sunset
The Unknown

JAMES PATTINSON

Soldier, Sail North

ROBERT HALE · LONDON

ISBN 978-0-7090-8823-3

Robert Hale Limited
Clerkenwell House
Clerkenwell Green
London EC1R 0HT

www.halebooks.com

2 4 6 8 10 9 7 5 3 1

Printed in Great Britain by the
MPG Books Group, Bodmin and King's Lynn

Contents

CONTENTS

CHAPTER ONE

Embarkation

As the Army lorry ground to a halt at the dockside nine men in battle-dress and greatcoats jumped down from the rear and stood for a few moments gazing up at the ship they had come to join. They saw a tramp steamer, somewhat old, somewhat battered, her grey paint blending with the grey mistiness of that December afternoon and her funnel blackened with soot.

She was a ship of some five thousand tons, and had had her fill of wandering about the sea-lanes of the world long before the War started. Now, after more than three years of dodging mines and torpedoes and bombs, she looked infinitely weary. She was like some aged charwoman condemned to work on long after she should have gone into honourable retirement. Grime had crept into her skin, and there was no getting it out. Nobody troubled any longer to chip the rust from her ironwork; it was painted over, and after a time it broke free from its covering and came out in red and yellow streaks, washed down by rain and sea-water.

At this moment her holds were empty and she stood high, her decks well above the level of the quay, so that her gangway rose at a steep angle and the men who were to leave Tilbury in her had to look upward to read her name.

They were silent, forming a little huddle of khaki, each one gazing at the ship and attempting to gauge her possibilities from that first brief inspection. The ship was important to them because it was to be their home—and their prison. In this ship they would live—eating, sleeping, working, playing, quarrelling, grumbling, laughing—their little world bounded by the iron walls of her hull. When they stepped aboard this ship they would set their feet upon the road to death, and the ship would be all that barred the way. If the ship died they would be likely to die with her; that was why they were there —to help the ship avoid death, to guard her through a perilous journey.

They were all men of the Maritime Royal Artillery, a branch of the Army of whose existence the general public was scarcely aware. Even some ship's officers still confused them with Royal Marines, a confusion which, though perhaps excusable, was resented by these soldier sailors in whom regimental pride was rendered none the less active by the fact that they were seldom with the regiment. Scattered across the liquid surface of the earth in small self-contained groups, usually free of commissioned ranks, they had developed a sturdy independence of outlook which at worst could make them embarrassingly impatient of authority and at best could imbue them with those qualities of hardihood and resource- fulness which distinguished the old soldiers of fortune. Soldiers they might be, but they had taken to the sea as men who had at last found their true element, as men of this island nation always will.

So they gazed up at their ship, their drab, weary ship; and suddenly one of them laughed.

"The *Golden Ray*! The s.s. *Golden Ray*! Damned if she don't look it! Proper ray of sunshine an' no mistake!"

The s.s. *Golden Ray* of Liverpool was silent and motion- less, made fast to the quay by wire hawsers looped over bollards, the oily flotsam of the dock crowding around her water-line. Giant cranes hovered over her like grotesque birds of prey waiting to peck at her entrails, and out of the opaque sky a flake or two of snow drifted waveringly down to fall lightly upon her cluttered decks.

"A rotten coal-burner! Everything covered with soot; you'll see."

"*Golden Ray*! My word, don't the name suit her!"

The sergeant stopped further comments, breaking in with his curt, incisive voice.

"All right! All right! Stop nattering and get the kit off. Let's have a bit of action."

The group broke up as the men moved to obey him, pulling kitbags and hammocks from the lorry and throwing them to the ground.

"Sergeant Willis!"

A young lieutenant wearing a trench-coat and peaked cap had walked round from the front of the lorry. He had a smooth, boyish face and a nervous manner.

"Sergeant, you'd better come on board with me and take a look at things."

Willis said, "Very good, sir," and followed the lieutenant up the gangway. A moment later he was stepping lightly down upon the iron deck which was to become so familiar to him in the months that lay ahead. It was a deck which had become overlaid with dock fungus—all that miscellaneous gear and refuse which, as soon as the ship was at sea, would be stowed away or thrown overboard. Willis looked around him, whistling softly through his teeth, waiting for the lieutenant to make a move.

For Willis this was to be the fourth voyage. His first ship had been a grain freighter; she had sailed in a North Atlantic convoy, had floated up the St Lawrence to Montreal, and there had taken on five thousand tons of wheat. The wheat had flowed into the holds like a yellow river, and dust had risen from it in a fine cloud that penetrated to every corner, lying thick upon bunk and chair and table. It had been hot in Montreal, and it had been good to see the lights again; in England one had almost forgotten what it was like to be without the black-out. But the stay in Montreal had been brief; three days and they were away again, dropping downstream past Sorel and Three Rivers and Quebec, past the mud-banks, the jetties, and the countless little wooden churches that looked so much like toys. At Halifax they had joined an east-bound convoy; three weeks later they were home. They had not seen a submarine or an enemy aircraft during either crossing.

Willis's second ship had been a tanker. They had sailed in convoy across the Atlantic, then alone down the American seaboard to the Gulf of Mexico. There had not even been shore leave; the ship had lain off-shore, and the oil had flowed out to them through a pipe-line. After two days they were away again to join a Halifax convoy and move eastward once more.

That had been a bad journey: ten ships had been sunk; two other tankers had gone up in flames. Willis had been thankful when it was over.

His third voyage had taken Willis to Buenos Aires and Rio de Janeiro. He had enjoyed that trip. The ship had been good, a Blue Star meat liner with a speed of seventeen knots. She had sailed on her own, relying on speed to keep her out of danger. Willis had had a fine time in Rio, that city of sunshine and gaiety, and though there had been a submarine scare on the way home, it had come to nothing. Willis had been disembarked when the ship docked at Avonmouth; he had returned to regiment and thence gone on leave. It was the usual routine.

Now he was embarking again, and this time he had a feeling that the going would be tough.

He remembered the words of the battery sergeant-major: " You've bought it this time. You're booked for the Russian run. Chance of a D.S.M., though. Malta and Russia for D.S.M.'s—no doubt about that."

Willis was not interested in medals; he took a realistic view and preferred a whole skin. But the prospect of a Russian convoy did not worry him. As a professional soldier he performed the duty assigned to him without fuss or bother, whatever that duty might be. It was his job.

The lieutenant, standing on the deck of the *Golden Ray* among the coils of rope, the paint-drums, the piles of rubbish, seemed at a loss. He was unsure of himself, hesitant. Willis waited; his face, bony, rather sunken below the cheek-bones, was expressionless, hiding his thoughts. Secretly he was contemptuous of the officer, a mere boy who had still been in the nursery when Willis was stamping out his lessons on the barrack square.

The lieutenant was looking for some one from whom he could obtain information; he kept slapping his leg with his cane and pulling nervously at an almost invisible moustache. His anxiety was relieved by the sight of a ship's officer who appeared from a doorway amidships and ran lightly down the ladder to the main deck. He came down the ladder sideways, his left hand, slightly above and slightly behind him, resting on the handrail. He was a young man, having two gold rings on the sleeves of his blue jacket with a gold diamond between them. The lieutenant saluted him perfunctorily.

" Could you tell me if the captain is aboard? "

The ship's officer shook his head. " The captain went ashore an hour ago and hasn't come off yet."

" Is the gunnery officer aboard? "

" I am the gunnery officer."

The lieutenant appeared relieved. " I've brought your new gun-team. Sergeant Willis is detachment commander."

The gunnery officer, who combined the duties attached to that post with the more normal ones of second mate, nodded to Willis. " I hope your men are good, sergeant. The last Bofors crew shot down a Heinkel. Think you can beat that? "

" Depends on whether we have the chance, sir."

The gunnery officer smiled somewhat wryly. " I'm afraid there's not much doubt that you will." He turned to the lieutenant. " I expect you'd like to see the gunners' quarters. They're aft. I'll show you."

He led the way along the deck and climbed a ladder to the poop. There were two guns mounted aft—a four-inch anti-submarine gun and, above it, on a tall mushroom-like pedestal, the Bofors. Both guns had their covers on and looked a little forlorn, like abandoned children.

The gunnery officer stooped to enter a small accommodation hatch, pulled aside a black-out curtain of heavy canvas, and began to descend a steep iron ladder. The lieutenant followed, and Willis, following the lieutenant, observed that they were going down into a deep, narrow hold whose length was roughly equal to the width of the ship at that point. The ringing of their boots on the rungs of the ladder echoed hollowly from the sides of the hold, and it seemed to Willis as though they were lowering themselves into a gigantic steel tank. The atmosphere had the cold clamminess of a tank and the odour of damp iron. On one bulkhead hung the spare propeller, looking immense at such close range, and it occurred to him to wonder how it had ever got there, and how, if it should be needed, it could be got out.

" This," said the gunnery officer, when they reached the foot of the ladder, "is the gunners' wash-place." He indicated a row of galvanized-iron basins ranged along one side and fitted with cold-water taps and waste-pipes. Then he pointed to two wooden cubicles thrust away in a corner. " Those," he said, " are the lavatories. We shall try to keep them from freezing with the help of hot water, but "—he raised his shoulders—" things have a habit of going wrong. They'll probably freeze."

A bulkhead separated the wash-place from the other part of the gunners' accommodation. There was a doorway between the two, but no door, the opening being closed by a black-out curtain of the same heavy canvas as the one above. Stepping over a high threshold, the three men passed through this doorway, and immediately came face to face with a round iron stove, the smoke-pipe from which led up through the ceiling. This stove was close to the starboard side of the ship, and in that side a port, tightly closed, let in a glimmer of daylight, a light which fortunately was augmented by an electric bulb set in the deckhead. By the aid of these two sources of light Willis was able to examine the cabin.

It was a long, narrow room formed by partitioning off a part of the hold. The compartment thus formed was some eight or nine feet wide and about forty feet long, its length being divided into three parts to provide a cabin for naval gunners on the port side, one for Army gunners on the starboard, and a common mess-room in between.

The bunks, which were of wood, were arranged in two tiers on either side of the cabin, with a passage between. In the starboard cabin there were eight bunks, and in the port cabin ten. In the mess-room was a table covered with brown linoleum.

The stove in the Army quarters was cold, but it had not been cleaned out. It stood upon a square concrete foundation with a raised rim, but this rim had not been equal to the task of preventing the migration of ashes. The floor, in fact, appeared to be covered with cinders and dust. Willis stirred some of the cinders with the toe of his boot, but said nothing. He had seen worse quarters, and he had seen better. What he liked least about these was their position. They were too far down, and the only way out was by one narrow iron ladder. He could imagine that ladder in an emergency, jammed with gunners all trying to get out at once. It was not a happy picture.

The gunnery officer was speaking. "It's no palace, of course; but the ship wasn't built to carry passengers."

The lieutenant said hurriedly, smacking his leg with his cane, "Oh, it's not so bad, not so bad really. After all, we've got to remember there's a war on, haven't we? "

All right for you, thought Willis; you're not going to live in it.

Aloud he said, " Do I sleep in here with the gunners, sir? "

Not that he minded sharing a cabin with the gunners; he had done it often enough; except on the bigger ships, it was the usual thing. Still, it was best to know.

" No," said the gunnery officer, " there's a two-berth cabin for the petty officer and sergeant at the end of the washplace." He smiled. " Not the end where the lavatories are."

Willis nodded, wondering what the petty officer would be like. The character of the man with whom you were to share a confined cabin for several months mattered not a little. It could make quite a difference.

They climbed back up the iron ladder and came out on to the poop. It had left off snowing, but the air was cold.

"You'll have to excuse me," said the gunnery officer. "No end of things to do. You'll find your way about."

They watched him stride away; then the lieutenant said, "We'll take a look at the gun, sergeant."

The Bofors platform stood about twelve feet above the deck, mounted on a slender stem. It was circular in shape, and when the barrel of the gun was depressed its trumpet-shaped flash-guard projected just beyond the three-foot shield that surrounded the platform. In the shield were ammunition recesses, and on one side of the platform, projecting towards the bridge, was a narrow extension on which the spare barrel rested. There was not much room for changing barrels, but that was not unusual.

Willis and the lieutenant lifted the cover from the gun.

"Dirty," said the lieutenant. "You'll have to get your men on this, sergeant."

Willis grunted. There had been no need to tell him that. It was always the same: you brought your gun into port looking like something that had slipped out of the drill-book, barrel shining, breech spotless, paintwork all freshly touched up, and then, when you joined another ship, you took over a weapon as filthy as this. The shore crews were smart enough when it came to examining the gun you brought in—no allowance for bad weather, salt spray, and the rest; but when you were taking over a gun it was different. Still, he was used to that now; he took it as a matter of course.

The lieutenant tested the elevating and traversing gear, and the slender barrel of the Bofors lifted and fell, swung left, then right.

"A little stiff. You'll have to put some grease in the bearings."

"How about anti-freeze oil and grease, sir?" asked Willis.

"You'll pick that up in Hull with your Arctic kit. Right?"

They pulled the cover on again and descended to the deck. The gunners had carried their kit aboard, and now it lay in an untidy pile on the cover of number four hatch. Dirty topees could be seen dangling from some of the kitbags, and Willis smiled grimly as he thought how small a need there was likely to be for tropical kit on this voyage. Yet it had to be carried.

He realized suddenly that the lieutenant was speaking. " I shall have to go now. You've got all you want? As I said, you'll draw Arctic kit in Hull."

He thrust out his hand. " Well, sergeant, best of luck! Come back safely."

He smiled as they shook hands, a shy, boyish smile; and in that last moment Willis felt his antagonism melting. The kid was not so bad really; just nervous; pushed into a job for which he had not been cut out.

" Good-bye, sir," said Willis, saluting.

The lieutenant went down the gangway rather faster than he should have done and climbed into the waiting lorry. The driver let in the clutch, and the vehicle moved slowly away.

Willis exhaled a long breath. He was always glad when this moment arrived, when he had the detachment to himself and no one else to give orders. He felt freer, less irked by superior authority.

" Come on, lads," he said. " Get cracking with that kit. I'll show you where we live."

He picked up a kitbag and led the way, and the men followed, each carrying a bundle. It was hard work, man-handling everything up to the poop and then down the ladder to the cabin; and there was some grumbling when the men saw their quarters.

" We had a better cabin than this on my last ship."

" Is that all there is to heat the place—that ruddy stove? "

" Proper pigsty, ain't it? "

Willis let them run on. He knew they would settle down and make the best of it in the end. Moving in was always a bad business; at first there seemed to be nothing but strangeness and discomfort, a feeling of being lost.

In his mind he began running over the immediate necessities. The steward would have to be found; from him they would draw their dry stores—tea, sugar, cheese, butter, jam. They would need hot water for the tea, fuel for the stove; they would have to find out about a cigarette issue.

The gunners were sorting themselves out among the bunks. Some preferred upper ones, some lower. There was a certain amount of argument, but it was friendly enough. Soon each man had taken a bunk and had flung his kit upon it.

Most of the men were new to Willis. Gunner Cowdrey was the only one he knew. Cowdrey had been with him on two trips—a good fellow, quiet, cheerful, conscientious; a man you could rely on. He would never make an N.C.O., of course; he was not that type; but not everybody could have stripes. What unlikely material the War made into soldiers! Cowdrey, for example—a small man, inclined to tubbiness, and bald as a rail. He was forty, a tailor in civilian life, married, but childless; Willis had learnt all this. Before the War Cowdrey had sat cross-legged on a table sewing clothes; now he helped to serve a gun that could pump out forty-millimetre shells at the rate of two a second; now he faced cold, discomfort, fatigue, and danger; yet his character had not changed; essentially he was the same inoffensive little tailor disguised in khaki.

Sometimes Willis marvelled at the way such men as Cowdrey could fall into the routine of Army life and endure the rigours of war service. For himself it was different: he was a professional, had been in the Army since he was a boy; it was his life, his career. Of course, the War had altered things for him too. It had meant farewell to the old regular habits, the barrack square, the display. But wherever he went, whatever he did, it was still his job, the work he had chosen and been trained to do; whereas men such as Cowdrey were still really tailors, mechanics, clerks, bus-conductors, shop assistants, fishmongers—anything but soldiers. It was amazing what good fighters the majority of them made.

Two sailors in dungarees of pale, washed-out blue had

wandered in from the mess-room. They stood in the door-way, regarding the soldiers with a slightly interested, slightly wary manner, rather like dogs meeting other dogs for the first time. One was a small man, not more than five feet six in height and lightly built, but wearing a thick black beard. The effect was somewhat grotesque; it was as though such a heavy upper growth on one so small and slender must surely render him top-heavy and make him liable to overbalance. He had a thin, piping voice that heightened the grotesquerie.

" You the new lot of pongos? " he asked.

Nobody seemed inclined to answer the inquiry. Possibly they resented the term ' pongo '; possibly the answer appeared too obvious.

" What's the ship like? " asked one of the gunners.

" It's a bastard," said the bearded sailor cheerfully. " You'll see."

" Never mind that," said Willis. " Can you tell us what time tea is? "

The other sailor, a fair-haired boy, still troubled by the pimples of adolescence, answered. " Should be ready now. We're just going for ours. If some of you fellows like to come along I'll show you where the galley is. You'll want to get that stove going to boil the water. There's a kettle somewhere about. There's a steam boiler out in the wash-place, but it don't work."

" Where do we get coal for the stove? "

" Draw it up from the stokehold."

" Andrews and Payne," said Willis, " you fetch the grub. Randall and Miller, take that bucket and get some coal. Scrounge some box-wood for kindling at the same time. We'll get properly organized to-morrow."

The galley was amidships, much of its space occupied by a black iron stove, the coal for which was kept in a bunker at one end. There was a sink full of greasy water, in which a galley-boy was making some pretence of washing pans and dishes, and on the stove stood a varied assortment of sooty boilers and saucepans.

The cook, who appeared to have spent so much time close to the stove that he had transferred much of its blackness to his own person, was tall and thin, and with a permanent stoop. He wore tight cotton trousers of a small black-and-white check pattern and a dirty singlet. A cigarette that had long since burnt itself out clung to his upper lip like a piece of brown fungus, moving erratically up and down when he opened his mouth to speak.

He was not in the best of tempers when Andrews and Payne asked for tea.

" Who the hell are you? " he snapped.

" Gunners; just come aboard."

" Two of you? "

" Nine."

The cigarette threatened to fly from its seating, but its adhesive power proved equal to the strain.

" Nine! Why, for crying out loud! How do you expect me to have grub for that lot? I wasn't told you were coming. I ain't got second sight; I only cook for them what I knows is aboard. Nine, you say. Some hope! You'll be unlucky, mate."

" Now, come on, Bert," said the pimply sailor, " you always have plenty of gash grub; you'll only chuck it away. Let the lads have some, and don't make such a fuss."

" I don't know," grumbled the cook. " I don't know what things is coming to, straight I don't. Nine extra all of a sudden like that. Don't give a man a chance."

Nevertheless he slapped some stew and potatoes into two enamel containers, which fitted, one above the other, in a metal carrier, found a loaf of bread and some cold spam, and handed these provisions to the two soldiers.

" That's the best I can do," he said. " I wasn't told."

When Andrews and Payne returned to the cabin they found that Randall and Miller had already brought the fuel and were busy lighting the stove. Like most of its kind, it smoked badly until it had warmed up, and it was slow in doing so. The air of the cabin became thick and choking.

Cowdrey had filled a bucket with fresh water from the after pump and was pouring some into an iron kettle. He took the lid off the stove and stood the kettle in its place.

" In an hour's time," he said, " she'll boil."

It was a pessimistic forecast. By the time they had eaten the stew the kettle was boiling. There was a tea-pot in the mess-room, and the sailors lent them some tea, sugar, and milk. Having eaten and drunk, they all began to feel better, to feel that they belonged to the ship.

After tea Willis went to the small cabin which the gunnery officer had said was for the petty officer and sergeant. It was extremely cramped, the two bunks taking up most of the space; but there were two metal cupboards and two drawers. Willis found that one cupboard and one drawer were filled with clothing, and surmised that his cabin-mate was already in occupation. Probably he was ashore.

Willis began unpacking his kit, stowing it in the empty cupboard and drawer. Then he unlashed his hammock and spread the mattress and blankets on the upper bunk, the one that was not in use, folding the hammock and stowing it at the foot of the bed.

He had just completed this task when he heard a noise and, looking up, saw a man standing in the doorway of the cabin. He was a stout man of about medium height with grey, spiky hair, cropped so close to his head that it looked like nothing so much as a door-mat that has been dusted with flour. His eyebrows were spiky too, and stood out on either side of his face like cat's whiskers. He had a heavy, razor-blue jowl and knobbly hands that seemed at one time or another to have been knocked about with a hammer. But his most striking feature, that which irresistibly drew the eye, was a large, rounded growth on the left side of his neck. It was red and smooth and shiny, and from its surface two or three coarse grey hairs grew like blades of grass growing out of an ant-hill. It was at once fascinating and repulsive.

He wore ordinary seaman's uniform—bell-bottom trousers and jumper—but from the crossed anchors on his sleeve Willis

could see that he was a petty officer. His age might have
been forty-five or a good deal more; it was difficult to tell.
His voice was gruff.

" Hullo!" he said. " You the new sergeant? "

" That's right," said Willis.

" I see you've moved in."

Willis nodded. " Didn't seem much sense in waiting. Got
to be done some time."

" Of course."

The petty officer moved into the cabin, hung his cap on
a peg behind the door, and began to roll himself a cigarette.
As an apparent afterthought he offered the tin of tobacco and
packet of papers to Willis.

" Smoke ticklers? "

" I like tailor-mades best," said Willis. " Thanks all the
same." He took a packet of cigarettes from his pocket.
" Have one of these."

The petty officer put the cigarette he had rolled in the
tobacco-tin and took one of those Willis had offered.

" For a change, then," he said.

He felt inside his blue jumper and hauled up a massive
brass petrol lighter. After much flicking of the wheel, which
was as big as a shilling, a flame was produced, and the two
men lit their cigarettes.

" My name's Donker—George to you."

" Mine's Bill Willis."

" The one who was here before was Briggs. Know him? "

" No."

" You ain't missed much. Proper pain in the neck. I've
got the bottom bunk. First come first served, hey? Anyway,
you're younger than what I am; I ain't built for climbing
these days. If it wasn't for this bleeding war I wouldn't be
in uniform now—not likely. I was on the Reserve, y'see; so
they lugged me back an' shoved me in Dems." He gave a
short, barking laugh. " Defensively Equipped Merchant
Ships! Now, I ask you! Me, what's served in the *Royal
Oak* and the *Hood*, pushed into Dems! Oh, well! "

He took a little smoke down the wrong way and coughed.
" You don't mind top bunk, do you? "

" I prefer it," said Willis.

Petty Officer Donker put his cigarette on the edge of an
ash-tray made from a tin-lid and began pulling off his jumper.
This, an operation of no little difficulty, was accompanied
by much puffing and groaning. His voice, muffled by the
material covering his head, jerked out information.

" You know she's sailing to-morrow? "

" I didn't; but it suits me."

" Picking up cargo at Immingham. That's a hole. Then we
shall proceed to Loch Ewe to join convoy. You been on the
Russian run before? "

" No."

Petty Officer Donker, the process of extricating himself
from the jumper completed, sat on the edge of his bunk and
delivered himself of a statement which Willis did not doubt
was completely true.

" It is," said Donker, " the bloodiest bloody trip of the
whole bloody lot. I'm telling you."

CHAPTER TWO

Coastal Convoy

THE s.s. *Golden Ray*, fussed over by two self-important tugs,
edged her way out from the encircling arms of the Tilbury
dock, through the lock gates, and into London river. There
the tugs abandoned her, and she set off downstream under
her own power, leaving Tilbury on the one hand and
Gravesend on the other, churning the thick river-water
to foam with her propeller only half submerged, and sending
miniature waves to slap against wooden piles, stir rich
slime, and rock any boats that might be moored against the
banks.

It was ten o'clock on a raw December morning, and a bitter

wind, cutting across the marshes, set up a high-pitched, wavering shriek in the rigging which seemed to have the effect of making the air at least ten degrees colder.

By midday the forts in the estuary of the river had come into view. Standing high above the water on their long steel legs, they looked like giant crabs, or, as Gunner Vernon thought, like the great fighting machines that Wells had given his Martians in *The War of the Worlds*.

Away to port, Southend pier crept out over the mud, searching for deep water. In sight of this symbol of happier days the *Golden Ray* let go her anchor and came to rest for the day.

At ten o'clock next morning the anchor came up, dripping mud, the engines began to turn over, and they were away. They joined a coastal convoy, one of those strange mixtures of shipping, marshalled into two lines, which might contain anything from a 400-ton collier to a 15,000-ton tanker. One lean destroyer flickered back and forth along the line of ships, thrusting her aquiline nose into the waves and flinging the white foam away on either side, while two motor-launches maintained a continuous thunder of high-powered diesel engines. Overhead in a clear sky of faded blue two Hurricanes flew round and round, until, their stretch of duty ended, they were relieved by two Spitfires. There was no excitement, nothing at all to stir the pulse; and there was the coast clearly visible on the port side, seeming no more than five hundred yards away. It was all so peaceful; there might have been no war on. But the guns were ready and the men were ready, and in every ship there were eyes scanning sea and sky; and in the destroyer the Asdic was sending its signal and waiting for the answer.

Willis had arranged his gun-team in three watches, with three men in each. With himself he took Randall and Andrews, who were the least experienced gunners. In the second watch he put Bombardier Padgett, Cowdrey, and Payne, and in the third watch Vernon, Miller, and Warby. Each watch did four hours on the gun and eight off.

Night fell. The accompanying aircraft returned to their base, and the convoy, so many dark shapes upon the dark bosom of the sea, crept steadily northward.

Sergeant Willis, with his two companions, Randall and Andrews, came off watch at midnight and was relieved by the bombardier's watch. A cold wind had been blowing from the east, and Willis felt tired and chilled. You fell out of the habit of watch-keeping when you went on leave, and it came hard when you started again. Four hours in a narrow gun-enclosure could creep damnably slowly, and the colder and darker it was the more slowly did the hours appear to go.

Willis clambered down the iron ladder and felt the immediate relief from the bitter wind and noise above deck. Here below were only the steady beat of the engines, the occasional rattle of the rudder-chains, and a rhythmic creaking of timbers. Here were men lying in narrow bunks, some snoring, some breathing quietly, all seeming strangely different at this hour under the shaded lamps that were kept on all night.

The relieving watch had made up the stove, and the kettle, a wire twisted through its handle and round the stove-pipe to prevent its falling off when the ship rolled, was boiling fiercely. Randall made cocoa, thick and sweet, and the three men gathered round the stove, sipping their drinks and warming themselves inside and out before going to their bunks.

" Well," said Willis, keeping his voice low to avoid waking the sleeping men, " we're away; but we'll be in port again to-morrow."

" It's going to be cold," said Andrews. " If it's like this here, what's it going to be like in the Arctic? "

" It won't be a picnic," said Willis, " but we shall pull through."

" We hope."

Randall had said nothing. All the time they had been on watch he had hardly spoken a word, but had stood hunched up, with hands in pockets, silent, unmoving. Willis hardly knew what to make of Randall. All the while he appeared to be looking inward, peering at some secret trouble. He did what he was told mechanically, like an automaton, having no interest in what he did. Willis had watched him at times unobserved and he had seen something that looked like terror lurking at the back of Randall's eyes; but Willis did not think it was the thought of submarines or bombs that had put the terror there. It was a deeper fear.

Andrews had something on his mind also; but Willis knew all about that because it was something Andrews was only too keen to speak about. It was a girl. Andrews had shown Willis her photograph; it was just an amateur snap and did not flatter the subject. But somehow the character came through. It was a gentle face, not truly beautiful, but having about it that which was deeper, more enduring than beauty. Willis was glad Andrews had a girl like that, for he was a good-looking youngster—tall, fair-haired, and athletically built—a decent kid.

Willis drained his cocoa, took the dirty mug into the mess-room, said, " Good night, lads," and, having removed just as much clothing as he deemed advisable, climbed over the sleeping body of Petty Officer Donker, and in two minutes was asleep.

The s.s. *Golden Ray* ploughed on through the night; dark figures moved upon her bridge and on the tiny, steel-surrounded platforms that supported her guns, while below them their shipmates slept; and below them again, under the water-line, grease-smeared troglodytes watched gauges, moved levers, oiled bearings, and flung coal into the roaring mouths of furnaces. Two bells, four bells, six bells, eight bells—and another watch was completed. The dark figures on bridge and gun-platform were joined by other dark figures; a few words were spoken; then the ones who had been on deck for four hours went below, and those others, fresh from the warmth of their bunks, began their own weary vigil, waiting for the dawn.

Two bells, four bells. And at four bells Sergeant Willis awoke and felt the call of nature. He cursed softly, clambered out of his bunk, and pulled on a pair of old gym-shoes. On his way through the wash-place he heard the sound of low voices coming from the gunners' cabin.

Willis was not a fool, and he realized that none of the gunners was likely to be wasting his precious hours of sleep by talking. Therefore he decided to investigate; and, investigating, he found Miller and Warby comfortably seated by the stove, their duffel-coats unbuttoned and their feet toasting in the hearth. They looked up with some surprise and a certain amount of consternation as Willis drew the black-out curtain aside and stepped into the cabin—Willis in gym-shoes, underpants, and shirt, a little tousled about the head and grim about the mouth.

When he spoke his voice was misleadingly quiet, but there was a keen edge to it. " May I ask," he said, " what you two think you're doing down here? Correct me if I'm wrong, but I was under the impression that you should be on watch."

The two gunners looked sheepish, but said nothing.

" I suppose," said Willis, laying on the sarcasm, " that you've both got such sharp eyesight you can sit down here and still see what's going on up top. Periscopic, X-ray eyesight, hey? Is that it? "

Miller got to his feet, fumbling with the toggles of his duffel-coat. " Ah, where's the sense in three bein' up there and getting froze? One's enough to keep watch."

Miller was a little man with a mumbling way of talking. At some time in his life he had received a blow on the nose that had put that organ permanently out of true. It was as though a pleasant odour to starboard had attracted the nose, and after wandering in that direction it had lost the power or the inclination to return. His face had an unhealthy pallor and was slightly pock-marked, and he had lost two of his front teeth, possibly in the same encounter that had spoilt the look of his nose. Altogether he was not a prepossessing individual, and had made a poor impression on his detachment commander.

Willis spoke curtly. " Get up on watch and stay there, both of you. I'll have more to say to you in the morning."

They obeyed him. Willis was not the kind of N.C.O. that men disobeyed lightly. He had the air of authority. Miller said something under his breath, but Warby went without a word. Willis knew there would be no trouble with Warby: he was a slow, plodding sort of fellow—a farm-worker in civilian life. But Miller was different: he certainly might cause trouble. It would be best to keep an eye on Miller.

Day climbed up over the rim of the sea, and with it came squalls of sleet. On the Bofors gun-platform no one had spoken for half an hour. Each of the three men appeared to be occupied with his own thoughts. Miller was sitting on one of the gun-seats, hands thrust into pockets, his head almost lost under the hood of his duffel-coat. He was whistling thinly and tunelessly, blowing through the gap in his front teeth.

Vernon was standing with his back resting against the barrel of the gun; every now and then the barrel would swing with the roll of the ship, and Vernon would lurch a step or two backward or forward.

Warby was standing in the recess where the spare barrel was kept. There was a rail running round this platform at a height of about four feet. Where this rail joined the gun-enclosure it was extended above the opening in the form of an inverted 'V' in order to form a barrel-stop and prevent accidents that in the excitement of action might cause damage to the forward parts of the ship.

"You know," said Warby, breaking the silence, "what we oughta do is tie some canvas to this here rail, so's to make a windbreak. Then we'd have somethin' to get behind."

Vernon eased himself away from the gun-barrel and walked round to the other side of the platform to see what Warby was talking about.

"You see," said Warby, "we could fix it round the three sides, here and here and here; and then we could sit on the barrel-box and be snug. Take it in turns—two in here, one keeping a look-out."

Vernon nodded. " I believe you've got something there. It'd be better than nothing."

Miller swivelled round on the gun-seat. " What about Sergeant bloody Willis? " he said. " You don't s'pose he'll let you rig up anything like that, do you? You might go to sleep behind a screen like that, 'stead of keeping your eyes peeled."

Warby was starting a cold, and his nose was running. He wiped it on the sleeve of his duffel-coat.

" Oh, the sergeant ain't that bad. Can't blame him for turning us out this morning."

" I should damn well think not," said Vernon. " It was asking for trouble, two of you going down. Did you expect him to let you stay there? "

" Ah, he's too regimental," grumbled Miller. " There won't be much rest with him in charge; you mark my words. It'll be all according to the drill-books. I wouldn't be surprised if he had us on P.T. every day."

Vernon began beating his hands to bring some warmth back into them. " According to Ben Cowdrey, the sergeant's all right. Ben should know; he's been with him some time."

" Ben's a creeper. You want to be careful what you say in front of him; it'll go straight to the sergeant."

" Nonsense! Ben isn't that sort. And I don't think there's much wrong with Willis either. You're just peeved because he caught you toasting yourself in front of the stove when you should have been on watch. In a way, I'm glad he did; and I'm glad he turfed you out. I shouldn't have thought much of him if he'd done anything else. After all, there's got to be some discipline, or everything falls to pieces."

Miller spat on the deck. " All right; all right. Even if you was a schoolmaster we don't want a lecture now; this ain't a class of snotty-nosed kids."

" I wish," said Vernon, " you'd stop that filthy habit of spitting. It's disgusting and it's unhealthy."

" Come off it," said Miller. " Where do you think you are? This ain't Buckingham Palace. It's about time you stopped being a sissy."

Vernon's face clouded. He took a pace towards Miller. " That'll be just about enough from you. Do you understand? "

Miller looked up at Vernon's face and laughed uneasily. " No offence, Harry. I was on'y joking. You can take a joke, can't yer? "

" Not that kind of joke. You'd better remember that."

" All right; I'm sorry."

The three men fell again into the silence of their own thoughts, watching the sea, feeling the lift and fall of the deck under their feet, the whip-lash of the wind on their faces. What a vast amount of time, thought Vernon, he had spent like this since the War started—just waiting, waiting, waiting! And millions of other fellows too. What a sum it must add up to, that wasted, empty time! Sometimes you wondered whether the War would ever end; you began to forget what it had been like not to be in uniform, what it had been like to go to bed every night and sleep through the whole eight or nine hours in a soft bed with clean, white sheets.

Miller felt a tooth begin to ache. The wind aggravated it, and the pain shot up into his head. He pulled the hood of his duffel-coat round his cheek and mumbled curses, wondering how much longer it would be before the watch was ended.

Warby was imagining the ship to be a ploughshare drawing a long, long furrow in the great field of the North Sea. Warby stood with his back to the stern looking forward, and imagined he had his hand upon this gigantic plough that drove on and on and never reached the headland. Here were no hedges, no distant trees on which to fix the gaze—only the endless sea rolling in long, white-crested waves like moving banks capped with the froth of lilies.

But the gulls were here. It was the same when he had ploughed the land at home; the gulls had followed him then, hovering and swooping, uttering their strident cries. He could hear the gulls now; it was the same sound, and it made him think of home. But when he looked back over the stern of the ship he saw that the furrow vanished as soon as it was made. There was no end to the labour, and it was all pointless.

Suddenly he felt very tired, as though the whole four hours of the watch had saved themselves up to drain away his energy at the last.

Promptly at eight bells Sergeant Willis, Randall, and Andrews crawled out of the skin of the ship and clambered up the vertical, swaying ladder of the gun-platform.

" All right, lads," said Willis. " Go and get your breakfast."

" Is it good? " asked Vernon.

" Bangers," said Andrews, " or curry."

Vernon sighed. " Unoriginal, terribly unoriginal."

The mess-table was a wasteland of dirty plates and mugs. A seven-pound tin of marmalade stood in the middle of the table, its lid roughly cut open and turned up like the one remaining petal of a giant tulip. The marmalade was flecked with butter where knives had dug into it; but the transaction had not been one-sided, for the slab of butter, lying in its paper wrapping, showed an equivalent lacing of marmalade. In the mess there were no such things as jam-spoons and butter-knives. Each man used his own knife both for cutting and foraging, digging here and there at the dictation of his needs. It was no place for the squeamish.

The bread, smeared with oily finger-marks, had been hacked clumsily with a knife that had never been designed for the task. Tea had been spilt on the table, and the loaf had slipped into the puddle, turning its underside to mush. The dishes of sausages and curry and rice had thoughtfully been placed near the mess-room stove to keep them warm; but this had resulted in one or two cinders falling into them. The room was thick with tobacco-smoke.

Vernon sat on the wooden form with his back to the bulkhead which separated the mess-room from the hold, and thought how greatly these conditions would have disgusted him only a few years ago. Yet now, coming off watch with the ferocious appetite that was the natural result of such a spell of duty, he could look upon the littered mess-table without a qualm, and, sweeping an open space amid the debris, settle down to a breakfast of half-warm sausages and stewed tea with all the relish of a gourmet partaking of the rarest delicacies.

So, thought Vernon, may a man's sensibilities be blunted; and so may any one of us descend closer and closer to the level of beasts. He wondered whether Warby or Miller had any such thoughts. Miller? Probably not. The fellow wolfed his food with noise and gusto, as though the chaos of the mess-table were his proper element. As for Warby, he ate stolidly, saying little, almost expressionless. You could never tell what Warby was thinking.

Curry and rice followed sausages; bread and marmalade followed curry. Then, pleasantly tight under the belt, they smoked, resting elbows on the table and feeling weariness creep up their bodies.

Then there was the washing-up to do. There was no sink, only a bucket of water on the table and another bucket on the deck for the refuse—the plate-scrapings, the tea-leaves, the unwanted food.

" We ought to keep a pig," said Warby. " Blessed if we don't throw away enough grub to feed one."

Miller sneered. " We've got enough to do wi'out looking after a ruddy pig. Where'd we keep it, anyway? "

" We could make a sty for it on deck."

" It'd be washed overboard in rough weather."

" Well, it was on'y a idea."

" You and your ideas! You'll be thinking of keeping chickens next."

" One ship I was on," said Vernon, " took on about twenty chickens in Buenos Aires to bring home to England. It was the Old Man's idea; he had a run fixed up with fish-netting on the top deck just abaft the after funnel—she was a meat liner, you understand—and had a little house made for them. Our cabin was next to the chicken-run, and half our time was spent rounding up those blessed fowls. They stank too."

" They would," said Miller. " What 'appened to them? "

" It was sad, really. Crossing the tropics, they thought summer had come and all went into the moult. Then, when we got farther north into cold weather, the poor devils were pretty well naked. Those which didn't peg out the cook had. None of them reached England."

Washing-up was one job Vernon could never become resigned to. He detested the greasy, filthy water and the damp, so-called drying-cloths which always acquired a dark-grey colour, gradually deepening almost to black as the voyage progressed. By all the rules the men ought to contract all sorts of diseases; yet they never seemed to do so.

He dried a plate which Miller handed to him, trying not to notice the bits of food still adhering to it.

" This is all confoundedly unhygienic," he remarked.

Miller, his hands and wrists covered by the greasy water in the bucket, sniffed. " What do you expect? You ain't at the Ritz now. It don't come so much of a change to some of us. We wasn't all so well off before the War—not by a long shot. I don't expect you ever knew what it was like to be hungry— real hungry, I mean—and not 'ave any money for food. I don't suppose you did, did you? "

Miller had become quite excited, so that he had forgotten to go on with the washing-up.

Vernon sighed. " I simply remarked that this is unhygienic. Whether I was hungry or you were hungry before the War makes no difference."

" It makes a difference to me."

" I mean it has no bearing on the present state of hygiene."

Miller rattled the knives and forks in the pail. " All right," he said, " but just remember we don't all come out of the top drawer; just remember that! "

Shortly after midday the *Golden Ray* and a few other vessels broke away from the convoy and headed for the mouth of the Humber. Some time later the *Golden Ray* came to rest in Immingham docks, to be invaded almost immediately by shore gangs, who rigged the derricks and loosened the hatch-covers ready for the start of loading on the following day.

The gunners, busy on their weapons, looked out over the docks and saw nothing but sheds and railway-lines, with here and there the tall necks of cranes thrusting up from the wilderness.

Payne voiced the general opinion. " Rotten hole," he said.

That evening Payne and Warby were sitting in a public house drinking mild beer and saying little when a man in a greasy cap spoke to them.

" You two lads are off the *Golden Ray*, aren't you? "

Neither Payne nor Warby answered.

The man closed one eye and opened it again. " All right, I know; I saw you down there."

He took a swig of beer and smacked his lips. " Here, drink up, lads; this one's on me."

Payne and Warby allowed him to take their mugs, and he brought them back foaming. He lowered his voice confidentially. " On the Russian run, hey? "

Payne said nothing. Warby lit a cigarette and puffed more smoke into the already overcharged air. The man in the cloth cap sat down, facing them across the bar table, resting his elbows on the polished wood of its top. Over his head on the opposite wall Payne could see a poster with the picture of a sinking ship; the stern was lifting out of the water and the bows had disappeared from sight. Under the picture Payne could read: " Careless Talk costs Lives." There was another poster which read: " Be like Dad; Keep Mum." And yet a third read: " Walls have Ears."

The man in the cloth cap leaned across the table and said, " Sooner you nor me, lads. Know what we're loading on your ship? Shells! Them and other things. None too healthy, I'd say. I hope you get through, though. They tell me it's a terrible run—terrible. Glad I don't have to go. But I did my bit in the last War—on the Somme; I wouldn't like another sample o' that, not for a pension. But they tell me it's right bad up there on the Russian run—Jerry planes and U-boats. They say there's a battleship up there, too; but of course it don't do to believe all you hear; there's that amount of rumours gets about you don't know where you are. Well, drink up, lads."

On board the s.s. *Golden Ray* four seamen gunners and three Army gunners were playing pontoon on the mess-room table. Gunner Cowdrey was lying on his bunk, his shoulders propped up on a folded duffel-coat and his bald head shining under the electric light. He was playing a mouth-organ, churning out tune after popular tune, pausing only to regain his breath and shake the moisture out of his instrument. Gunner Andrews was reading a letter. He had read it before, and he would read it again; and there would still be delight in doing so. The letter began: "George Darling, Just so you don't forget—I love you——" It was a long letter. Vernon was engrossed in a book, and Bombardier Padgett was making toast.

Randall, lying on his bunk with his eyes closed, heard the sound of Cowdrey's mouth-organ, the voices of the pontoon-players, and the noise of Padgett poking the fire. Randall heard them all, and they were like waves beating against the shell of his own torment.

CHAPTER THREE

Homecoming

LOADING began early on the following day. Randall borrowed a newspaper from one of the stevedores and glanced quickly through it, his eyes flitting over the headlines, searching for something he feared to discover. But it was not there. War news and more war news, and little else in the few sheets to which all papers had shrunk. Randall folded the newspaper, thrust it into his pocket, and followed the others up to the gun-deck.

Five hundred extra rounds of forty-millimetre ammunition had come aboard, and another spare barrel for the Bofors. They now had three barrels and 1500 rounds to put through them. The morning was spent stowing ammunition and man-handling the new barrel into position.

During mid-morning ' smoke-o,' as he sat in the mess sipping hot tea, Randall went through the newspaper more carefully, making sure he had missed nothing. No, it was not there—not even in a small paragraph tucked away at the foot of a column. That meant the discovery had not yet been made. But did it? Would it have been a big enough thing to force its way in among the far more important news of the War? Possibly not. Besides, how could he tell that it had not been in yesterday, when they had been at sea?

Randall discovered suddenly that he was being spoken to. Payne was speaking. Randall tried to pull himself together, to focus his attention on what was going on around him, to drag his mind away from that other matter which drew it irresistibly.

" What's that? What did you say? "

" I said, lend us your paper. You're in a dream, aren't you? Still thinking about her? You'd better forget her for two or three months." Payne laughed.

Randall pushed the paper across the mess-table. Forget her! Ah, if only he could! Forgetfulness would be as balm to his soul; it would be release from the hell of fear in which his mind was imprisoned. But he could not forget her—never, never. Waking, she was there in his mind; sleeping, she was in his dreams—in those nightmares from which he awoke, sweating and trembling.

How many, many times in his mind he had gone over the events of the past two weeks! Only two weeks! Surely it could not be as short a time as that! Yet, so it was. Two weeks ago he had been happy. In those two weeks his world had crashed about his ears.

The babel of voices in the mess-room went on around him, and Randall sat there—alone—more alone than he had ever been. He felt that between himself and these others a wall had grown, a wall that he had been instrumental in building and that he could not now pull down. The din of voices surged around him like a foaming sea, and he was an island, isolated, deserted.

His gaze rested on the head of a rivet; round the rivet was a circle of rust, a red stain upon the white paint of the bulkhead. But Randall did not see the rivet or the rust, for his mind was away again, reliving the events of the past fortnight from the moment when he boarded the train at Southport that was to take him on the first stage of his journey to Yarmouth.

Randall had eight days of leave to look forward to, and his heart was happy. Two days earlier his ship had docked in Liverpool after a ten-month voyage to Australia and New Zealand. Randall had sugar and tea and butter in his kitbag and twenty-five pounds of back-pay in his wallet. He had ten pairs of silk stockings, a silk nightdress, a pair of embroidered slippers, and a crocodile-leather handbag; and he was happy because he was going home to his wife after ten months. Add two weeks to that period, and you had the length of time he had been married. So he was happy.

There were no taxis at Liverpool Exchange; so Randall had to carry his kitbag across to Lime Street Station. It was hard work, thus loaded, toiling up the last slope towards the entrance, the din of tramcars sounding in his ears and a thin drizzle of rain falling. Then he was under the arch of the station, mingling with the crowds of khaki- and blue-clad men and women, the lucky ones departing on leave, the unlucky ones coming back.

Randall had two hours to wait for his train. He climbed up to the Y.M.C.A. canteen, which was above the R.T.O. office, and waited in a queue for sausage-and-mash and a cup of tea. He ate his meal at a dirty table, which he shared with five other men—three sappers, a Royal Marine, and a leading

seaman. He scarcely tasted what he was eating, because the
joy of going home was like a ferment within him, a strange,
exultant feeling in his stomach and chest that swept away the
taste of food. He ate mechanically, washing down the solids
with gulps of tea, and began to imagine how Lily would greet
him, the words she would speak. He pictured the surprise in
her eyes turning to delight. He had a little speech prepared;
it was the sort of thing they said on the films: " Here's the
man you married. Remember me? " In his mind he never got
any further than that because that was the point at which she
came into his arms and he kissed her.

" Pass the salt, mate," said the Royal Marine.

Randall came out of his dream and pushed the salt-cellar
along the table. The Marine shook salt on to his potatoes.

" Going on leave, mate? "

Randall said, " Yes; eight days."

" Lucky bastard!" said the Marine. " I've just had mine;
it's a sod coming back. It's all right going, but it's a sod
coming back. Married? "

Randall nodded. " I got married on my last leave—ten
months ago."

The Marine whistled. " Ten months; that's a long time.
You bin abroad? "

" Australia. I'm in the Maritime."

" Oh, merchant ships; that lark. Well, she'll be glad to see
you. No need to knock at the front door and run round to
the back, eh? "

The Marine laughed and applied himself to fried spam;
but his words had called up a tiny cloud on the horizon of
Randall's happiness. Of course he did not have to knock at
the front door and run round to the back; he could trust
Lily; he had never for a moment thought of distrusting her.
But why did the Marine have to make such a remark? It was
as though a dirty finger had been rubbed across a clean page;
the smear remained.

Randall finished the last of his tea, recovered the deposit
on his knife and fork, and went downstairs again to the

sombre platforms where human beings swirled and eddied like flotsam borne upon the evil tides of war. Already, though there was still an hour to wait, a queue was forming for his train. He attached himself to the queue, in front of him a tall and very beautiful Wren, behind him a short and extraordinarily ugly infantryman. They waited with that dead, unfeeling, infinitely elastic patience to which people had become accustomed. They had almost forgotten that it had not always been like this; they scarcely dared to hope that it would not always be so.

Randall was lucky; he found a seat in the train. The Wren sat opposite him, a table between them. Between Liverpool and Crewe Randall told the Wren all about himself. She was sympathetic. Randall thought her pretty—not as pretty as Lily, of course, but nice, real nice. She seemed to understand just how he felt, going home after being so long away. He showed her the photograph of Lily and himself taken on their wedding-day. It was not a good photograph really; Joe had taken it with a box camera and the day had been cloudy, so that it had not come out too clearly. But the Wren said she could see what it should have been like, and she thought Lily looked sweet.

Randall was pleased. He was so pleased he gave the Wren one of his pairs of silk stockings. She refused to take them at first, but he could see that she wanted them, and in the end he persuaded her. He had to change trains at Rugby and leave the Wren. The rest of his journey was less comfortable.

At Peterborough he had four hours to wait. It was the middle of the night and cold. While he waited he smoked a whole packet of cigarettes, and his tongue was like a piece of cracked leather. But he was patient; he had waited ten months; what were a few more hours?

He arrived at Yarmouth at ten in the morning, and it was raining. Walking over Vauxhall bridge with his kitbag on his shoulder, he could see the raindrops dimpling the surface of the river. The water looked dark and cold, as it always did, even in summer; and the rain was cold too, running down off the hand that supported the kitbag, under his sleeve and down his arm. He could feel it trickling down towards the elbow and feeling its way along to his armpit. But the rain did not worry him. He was nearly home now. Soon he would be seeing Lily. His heart jumped.

But she might be out; she might be shopping. He had not let her know he was coming; he had meant to send a telegram, but the post-offices had always been shut when he had the time, and so it had never been done. It'll be a surprise for her, he had thought, I'll just come on her sudden like and hear what she says.

The house was the end one of a row. It was not much of a place, but they had been lucky to find a house of any sort, one of their own. And, as they had both said, it would only be for the duration; when the War was over they would be able to find something better. Neither of them had ever mentioned the possibility that they might not need a house after the War, but the idea had sometimes come into Randall's mind, nagging him. For he wanted very much to come back; he was only twenty-two, and life seemed particularly sweet to him, so sweet that he wanted to live it out to the full. Yet there were a lot of fellows of his age who were not going to taste much more of life, and there was no telling that the cards might not run against him also. Some men said if the bullet had your number on it there was nothing you could do. That was fatalism. In a way, of course, it was true; but he had never cared for that kind of outlook. Somehow he had a feeling that he would pull through. There might be no reason why he should do so; but he had the feeling, nevertheless. It was a comforting feeling.

Randall pushed open the gate of the tiny front garden, a garden about ten feet square with a path of crazy paving and weeds springing up between the slabs, and tried the front door. It was locked. Randall put down his kitbag on the doorstep and pressed the bell. He could hear it ringing inside the house; then he took his finger off the button and waited, listening for the sound of his wife's footsteps.

The rain had stopped, and a beam of sunlight was pushing its way through the banked clouds, glinting on the dripping road. A horse and trolley clattered past, the driver sitting on one side, his feet dangling. Randall watched it to the end of the road, the sound dying gradually away. Then he rang again.

He waited two minutes, and then rang a third time. Then, as there was still no answer, he left his kitbag on the front doorstep and walked round to the back of the house. At the back was a tiny yard, separated from the road by a brick wall, and from the next property by a wooden fence, falling into disrepair. Jutting out from the house was a shed which was used as a coal store; by the shed stood two dustbins and on the shed wall hung a galvanized-iron wash-tub.

Randall tried the back door, but it was locked. So he rapped with his knuckles, not because he thought there was now any likelihood of Lily's being in, but because he had not yet thought of anything else to do. He had just stopped knocking when a voice said, " You'll have to knock harder than that if you want to wake her up."

Turning his head, Randall saw a plump, middle-aged woman leaning over the fence. He remembered her at once; it was Mrs Hawkins, their neighbour.

" What do you mean—wake her? " he asked. " Doesn't she get up before this? "

Mrs Hawkins shook her head. " Not as a rule. Well, it stands to reason, don't it? " She was about to say more, but something in Randall's expression seemed to jog her memory, and she cried, " Why, it's Mr Randall, isn't it? It's bin such a long time, I'd almost forgot you. I must say you're looking well. 'Course they feed you well in the Army. Better than what we have to put up with. Still, I'm glad to see you home again. Mrs Randall didn't tell me you was coming."

" She didn't know," said Randall. " I couldn't let her know. It'll be a surprise for her."

" It'll be that all right," said Mrs Hawkins.

" You think she's in? "

" Oh, bet your life! Give a good old bang on the door."

Randall did as suggested, while his adviser rested her elbows on the fence and watched with every appearance of deep interest. After a while there were sounds inside the house. A bolt was drawn back, and the door opened.

In the long months of imagining this reunion Randall had never pictured his wife greeting him like this—sleep clinging to her eyes, her hair in curlers, an old blue dressing-gown flung over her pyjamas, and her feet thrust into worn-out slippers. His mental picture had been idealized, the picture of Lily as she had been on their wedding-day, an excited, happy, nervous girl. Slovenliness had formed no part of that picture.

There was a sulky look on her face as she opened the door, as though she resented being dragged out of bed at half-past ten in the morning. Then, as she saw who it was who had awakened her, surprise drove the other expression away.

" You!" she said. " But how? When? "

Randall had a feeling that Mrs Hawkins was still leaning over the fence, and he had no desire for onlookers at this moment. He walked in and closed the door behind him, standing in the tiny kitchen, with its smell of stale food, facing the girl he had married ten months ago.

" Well," he said, " aren't you pleased to see me? "

" Of course I'm pleased, Sid! But why didn't you let me know you was coming? Springing on me sudden like this! Give me a shock."

" Never mind the shock, Lil. Give me a kiss, a real big kiss. God! I've waited long enough for it."

When he had her in his arms and her lips warm on his, Randall forgot that his home-coming was not just as he had planned it. He rested his cheek against hers, and felt all the weariness of his journey dropping away from him. He was home again, home for eight days.

" Why," she said, " you haven't shaved; you're like a hedgehog."

" I've been travelling all night."

" Well, you'd better shave now. I'll put some water on."

" Never mind that," he said. " There's plenty of time for that. Let's have some breakfast. I haven't eaten for fifteen hours."

Lily said, " All right; I'll cook some in a jiff; but I must go and do meself up first. I look a fright."

" You couldn't," said Randall, " not as long as you're you."

She patted him on the cheek and went upstairs, leaving behind her the vague odour of her body to mingle with the sour smells of the kitchen. Randall suddenly remembered his kitbag and went to fetch it. He unpacked the silk stockings, the nightdress, the slippers, and the handbag, laying them on the table so that Lily would see them when she came down. Then he washed his face and hands at the sink and dried them on the roller towel. He felt better after that, fresher. He lit a cigarette and waited for Lily to come down again.

When she did return she looked different, more like the picture. The curlers were out of her hair; she had touched up her lips with lipstick, and she was wearing a pleated skirt and a jumper which accentuated her figure. Randall's heart gave a leap when he saw her; but he was nervous. In a way it was as though they were strangers; it was like starting all over again. Still, he would not grumble at that—not if it was as enjoyable as the first time.

Lily said, " Give me a cigarette, will you? " Then she saw the things on the table, and she uttered a little cry of surprise and delight, her eyes sparkling. She took one of the stockings out of its cellophane packet and pushed her hand into it, spreading out her fingers to allow the light to shine through the silk. She drew her breath in a long sigh of rapture.

" Silk! Real silk!"

Randall grinned. " So's the nightdress."

She lifted the nightdress by its shoulder-straps and held it against her body.

" I hope it fits," said Randall. " I can't take it back."

" It'll fit," said Lily. " Where did you get it? "

" Sydney—Australia."

" All the way from Australia! Fancy! You can't get things like this in England now, you know."

" I know. That's why I got them in Australia. There's a handbag and slippers too. Look."

She folded the nightdress and took the bag in one hand and the slippers in the other, looking at each in turn.

" You must have spent a lot of money," she said.

" I earned some," Randall explained. " I worked on the ship and earned some on top of my pay. I've got plenty left."

He opened his wallet and showed her the wad of notes. " We'll have a good time while I'm home. It won't be long, but we'll have a good time while it lasts. What do you say? "

" Of course," she said; " of course." But she said it vaguely, as though her mind were not on what she was saying, as though it had drifted off at a tangent. Suddenly she said, " Well, Sid, what about that cigarette? "

He gave her one and lit it for her. " You didn't used to smoke," he said. " When did you start? "

" Didn't I? " She seemed suddenly to be on the defensive; she spoke with an edge of defiance to her tone. " Well, I got to pass the time somehow, haven't I? You aren't going to object to me smoking, are you? "

Randall was surprised at the effect his words had had. " I don't object at all. I only said you didn't used to smoke."

" Well, I do now."

She took an overall from a peg, and put it on over her jumper and skirt. " Do you mind sausages? That's about all there is. I didn't know you was coming, or I'd have had something in."

" Sausages will do me fine."

He was still wondering why she had spoken like that just because he had remarked on her smoking. Of course he had no objection; why should he? He smoked himself. So why should Lily not smoke? But there had been no reason for her to speak like that; quite sharp, she had been. It was just as though she had a feeling of guilt. Because she had taken to smoking? The whole thing was ridiculous. He brushed it from his mind and watched his wife frying sausages on the gas-stove.

" Where would you like to go to-night? " asked Randall. " Pictures? Theatre? Pub? "

Lily shook the ash from her cigarette so that it should not fall into the frying-pan, and spoke with the butt still in her mouth. She was holding the handle of the pan in one hand and moving the sausages with a fork.

" I'm on at the canteen to-night," she said.

Randall almost shouted: " What? "

" I'm on at the canteen."

" What canteen? "

" The Forces canteen. Didn't I tell you in my letters? I help there."

" You didn't tell me." Randall's voice was hard and angry, though he was trying to keep the anger out of it. " What made you take on that job? "

" Well, I had to do something, didn't I? You didn't expect me to sit here twiddling my thumbs till you came back. Besides, it's work of national importance. Somebody's got to do it. I expect you're glad enough of a canteen yourself now and then."

Randall knew that what Lily said was true; somebody had to do canteen work. He knew it would be unreasonable if he were to object to Lily doing it while he was away. She had nothing else to do; it was not as though there were any children. But, unreasonable or not, he did not like it. He would have preferred her to take any other job than that. Yet, what was his objection, reduced to essentials? It was simply a dislike of having her serving sailors and soldiers and airmen; being jollied by them, cracking jokes with them, just being friendly to them. He wanted her to be his, his alone, and the root of his objection was jealousy. He knew it, but the knowledge made the objection no less strong.

" How long have you been doing this? "

" Six months; thereabouts."

" Oh! "

He lit himself another cigarette from the stump of the old and sat for a time smoking in silence. Then he said, " Can't you get off for this week? It's not often I'm home."

" I'll try," said Lily. " I expect I can; but it would have bin easier if you'd let me know you was coming."

" I couldn't—not until we docked. I didn't know even then. I might not have got leave."

" All right; I'll ask. I expect it'll be O.K."

Randall slept most of the afternoon. He had not meant to sleep; sleeping was a waste of his all too short hours of leave; but sitting in an armchair in front of the living-room fire sleep took hold of him, and he dozed. When he awoke it was nearly five o'clock. He listened for sounds of Lily moving about the house; but there were none, and he supposed that she had gone down to the canteen, as she had said she would, to see about having the week off.

Randall fingered his chin, and the roughness reminded him that he had not yet shaved. He had better do so at once, for he could not go out in the evening with thirty-six hours' growth on his face. He went to the kitchen, drew the black-out curtains, and switched the light on. Then he filled a kettle with water and set it on the gas-stove to heat.

Waiting for the kettle to boil, Randall had time to examine the kitchen more closely than he had done before. There was no hiding the fact that it was in a mess, dirty, untidy, as though it had not been swept up or scrubbed out for months. In one corner was a basket of soiled linen; under the sink were one or two unwashed saucepans, and beside them a pail full to the brim with potato-peelings, tea-leaves, and other garbage. Randall drew his finger along one of the shelves of the dresser and raised a little mound of dust like the terminal moraine of a glacier.

He sighed and prepared to shave.

Lily came back just as he was drying his face.

" It's O.K.," she said. " No more canteen for me till your leave's finished."

Randall hung the towel he had been using on a cord over

the stove. "They couldn't very well refuse, could they?"

"No; but it puts more work on the others." She began taking off her coat. "Any plans for to-night?"

"I thought we might just pop down to the Grapes for an hour or two. I don't feel like doing a lot to-night. Too tired."

The suggestion did not appear to please her. She pouted. "Not the Grapes, Sid. Some other place."

"Why, what's wrong with the Grapes?" asked Randall. "We always used to go there, and it's close and handy. Tell you what. We'll go there to-night and try some other place another night—eh, Lil?"

He put his arm round her waist as he said it, but she did not respond to his gesture of affection, and he felt rebuffed.

"All right," she said; "do what you like. It's your leave. Don't mind me."

"Now, Lil," he said, "don't talk like that; it's your leave too, in a way. I don't want to do anything you don't like; you know that. If you'd rather not go to the Grapes we won't go there. You've only got to say the word."

"Oh, no," she said, "you want to go to the old Grapes, so we'll go."

She slipped away from his arm and began to fill the kettle for tea. Randall wondered what was going wrong; this did not seem like the wife he had left ten months ago. She seemed short-tempered, ready to go up in the air at a word. It worried him.

"What's wrong, Lil?" he asked.

She looked at him sharply. "Wrong? What should be wrong?" Then, as though feeling that she was not behaving fairly to him, she kissed him on the cheek. "I'm sorry," she said. "I shouldn't have spoke to you like that. You mustn't take no notice of what I say; I don't always think. But you know I love you, Sid dear; you know that, don't you? There's never bin nobody else but you, Sid. Truly!"

Randall said, "I know, Lil; I know. It's the same with me too."

The bar of the Grapes hotel was so crowded when Randall and Lily arrived that they had to edge their way through the press inch by inch. It was a crowd made up predominantly of blue and khaki, and over its head hung a thick haze of tobacco-smoke. Coming from the cold darkness outside, one burst suddenly into bright light, warmth, and noise, the buzz of conversation, the clink of glasses, and brief gusts of laughter. It was a crowd trying to forget for a few hours the guns, the aircraft, and the ships—trying to do so, but never really succeeding.

" What'll you have, Lil—when I can get it? "

" A gin and tonic, please, Sid."

Randall elbowed his way to a strategic position at the bar. " Thank you," he said; " thank you "—dodging mugs of beer, ducking under lifted arms. " Thank you; thank you."

At last he caught the eye of Percy, the barman, who had been working in that hotel for as long as Randall could remember.

" Hullo, Sid," Percy said. " On leave? "

" Eight days," said Randall.

" And very nice too," Percy said. " Where've you been this time? "

" Australia."

" Australia, have you? That's a long way. Well, what's it to be? "

" Gin and tonic and a pint of half-and-half," said Randall. He had a feeling that Percy was really not interested in where he had been. If he never came back again Percy would not lose any sleep. Well, that was how it was; he was nothing to Percy; just another customer; so why should Percy worry?

He paid for the drinks and edged his way back to where Lily was standing. It was a tricky job with the gin in one hand and the pint mug of beer in the other. A sailor jogged his elbow, and some of the beer was spilt; it splashed a sergeant-pilot who was standing close by.

" Sorry," said Randall. " I'm sorry."

" You want to be more careful," the airman said. He

looked down at his trouser-leg. "You want to mind where you're going."

"I said I was sorry."

"I should think so, too, splashing beer over people."

Randall left him still complaining.

Lily was standing by the wall, almost flattened against it. She was gazing across the room, as though searching for somebody. Randall had to speak to her before she noticed him.

"Here you are," said Randall. "Here's your gin."

"What a crush, Sid!" She took the glass. "Seen anyone you know?"

Randall shook his head. "Only Percy."

He took a pull at his beer, and as he lowered the mug he heard a voice say, "Why, hullo, Lil! Fancy meeting you here!"

The remark was made in a bantering tone, as though the speaker really felt no surprise at seeing Randall's wife in those surroundings. Turning, Randall saw a sergeant grinning at Lily, a heavily built man with close-cropped black hair and a neatly trimmed moustache. He had thick eyebrows which met across the bridge of his nose, and when he smiled there was a flash of white teeth. Randall disliked him intensely from the first moment.

Lily spoke quickly, as though she were afraid of what the sergeant might say next. "You haven't met my husband, have you? Sid, this is Sergeant Wilson. He comes to the canteen."

"Your husband! Oh, better watch my step!" He laughed, and it occurred to Randall that the fellow had already had as much drink as was good for him. Then he put out his hand. "I was only joking. Johnnie Wilson's little joke, eh? Pleesetermeecher!"

The sergeant's hand was large and moist; he squeezed Randall's hand very tightly, perhaps to show his strength. Then he said, "I see you're in the Artillery, too."

"Yes," said Randall.

" He's got eight days' leave," said Lily. " Eight days. I shan't be at the canteen while he's home."

" Oh," said Wilson, " that's a pity. We shall miss our Lil."

Randall resented the way he said " our Lil." What right had the fellow to talk like that? He stood glumly silent and waited for the sergeant to move on. This was what happened when your wife helped in a canteen; every Tom, Dick, and Harry who took a cup of tea out of her hands thought he had the right to call her by her Christian name. There was too much familiarity—altogether too much.

Sergeant Wilson appeared to sense a touch of frost in the atmosphere. " Well," he said, " I must be moving. Got to see a man about a dog." He winked at Lily. " I can see I'm one too many here. Eight days! O.K." He laughed and began to plough his way towards the bar.

" That," said Randall, " is the sort of man I don't like. He's got a nerve—calling you Lil."

" But they all do, Sid. It don't mean anything."

" Well, I don't like it. I wish you didn't go there."

" Now, Sid, we've bin over that once. Don't let's say any more about it now. Give me a cigarette, there's a dear. I'm dying for a smoke."

Randall put his mug on a window-ledge and took a packet of cigarettes out of his pocket, handing them to his wife.

" It's not that I don't trust you, Lil; it's not that—— "

She answered quickly, " I should think not, indeed. Not trust me! Why, there's a thing to say! What do you think I am? "

" Now, now, Lil," he said, " don't take on. I didn't mean anything. It's only that I've been away so long, and—— "

" And what? "

Oh, God! he thought. This isn't how it ought to be; this isn't how it ought to be at all. What's gone wrong? What's gone wrong?

He struck a match for her cigarette. But she just stared at him, and the match burned down to his fingers.

" Let's forget it, shall we, Lil? Let's forget all about it."

" I don't know what it is you want to forget," she said. " I don't know if you're trying to accuse me of something. If so, you'd better say it straight out."

" Lil," Randall said desperately, " I'm not accusing you of anything."

A man bumped into his back, thrusting him forward, close up against his wife.

" Sorry, chum," said the man. " What a crowd! Can't see to move, can you? "

Randall thought: This is a fine place to quarrel in, with scores of people milling around. But nobody was taking any notice of them. People were interested only in themselves.

" Lil," he said, " let's go home."

CHAPTER FOUR
Nightmare

THE first morning of his leave Randall spent in cleaning up the house. He began in the kitchen; he scrubbed the floor, took everything off the dresser and scrubbed that too, scoured all the pots and pans, and ended by polishing the brass water-tap. Later he would clean the other rooms. Randall was a man who detested dirt and untidiness; on parade he had often been complimented on his smart turn-out, the gleaming polish of his boots, the glitter of his brasses. Therefore he could not bear to see his own house dirty and slovenly. Therefore he swept and scrubbed and polished.

Lily watched him, not offering to help. She seemed to be amused that he should think such labour necessary or even desirable.

" Where does it get you? " she asked. " Couple of days and it's as bad again."

He answered cheerfully, " Now, Lil, that's not the way to look at things. Think what a state the house would be in if we never did any cleaning."

" Oh, well," she said, " if you want to do it, nobody's going
to stop you. But you needn't think I'm ever going to wear
myself out doing that sort of work. I'm not a char."

In the afternoon Randall went for a walk. Lily refused
to go with him because she wanted to wash her hair. So he
went alone. He walked along the promenade, thinking how
different it was from what it had been in peace-time. The
sands were deserted, bleak and cold; the pleasure beach was
silent, falling into decay, with bits of canvas flapping miser-
ably in the wind; shops and amusement arcades were boarded
up; here and there a house had been taken over by the Army.
It looked what it was—a town at war.

Coming back along the river-bank he saw that where once
the herring fleet had floated, three ships abreast, were now
only naval craft; and a long stretch of the wharves had
been wired off to keep the public away. Many times he
saw where bombs had fallen, tearing great gaps amid the
buildings.

He went home feeling depressed by what he had seen.

The days of Randall's leave flickered past like the pictures
in a peep-show, gone before he could grasp the reality of
them. Sometimes he wondered whether he really understood
Lily; she was like a weather-vane on a day of light and
variable breezes, never the same for two hours in succession.
At times she was sweet to him, and he felt that he was living
in some seventh heaven of delight; then she would become
sulky and he would not know what to say to her, since everything he said seemed to bring only a bitter answer. Then he
would become bitter too, and they would both say things
they did not mean, wounding one another with words.

Many times Randall told himself that this was not the
leave he had planned. There was always a kind of tension in
the air, as there is when a thunderstorm is brewing. Randall
felt the tension and hated it. Yet he hated more to think of
going back. Lily and he might quarrel; he might doubt
whether he understood her; but of one thing he never had any

doubt—that he loved her. And, loving her, he wanted to be with her always. Yet to-morrow he must go back.

Hell! he thought. To hell with war!

He turned over in the bed and felt his wife lying warm beside him. He wondered whether she were awake, and whether she too were thinking that this was to be their last night together for who could tell how many months.

He whispered, " Lily, are you asleep? "

She murmured something he did not properly hear, muttered words from the country that lies between waking and sleeping and belongs to neither.

The room was very dark; there was not even a glimmer of light from the window, since the black-out curtain was still covering it. Randall felt that he and Lily were in a box, cut off from the rest of the world—he and she complete in themselves. That was how it ought to be. He wanted to stay in the box for ever; it was warm and soft and safe; and the darkness pressed in on all sides like black cotton-wool, a shield, a covering, a defence against all that was harsh and unpleasant.

Randall's mind was wandering, hovering on the borders of sleep. He imagined suddenly that he was alone. He was still in the box, but now he was alone; and the box was no longer a haven, a sanctuary of peace, but a prison. The darkness had become thick and heavy, suffocating him; he was shut in, and he could never get out—never.

Randall was afraid. In his fear he thrust out a hand, and the hand found his wife. With that contact his mind came back out of the dark cavern into which it had wandered, and relief flooded in upon him.

" Lily," he said; " Lily, my darling! "

He heard her long, sighing breath close beside him, and he loved her; he loved her more than ever now, because he knew that to-morrow he must go back to the billet and the gun-drill, the crowded wash-place, the wire bed, the filthy blankets, the coarse jokes—all the strange ingredients of a soldier's life. He must go back to all that.

Yet he must have this memory to take with him, something of this to hold on to in the months ahead.

"Lily," he said, "you do love me, don't you, Lil? "

She was still half asleep, and her words were muffled; but he heard them.

She said, " Of course I love you, Johnnie."

Suddenly the darkness was a blinding, flaming hell to Randall. His hand wrenched Lily into wakefulness. His voice was high and unsteady.

"What did you call me? " he cried.

Lily could not see her husband, but his voice and his hand alarmed her. Yet she did not realize what had caused his emotion, because sleep was still clogging her brain.

" You called me Johnnie." The words were bitter, angry. " You called me Johnnie."

He shook her, rattling the bed, driving the sleep out of her brain.

" You called me Johnnie."

" Don't," she protested. " Don't, Sid."

" You called me Johnnie." That one fact appeared to have seized upon his mind, holding it completely, driving out every other thought.

" You called me Johnnie."

Lily tried to push his hand away; the fingers were biting into her arm, hurting her.

" Don't be silly, Sid. You've bin dreaming. Why should I call you that? "

" That's what I want to know. That's what I mean to find out. Who do you know of the name of Johnnie? Tell me! Who is it? "

She tried to laugh, but the attempt was nearer hysteria than genuine laughter. She had never known Sid to be in such a fury.

" I don't know nobody called Johnnie. You bin dreaming, I tell you."

Randall said harshly, "I wasn't dreaming; but you were, and you called me Johnnie. Who's Johnnie? That's what I want to know."

His fingers tightened on her arm so that she cried out with the pain. "Sid, let me go; you're hurting me. I tell you I don't know anybody called Johnnie; I swear I don't."

Randall was stirring his memory, flogging it into activity. Johnnie! Where had he heard that name before? It had been recently; he was sure of that. Where had it been? Johnnie! Johnnie! He loosed his grip on Lily's arm and began to think back over the days, methodically searching for a man called Johnnie.

And suddenly he found what he was looking for; he found it on the first evening of his leave in the smoky, clamorous atmosphere of the Grapes hotel. A sergeant with a black moustache! Johnnie Wilson!

He grasped his wife's arm again, his fingers sinking into the soft flesh. "What you been up to while I was away? Come on; tell me."

She tried to wrench her arm away, but the grip tightened.

"I don't know what you mean."

"Oh, yes, you do. This Johnnie—Johnnie Wilson. That's what I mean. You've been playing around with him, haven't you? Tell me! Tell me!"

"Let go of me!" she cried. "Sid, let go of me, you damn fool!"

But he would not release his grip, and suddenly she bit him in the hand. He cried out, and the grip relaxed.

"You little devil!"

"Serves you right. I told you you was hurting me."

He sucked his hand, feeling the hot taste of blood where her teeth had broken the skin. His anger had left him, and he felt weak and unhappy, like a child that has been beaten.

"Lil," he pleaded, "Lil, tell me it isn't true. I'll believe anything you say, Lil; but just tell me."

Detecting his altered tone, her fear left her, and she became sulky, determined to goad him, determined to take her revenge upon him.

"You're a damn fool," she said. "What you expect me to do while you're away for months on end? Sit at home and

sew? I got better things to do than that. I got my life to
live."

"Lil," he said hoarsely, "you don't mean it. You're
joking."

She loaded her voice with sarcasm. "Oh, yes, of course;
hear me laugh!" Then she changed her tone. She spoke
rapidly, defiantly, as though trying to convince, not Randall,
but herself, that she was in the right. "How do I know what
you get up to while you're away? Of course you're Mr
Righteous, but I bet you bin with women since you was home
last. I know soldiers; they're all alike. Of course they can do
what they please, and it's all right. But wives! Oh, that's
different. Well, I don't see it. I say a wife has got as much
right to have a good time when her husband's not there to
give it to her as what he has. We're only young once. So we've
got to enjoy ourselves while we can. You can't expect—— "

"Lil!"

The cry silenced her. It was not Sid's voice at all. It was
just as though a demon had got into him and was shouting
through his mouth.

"Lil! You whore!"

Randall's hands seemed to move of their own will; he
could not have held them back if he had wished. They felt
for Lily's throat and closed upon it. She cried out, but the
cry was strangled as the hands pressed more tightly.

Inside Randall's brain the blood was pulsing and hammer-
ing, driving out his sanity. When it ceased to hammer Lily
was dead.

When he was sure that she was dead, when he was sure
that all his frenzied efforts to revive her were in vain, Randall
dressed himself and went downstairs. Strangely, now that the
thing was done, now that he knew he had murdered his wife,
he felt remarkably calm. It might be that this was simply a
numbness of the senses caused by the shock, just as a limb
is numbed by the immediate shock of a wound. It might be
that pain would come later; but for the moment he was calm.

He went into the kitchen, boiled a kettle, and made a pot of tea. It was cold in the kitchen, so he fetched the electric fire from the drawing-room and switched it on. Then he sat, drinking tea and smoking, while he tried to decide what to do.

When day broke Randall had reached his decision. He went upstairs and lifted Lily's body from the bed, surprised to find how light she was. The eyes, wide open and staring, worried him; but he avoided looking at them, and carried the body to a cupboard let into the wall of the bedroom beside the fireplace. In the cupboard were Lily's dresses and coats, and it came into Randall's mind that at least she would not be lost for a change of clothing. It was a foolish thought, and he tried to drive it out; but it persisted.

The cupboard was large; the body lay with its lower half along the floor and its back propped up against the wall. Randall took a last look at what had been his wife, and imagined that the eyes stared back at him accusingly. He shuddered and closed the cupboard door. Then he locked it and dropped the key into his pocket.

Randall breakfasted on coffee and cigarette-smoke. He had no stomach for food. Why, he thought, has this happened to me? I didn't deserve this. Why did it have to happen to me? Why? Why?

There were times when he did not believe that it had really happened. Then he would sit listening for Lily's step on the stairs and the sound of her voice. But they never came; and the misery would flood in upon him again in a black wave of despair. Ah, why had this happened to him?

But his plan was made, and he meant to carry it out; though, at best, it was no more than a makeshift. There was no future in it, he told himself wryly; but he could think of nothing else to do.

When, through the kitchen window, he saw Mrs Hawkins in her backyard Randall picked up a bucket of rubbish and went out to the dustbin.

" 'Morning, Mrs Hawkins," he said, trying to keep his voice steady.

" 'Morning, Mr Randall." Mrs Hawkins was hanging clothes on a line. Her voice was muffled by the peg that she was holding between her teeth. " Going back to-day, aren't you? "

" That's right. Got to be back to-morrow morning, so I shall have to take the evening train. Mrs Randall's coming with me."

Mrs Hawkins's eyebrows went up in surprise. She took the peg out of her mouth. " She is? She never told me, an' I was talking to her on'y yesterday. Never mentioned a word of it then, she didn't."

" We didn't decide until yesterday evening," said Randall. " It seemed a good idea. I can get rooms for her in Southport, and maybe get a sleeping-out pass. It'll be better than the billets."

Mrs Hawkins agreed. " 'Course it will. Make the most of your time, I say. You don't know how long it'll last. I suppose Mrs Randall will be coming home when you go off on your ship."

Randall pushed the lid of the dustbin down into place, avoiding Mrs Hawkins's eyes. " It depends. She might get a job up there; plenty of 'em going, and good money. We'll see how things pan out."

" Well," said Mrs Hawkins, " I s'pose she'll come and have a word afore you go. Or should I pop in and see her? "

" She's in bed," said Randall hastily. " We had a late night; but she'll come and see you before we go."

" I'll be expecting her," said Mrs Hawkins.

Randall was sweating when he went indoors, though it was a cold day; and he felt weak and sick. He wished there had been some brandy or whisky in the house, for he felt in need of a stimulant; but there was nothing of that sort. And even if there had been he would not have dared to touch it, for fear it might loosen his tongue. In future his tongue would have to be under control—always. He must not make a slip.

When he had shaved he packed his kitbag and stood it in the hall. Then he went out, locking the house behind him.

First he visited the baker and cancelled the bread order; then he went to the dairy and told the dairyman that Mrs Randall would not require any more milk for the present. He stopped the daily paper, and in turn called on the butcher and grocer. To each he gave the same story: his wife was going back north with him.

Neither he nor Lily had any relations in Yarmouth. There were a few slight acquaintances; but he felt he could safely leave it to Mrs Hawkins to inform them of what had happened, or at least of what Mrs Hawkins supposed had happened.

On his way home Randall called at the canteen where Lily had helped. It had just opened, and there were few other Servicemen in the place. He found the lady in charge and told her who he was.

" My name's Randall. My wife helps here."

The lady had perfectly white hair and thin features. She wore heavy ear-rings, and her neck seemed to be a bundle of wires with a loose skin covering. Randall noticed these things as he felt the sweat pricking out on his forehead again.

She said, " Lily Randall. Why, of course. You've been home on leave. I hope you're having a good time."

Randall said, " I go back to-day. My wife's coming with me. I thought I'd better come and tell you; she may not have time; there's a lot to do."

A shadow passed over the white-haired lady's face. " Oh, dear! This is most awkward. If only I had known sooner."

" We didn't decide until last night," said Randall. " We couldn't let you know before we knew ourselves."

" No, no! Of course not. However, it is awkward."

Randall forced himself to eat some dinner. It was no good going without food and then fainting; that would not help. He found some cold meat and pickles and ate as much as he could. Then he made a pot of tea and drank four cups; there was no need to save the sugar any longer. Afterwards he washed up and put the things neatly away, drawing from these ordinary, humdrum actions a store of nervous strength.

He did not go upstairs. He felt that never again would he dare to enter that part of the house. He was finished with that for ever.

A loud knock on the back door startled him. When he opened it he found Mrs Hawkins standing on the doorstep.

" I thought I'd just come and see if there was anything I could do," she said. " Mrs Randall 'asn't been to see me."

" She's down the town," said Randall. " I expected her back, but maybe she's been held up."

" Oh," said Mrs Hawkins; " oh, well." Her gaze moved about the kitchen, with its new cleanliness. " You've made a change here since you been home, an' no mistake. Real spick-and-span. That's Army spit and polish, I s'pose. My old man used to be like that when he was alive; guardsman, he was; reg'lar. 'Course, the Army was different in his day."

Randall felt the smile setting rigid on his face. Why don't you go? Why don't you go? he thought. Go, go, go!

Mrs Hawkins hovered on the doorstep. " You'll be travelling all night, I s'pose. Wouldn't like that meself; never did like long train journeys, anyway. And what a crush these days! Lucky if you get a seat. You'll be having a taxi to the station, of course."

" No," said Randall, " we're going to walk."

" With all your luggage? You'd be better with a car."

" I've taken the luggage to the station," lied Randall. " We'd rather walk."

" It might rain."

" We'll risk that."

Mrs Hawkins started to move away. " Well, if there's anything I can do to help you've only got to say the word."

" No, there's nothing, nothing, really. Thanks all the same."

" And Mrs Randall will pop in before you go? "

" Yes, yes, I expect so. But we may be pushed for time."

When he had closed the door Randall leaned against it for some minutes, feeling mentally and physically exhausted. The cheap tin clock on the kitchen mantelpiece made the only sound in the house; it ticked away the seconds with a loud, monotonous beat that seemed to drive its way into Randall's brain, mocking him, laughing at him. *Tick-tock, tick-tock*; your wife is dead. *Tick-tock, tick-tock*; dead in the room upstairs. *Tick-tock, tick-tock*; you killed her. *Tick-tock, tick-tock*; they'll hang you.

Randall saw by the hands of the clock that it was only half-past two, and his train did not leave for nearly five hours. To help pass the time he got out his cleaning-gear and began to polish his cap-badge and the buttons of his greatcoat. When he had finished the brasses he took off his boots and started on them, working spittle into the toe-caps with a toothbrush-handle, then rubbing them with a soft cloth until they shone like black glass. Absorbed in this task, he forgot the ticking of the clock; but when he had finished the time was still only half-past three, and as he sat idle the clock again began to mock him with its *tick-tock, tick-tock, tick-tock*.

To get away from the clock he went into the front room and stared morosely out of the window at the darkening street. One or two people hurried past, muffled up against the cold, and Randall envied them. They had not his trouble weighing heavily upon them; they were free and happy. And yesterday he had been like them—only yesterday, so short a while ago. He could have wept with self-pity.

Shadows were creeping into the house, and Randall was afraid, his mind haunted by the silent occupant of the cup-board upstairs. He imagined he heard sounds, rustlings, whisperings, muffled laughter. He caught himself listening straining his ears for the sound of a footstep, a chuckle, any-thing. The hair prickled on his scalp, and he shivered in the cold room.

" Oh, God," he whispered, " oh, God, give me back yester-day!"

At five o'clock the air-raid siren gave out its wailing, banshee note, and Randall welcomed it because he knew it would send Mrs Hawkins scuttling to her Anderson shelter, there to remain until the All Clear. So there would be no danger of her seeing him leave without Lily; nor would she think it so strange that Lily did not come to say good-bye. Randall waited ten minutes; then, having bolted the back door, he let himself out at the front and locked that door behind him. Having put the key in his pocket, he shouldered his kitbag and began walking towards the station.

Searchlight beams were slashing the sky, weaving bright, silver patterns upon its sombre background. Somewhere there was the throb of aeroplane engines; in the distance a gun barked, and its shell burst between the questing beams in a brief glitter of light.

Randall walked on, half hoping that a bomb might kill him and end his misery. For the first time he had no fear of an air-raid; a greater fear had thrust out the lesser.

Before he reached the station the All Clear had sounded. His train was only twenty minutes late in starting, and then he was moving smoothly away from the scene of his crime, moving away into the night. He lay back in his corner and tried to sleep.

Now that Randall was away from the house a strange desire began to grow in him, gathering strength as he fell again into the routine of Army life. He wanted to go back and see whether anyone had been to the house. Every minute he expected to feel the heavy hand of a policeman falling on his shoulder. He wondered whether the secret of the cupboard had been discovered. He wanted to go back and make sure that Lily was still where he had left her.

The first night in billets, lying between rough grey blankets on a palliasse stuffed with straw, he dreamed that he was in Yarmouth, walking towards his own house. He dreamed that he unlocked the front door and let himself in, and stood for a moment listening. There was no sound—no sound at all. He knew that he was searching for some one, though who it was he could not remember. He went into the kitchen, but there was no one there—only a tin clock, which leered at him with its grotesque white face, suddenly appearing to cover the entire wall. He hated the clock and feared it, and as he retreated from the kitchen the clock began' to strike in tremendous, vibrating strokes. He thrust his fingers in his ears and ran into the front room; but there was no one there either —only a frigid cold which set his teeth chattering. He glanced out of the window and saw a policeman standing in the road, watching the house with large, glowing eyes. Randall pulled the curtains across the window, but the eyes shone through, and in terror he ran from the room and mounted the stairs.

Now he was in the bedroom and still searching. He looked under the bed, in the drawers of the dressing-table, and in the wardrobe. Finally he opened the cupboard door, and as he did so a skeleton fell out upon him. Then the luminous eyes were in the room and a hand was on his shoulder. He screamed, and woke to find himself drenched from head to foot in sweat.

For a time the shreds of his dream clung to him, and he could feel his heart beating with loud hammer-blows. Then the rhythmic breathing of the other sleepers, interspersed with snores and whistles, brought him back to reality. He was surprised that his screaming had awakened no one, for it had seemed piercingly loud in his dream. But the twelve other men in the room slept on undisturbed, and Randall envied them their untroubled slumber, for he would sleep no more that night. Through the long, dragging hours he lay staring up into the darkness, and at the morning cry of " Wakey, wakey!" crawled from his blankets, haggard and weary, to begin another day.

Randall had been back at Southport for only four days when he was warned for embarkation and found himself in Sergeant Willis's nine-man gun-team. Russia! He welcomed the prospect of that bitter journey, and hoped that he would never return.

CHAPTER FIVE
Outward Bound

FOR seven days the four great mouths of the s.s. *Golden Ray* gaped wide; for seven days into her capacious stomach poured a strange, miscellaneous cargo. Coal formed the base, and above this were piled, in successive layers, barrels of fat, boiler-plates, coils of wire, high-explosive shells, depth-charges, machinery, and chemicals. Then, when nothing else could be wedged into the holds, the hatches were battened down and several tanks were lowered on to the decks and lashed there with wire ropes, effectively blocking the way forward and aft, except for a narrow passage along the rails, made hazardous in the dark by tautly stretched hawsers. Finally, the derrick-booms were lowered into their cradles, and the *Golden Ray* was ready to go.

On the third day Sergeant Willis and his men travelled to Hull to draw their Arctic kit. They went by tram to Grimsby, and thence by ferry across the Humber. Then they were met by an Army lorry which conveyed them to the naval depot from which the kit was to be issued. This outfit consisted of heavy leather sea-boots, a sheepskin jerkin, a hooded waterproof type of duffel-coat, a pair of fleece-lined gloves, a Balaclava helmet, and a fleece-lined bed-cover. With this gear they struggled back to the ship, to arrive late in the evening, cold, hungry, and disgruntled, to find the fire dead and their cabin icy.

On the following morning the captain sent a message to Petty Officer Donker and Sergeant Willis that he desired their presence in his cabin.

"Pep talk," said Donker. "Get one at the start of every trip. Old boy likes to hear 'isself talk."

Captain Pownall was a man who had seen more years at sea than were, in the normal course of events, likely to lie ahead of him. His head, which was entirely bald, bore upon its surface a number of dark, scabby patches, like an unhealthy apple, and these patches were matched by others on his face. His face was thin and long, an area of bulges and hollows like a stretch of country that has been ravaged by battle. His eyebrows were bushy, still retaining some faint traces of their original copper hue, and they overshadowed a pair of almost colourless eyes that in course of time appeared to have sunk deeper and deeper into his head, as though seeking therein what they no longer hoped to find outside. His lips were thin and had about them an unhealthy, bluish tinge. His smile, which was a rarity, had never been known to affect more than one half of his face; it consisted of a twisting up of the left side of the mouth and a slight closing of the left eye. To the sensitive it appeared more a sneer than a smile; but at that it was preferable to his frown.

Captain Pownall had a long, lean, creaking figure which had once been over six feet in height, but which a permanent stoop had reduced to well below that mark. Willis noticed that he wore the ribbon of the D.S.O.

While he talked he moved restlessly about the cabin, fingering a book here, a writing-pad there, as though to be still were foreign to his nature. Occasionally he would pause for a moment and shoot a glance at the petty officer and sergeant in order to thrust home some point of his discourse. He had a harsh, grating voice which seemed to go well with his appearance.

" I don't need to tell you two men," he said, " where we're going; it's common knowledge—too common. Every dockside worker knows, and half the prostitutes in Hull and Grimsby besides, I shouldn't wonder. That's security for you."

He had taken up a book from his desk and was flicking over the pages, more, it seemed, to give his fingers employment than for anything he might find there.

" You," he said, fixing his gaze on Willis, " you, sergeant, are coming with us for the first time. The petty officer has been with us before; he knows what it is like."

Donker nodded vigorously, corroborating the captain's statement, and managing to convey by the extreme vehemence of his nodding and the expression on his face that he did indeed know only too well.

" The petty officer," continued Captain Pownall, gazing all the time at Willis and ignoring the person of whom he was speaking, " knows that a convoy to Russia is just about the most uncomfortable, coldest, and most dangerous voyage we are called upon to make. At this time of the year the weather is likely to be at its vilest. That will be the least of our troubles."

He closed the book with a snap and began to pace backward and forward across the carpet, as though he were on the bridge.

" We shall not be able to travel very far north because of pack-ice; rounding North Cape we shall be within the easiest distance of German aircraft bases in Norway, and we are likely to be heavily attacked. There will be submarines as well, and possibly surface raiders; but I don't expect you gunners to do a lot about them; they're jobs for the escort. Aircraft are different; they're your meat, and I shall expect all your men to be on their toes. Keep a sharp look-out and have the guns ready for instant action. Is that understood? "

He had come to a halt again in the middle of the cabin, and was staring at the two men from under his shaggy eyebrows. Willis and Donker answered " Yessir " in unison.

" Very well. That is all I wished to say."

As he and the petty officer left the cabin Willis noticed that Captain Pownall was already seated at his desk and scribbling furiously on a writing-pad. Willis closed the door silently.

" Usual stuff," said Petty Officer Donker. " He thinks 'is little pow-wow keeps us up to the mark. Well, it pleases 'im, and it don't do no harm."

" Know how he got his D.S.O.? " asked Willis.

" That? " said Donker. " Why, yes. It was some time back, off the West Indies. His ship got sunk by a U-boat. They was in the lifeboat forty days—nearly died of thirst. The Old

Man it was who kept 'em going. He's better than he looks, you know."

" You seem to know all about it."

Petty Officer Donker fingered the lump on his neck caressingly. " I ought to," he said. " I was there."

Before going back aft Sergeant Willis took it into his head to climb up to that highest part of the superstructure, known as ' Monkey Island.' From this vantage-point he had a view of the entire ship's armament—a bird's-eye view. Away forward, almost in the bows, was the twelve-pounder. Willis had a poor opinion of the effectiveness of that weapon—at least against aircraft. Its rate of fire was too low, and there was no tracer by which to observe the path of the shells. It was an old-fashioned gun, like the four-inch on the stern. Yet he supposed Donker loved it; it was strange how these old shellbacks clung to the weapons of their salad days, having for them the same affection they had for ancient ships, long past their prime. In a way it was touching.

Willis could see the paravanes lying one on either side of number one hatch, looking like elongated eggs with fins attached to their pointed ends. They were for protection against mines, but he had seldom seen them used. Then, on either side of the bridge, were Oerlikon guns, twenty-millimetre automatics. Willis approved of them; next to the Bofors they were, in his opinion, the best anti-aircraft guns carried by merchant ships. It was strange, he mused, that those two peerless light-anti-aircraft weapons should both have been designed in neutral countries—the Bofors in Sweden, the Oerlikon in Switzerland. He supposed the Swedes and Swiss had the time for such intricate work.

On either side of the boat-deck were racks of explosive rockets—racks known irreverently as pig-troughs. And about as much use, thought Willis. A lot of noise and damn-all to show for it. Well, they were Donker's worry, and he believed that Donker had put the apprentices in charge of them. Willis hoped those youthful heroes would not blow themselves up. Rockets were inclined to be dangerous things—for their users.

Aft were two more Oerlikons, then the Bofors and the four-inch. Lashed to the poop-deck near the taffrail were eight smoke-floats.

" Regular little man-o'-war," muttered Willis, as he made his way aft.

The several members of Willis's detachment prepared for the voyage each in his own manner. Vernon went to Grimsby and bought himself a number of books by Russian authors: Dostoevski's *The Brothers Karamazov*, Chekhov's plays and stories, Tolstoy's *War and Peace*, and Turgenev's *Fathers and Sons*. He had for a long time been intending to study Russian literature, and the present seemed a singularly appropriate time to begin. In addition he picked up a copy of Housman's *A Shropshire Lad* and an anthology of English verse. Thus equipped, with his unspillable ink-bottle replenished and an exercise-book in which to write, he felt that any spare time there might be on the voyage should not be difficult to pass away.

Bombardier Padgett's choice of literature bore little resemblance to that of Gunner Vernon. Padgett had been a keen amateur weight-lifter before the War, and his torso proclaimed the fact. When Padgett was stripped down the muscles could be seen rippling all over his body as he tensed and relaxed them. He was a walking advertisement for physical culture, and physical culture was his supreme interest in life. To Padgett the body was all-important, a living sculpture to be carved out of the basic material given to every normal man. In his view neglect of the body was a crime for which there was no excuse. Muscles, tendons, sinews, chest measurements—these were the themes of Padgett's conversation; these were the objects of his labour.

Padgett bought two books to see him through the voyage. One was called *Building the Body Beautiful*, with 150 full-page photographs and ten tables of exercises; the other was *Strength through Diet*. With these two volumes he expected to spend many an interesting and instructive hour.

Gunner Payne bought a pile of Wild West magazines. For

him the stage-coach still rolled across the Texan prairies;
six-guns barked out their messages of death; and Zane Grey
was the greatest writer that ever lived. In some ways Payne
had never grown up.

None of the others bought any books; there was a small
library on the ship supplied by the Missions to Seamen, and
this they relied on for any reading matter they might desire.
Cowdrey had brought a game called Monopoly back with him
when he came off leave, and while the ship lay in port he
often collected enough gunners to play a round. It made a
change from nap.

Miller never did any reading. He had once tried to read
a book by Karl Marx called *Das Kapital*, because the comrades were all supposed to be familiar with it; but he had not
made much headway, and in the end he had given it up. He
had sometimes read the *Daily Worker*; but that had been
before he joined the Army. Now he read nothing.

Willis did not read much either. His life had always been
one of action, and he had never had any time for that faint
mirror of reality that lay in a printed page. Army manuals,
handbooks of gunnery—these were the only books he
respected or understood—books that served a purpose—
books of fact, not of erotic nonsense or synthetic adventure.
Life was real to Sergeant Willis, and he had never felt the
need for escape into a fictional world of make-believe.

Randall read only the newspapers, skimming fearfully
through them, and, having failed to find that which he feared,
threw them aside and waited for another day to pass.

So they all waited as the s.s. *Golden Ray* sank lower under
her cargo, until, on the ninth day after their arrival, the ties
of Immingham were cast off, and they made once more for
the open sea to join a north-bound convoy. So north they
went, creeping along the coast past Flamborough Head, past
the mouth of the Tyne, past the Firth of Forth; still northward past Peterhead and Fraserburgh, round John o' Groats
and through the Pentland Firth; sometimes in daylight, sometimes in darkness, but moving on, moving on without pause;

westward through the Pentland Firth, westward to Cape Wrath; then southward down the Minch, with the jagged coast of Sutherland and Ross and Cromarty to port, until they came to a narrow inlet leading to a stretch of hill-surrounded water, and here they sought shelter. The antisubmarine boom opened to let them pass; they steamed in past the ships which operated the net and dropped anchor in Loch Ewe. The net closed behind them, and they lay at the foot of the snow-bound hills and waited.

And other ships nosed their way into the loch, other ships low in the water with cargo; and these too dropped their anchors and waited under the white, silent hills, while the gulls hovered and swooped and quarrelled, filling the air with the sound of their raucous voices.

And Petty Officer Donker, leaning over the taffrail, noticed with satisfaction that there were three tankers among the ships; for he knew from experience that tankers were favoured targets for U-boats. And Donker reasoned that for every torpedo aimed at a tanker there would be one less for the *Golden Ray*. Therefore he smiled and rubbed the knob on his neck for pleasure.

"Tankers," said Petty Officer Donker, "are what I like to steer clear of. Hell-ships," said Petty Officer Donker; "hell-ships!"

But Gunner Payne, who was also leaning over the taffrail, disagreed. In his opinion tankers had their good points, and he had sailed in two, so ought to know.

"They feed well," said Payne. "They feed damn well. None of the sort of muck we get on this tub. They have cooks in tankers—real cooks—and good quarters."

Petty Officer Donker cleared his throat and spat. His spittle dropped into the placid water of the loch and sent ripples circling away from it, sinking gradually once more to their former level.

"They can keep their food and their quarters," he said. "They ain't safe. You don't tell me you like sleeping on ten thousand tons of high octane ready to go up like a volcano."

" Well," said Payne, " it's a bit nerve-racking if you think about it. No smoking on deck and no hobnailed boots. Best thing is not to think about it."

" Easier said than done."

" Oh, I don't know. You get used to anything."

Donker, still staring at the vessels in the anchorage, drew up more information from the well of his experience.

" There's a Blue Funnel boat; they've lost a deal of ships, one way and another. Used to be in the Java and Sumatra trade, a lot of 'em. Tea! Boxes and boxes of it. My word! That one on the far side is a Harrison—Harrison, T. and J.; wonder which one she is; might be the *Adviser* or the *Settler* —that type. Ha! See that one over there; that's one of the Strick line; bit off their old run, this; Persian Gulf's more their home. One of them tankers is a Norwegian. Wonder what she's carrying to Russia."

A motor-launch, heading for the *Golden Ray* and flying the Blue Ensign, put a stop to Donker's lecture.

" More trouble," he grumbled. " More bastard shore staff."

He pushed himself off the rail and went to see that all hands were occupied.

While the ship was in Loch Ewe Sergeant Willis was not idle, and he did not allow his men to be idle either. It was gun-drill, gun-drill, gun-drill, until each man fitted into the pattern of the team as the portions of a jig-saw puzzle fit into the whole. Willis's voice, trained on the barrack square, was loud and penetrating. It penetrated to the ears of Captain Pownall; and more than once that taciturn man paused in his affairs to glance aft and watch the gunners leaping to their posts. And at these times the master would nod his head in satisfaction, supposing that his brief lecture had not been in vain.

The days passed. Snow, scudding across the loch, was followed by clear skies, and they in turn were followed by sleet and boisterous winds, which lashed the surface of the water into miniature waves that ran foaming up to beat futilely against the edges of the land. The s.s. *Golden Ray* pulled at her anchor, like a dog unwillingly chained to its kennel, as though impatient to be gone. But the gunners, staring up at the bleak hills, hoped for another night at anchor with peaceful sleep and no watches.

But after four days the boom opened, and one after another the ships filed out of the loch, turned to starboard, and headed north. The dark journey had begun.

It was three o'clock in the afternoon, and already the light was failing. A strong beam wind brought scuds of rain, and the sea heaved. The s.s. *Golden Ray* swung like a pendulum, biting her way through the grey sea and casting up founts of spray. Ahead of her went the Blue Funnel steamer; astern lay one of the tankers; and this was the start of the journey.

Sergeant Willis was on watch with Randall and Andrews. Andrews was feeling sick. He knew that in a few days he would be all right again; he was always sick at the start of a voyage if the sea was at all rough, but the sickness never lasted many days. But the knowledge that his sickness would leave him to-morrow or the next day was little consolation. All he could think about now was that he was sick; his head was heavy; his eyes ached, and hot liquid kept rising in his throat; swallow as he might, it rose again. He longed for the watch to end, so that he could crawl into his bunk and sleep; but the watch had only just begun.

Randall was staring at the coast of Scotland, a vague outline on the starboard beam. He was glad that they were under way; he felt that he had severed his last link with home and that he would never return. Somewhere in those far northern waters he would find forgetfulness and oblivion. Let the law search for him how it might, it would never find him.

Sergeant Willis was thinking: Two weeks! Two weeks, and we should be there—either there or meat for fishes. If only we knew what was waiting for us. But perhaps it's best not to know. Yes, certainly, best not.

Suddenly the telephone-bell rang. Willis spoke into the mouthpiece. " Bofors gun-position here."

A metallic voice sounded in his ear. " Bridge here. Just testing. Just testing. O.K.? "

" O.K."

Willis put the telephone back in its waterproof box and began pacing up and down a ten-foot stretch of gun-platform, leaning against the roll of the ship. Fourteen days, he thought. Where shall we be in fourteen days?

A Whitley bomber of Coastal Command was flying round the convoy, keeping watch upon the water. Now and then it winked at the ships in a series of flashes, long and short, short and long. And from the bridge of the commodore's ship a signal rating, steadying himself on wide-parted legs, flashed back an answer. It was all so usual; it was just the way every convoy began its journey; and nobody thought what a miracle of planning and organization it all was. But twenty merchant ships in four columns lay upon the heaving bosom of the sea, keeping the pattern of their movement, like chessmen lying on a board, while round them the steel ring of corvettes and destroyers kept watch and ward.

At dusk the Whitley left them, and through the night they pushed on, northward, ever north, still keeping their positions on the chessboard, dark shapes showing no light from blacked-out ports, no glimmer from wheel-house or galley or cabin, dark shapes moving upon a dark and restless sea. The watches changed and changed again; and dawn came, and with the dawn a Lockheed Hudson, sweeping up from the land and winking its greeting. And the convoy winked back in answer and moved on, moved on.

On the third day the carpenter slipped on the deck-ice and sprained his ankle. It was not the first mishap, for Vernon had already made a sad mess of his left thumb. He had been taking cleaning-rags from one of the lockers, an iron locker with a lid weighing a quarter of a hundredweight. Vernon had omitted to fasten the lid back, and a sudden roll of the ship upset its equilibrium. Twenty-eight pounds of iron caught his shoulder a glancing blow and fell upon his thumb.

After the first fierce shock of pain Vernon felt surprisingly little beyond a dull ache, but, looking down at his thumb, he saw that the end had been flattened and mangled. It seemed unreal, something that did not belong to him; but he felt sick and weak and was glad to sit down on the locker until he should recover.

Miller and Warby looked at the thumb, as men may inspect a strange specimen. Miller shook his head.

" Now you've done it," he remarked. " Proper mess you've made of that. Does it 'urt? "

" It does," said Vernon. " Try it yourself some time."

The blood was dripping from the end of the thumb and making red splashes on the deck. Vernon took a handkerchief from the pocket of his coat and wrapped it round the wound. The handkerchief was black with oil, but soon the red was showing through.

" Good thing I had my anti-tetanus injection the other week," he said.

" You'd better go along to the steward with that," said Warby. " Are you feeling all right? Want me to come with you? "

" I'm all right," said Vernon. " But I think I had better see the steward."

His legs felt weak as he climbed over the side of the gun-platform, and it was difficult steadying himself with one hand; but he would not admit his weakness to the two watching him.

" I'll be all right," he said. And he thought: I've got to be. This is only the start.

The steward was ' doctor ' on board the *Golden Ray*. Often it had occurred to Vernon during his time at sea in cargo vessels that it would go hard if one were seriously ill or injured far from land with only an amateur to doctor one. Supposing one had acute appendicitis? What then? That, like many other things, was better not thought about.

The steward of the *Golden Ray* reminded Vernon of Harold Lloyd; he wore the same type of black-rimmed spectacles, and he had the same gullible, inoffensive look. In the case of the steward, whose name was Carter, looks were misleading.

Carter looked at Vernon's thumb and did not like it. " How did you do this? " he asked.

" Shell-locker. Lid fell on it."

" Nasty, very nasty. Hurt much? "

" Enough."

The steward sat Vernon in a chair and went away for a bowl of hot water. The steward's cabin was comfortable; it compared very favourably with the gunners' quarters. Vernon noticed that there were sheets on the bed and coloured curtains over the port-hole. There was a desk and one or two wooden lockers and three chairs. In one corner was a small bookcase. One of the books was *Shakespeare's Sonnets*. That surprised Vernon; but he had knocked about the world enough to know that people were always surprising. A man's mind was his own, something secret, impenetrable. Sometimes a tiny corner of it might be revealed, and then it was often the unexpected.

Vernon began to feel sick again, and had difficulty in preventing the revolution of the cabin. He closed his eyes.

" All right," said the steward. " Dip your thumb in this; it's antiseptic."

Vernon dipped his thumb in the bowl, and pain shot up from the tip like a tongue of flame. The water turned red.

" This'll be awkward for you on the gun," said Carter.

Vernon knew it would. Hell! he thought. Why did this have to happen? Hell!

The pain ebbed. The steward was drying the thumb on a piece of gauze; then, not unskilfully, he bandaged it. He seemed pleased with his work, looking down at it with a halfsmile on his face, as though congratulating himself.

" Thanks," said Vernon. " Thank you."

The steward went to a locker and took down a bottle of rum and a glass. He poured a liberal tot and handed it to Vernon.

" Here! Drink this. It'll make you feel better."

Sergeant Willis was annoyed. " Of all the bloody silly things to do! I suppose now you expect to be excused duty. Mucks everything up."

Willis's tone nettled Vernon. " I don't expect anything of the sort. I'm capable of doing watches, and I can still lay the gun."

Willis felt that he had been unjust. After all, a man did not smash up his thumb on purpose, and Vernon must be feeling a bit sick. Still, it did make things awkward; there were a lot of jobs a man with a smashed thumb could not do. But worse things could have happened—and probably would. When he spoke again his tone was less acid.

" All right; we'll see about that. But there's no need for you to go on watch to-night; two men will be enough. Get some sleep into you; you'll need it. For that matter, we all shall."

When the carpenter slipped on the ice Vernon had got used to having a bandaged thumb. It would not go into his glove. But Cowdrey slit the thumb of the glove and enlarged it with a strip of blanket. It was a neat job of work, and Vernon was grateful. Cowdrey thought nothing of it; he would have done the same for anyone; but the simple act of kindness warmed Vernon's heart. It was strange how such conditions, cramped, uncomfortable, dangerous, often brought out qualities of decency and kindliness in men, so that they pulled together for the good of all. Here was true comradeship growing from the common need, the common suffering.

On the third day the carpenter slipped on the deck-ice and sprained his ankle; and five minutes later an American freighter in one of the outer columns began firing into the sea with all guns that could be brought to bear.

Bombardier Padgett, who was on watch on the Bofors, peered through his binoculars, but could discern nothing in the water which might have caused this burst of fire, and was mystified. For two minutes the firing continued, then ceased as abruptly as it had begun.

" So what? " said Padgett.

Others, perhaps, were asking the same question, for a destroyer, bow-wave creaming back from its razor stem, rushed to the scene and dropped two depth-charges. Then she raced to the head of the column and made a report to the commodore through her loud-hailer. The words floated across and could be heard clearly by the gun-crews of the *Golden Ray*. There was a satirical quality about them which brought grim smiles to many faces.

" The *Silas P. Manderson* reports having bumped a U-boat and fired upon it. I can detect nothing, but have dropped two depth-charges for purposes of morale-boosting. It is my belief that imagination played a major part in this epic engagement."

The loud-hailer switched off with a click, the propellers of the destroyer churned the sea to foam, and she swept away in a wide curve to take up her position again in the defensive ring.

"Just like the Navy," Padgett observed. "Disbelieving shower. Lot of ruddy Thomases."

" If you believed everything the Yanks told you you'd have the jitters proper," said Cowdrey. " Trigger-happy! That's what they are."

"Pays to be on this job," said Payne. "Shoot first and ask questions after; that's the best motto."

" And run out of ammo half-way to Russia. Lot of sense in that!"

" All the same, you can't be too careful."

On the third day the carpenter slipped on the deck-ice, and his swearing could be heard from poop to bridge.

CHAPTER SIX

Arctic Convoy

WHEN daylight came on the fourth day there was, for the first time, no escorting aircraft. It made the men in the ships feel lonely not to see the familiar shape of the Catalina flying-boat that had been with them on the previous day. It was as though that last link with home had been cut, and they were alone on the dark and dreary Arctic Ocean. The cold was hardening now, closing on them with steely fingers, feeling for the blood in their veins; it took the wind for an ally and came shrieking down from the North Pole, from the regions of eternal ice. Snow came with it too, and the ships became pale ghosts, moving on under the iron dome of the sky into a world of death and darkness, moving on towards the rim of the ice.

Daylight came late, a weak shadow of its southern self, and stayed only an hour or two. The sun, barely peeping above the grey horizon, rolled for a brief while upon the lip of the ocean and then sank to rest. It had no power to warm the men on watch, and they could observe it with undazzled eyes, observe it appear and disappear, like a new penny thrust up through the slot of a money-box, only to be withdrawn again.

At night the aurora borealis flickered across the sky, its streamers twisting like cold flames, changing colour, growing and fading, casting an eerie glow over the vessels of the convoy and holding all who watched them spellbound by their wonder. It was as though a great luminous hand had been thrust up over the northern horizon, its fingers groping across the heavens; at any moment it seemed those fingers might fall upon the convoy and force it down into the bottomless depths of the sea.

Then came the moon, hanging like a child's plaything amid the drifting stars, and washing the ships with silver.

Vernon, for the first time in his life, was wearing long woollen underpants; the gunners called them John L. Sullivans. He was glad to wear them, glad to wear a thick vest, a flannel shirt, two pullovers, battle-blouse, lambswool jerkin, Army greatcoat, and duffel-coat; glad to wear two woollen Balaclava helmets under the hood of his coat, two pairs of trousers, and thick sea-boot stockings and leather sea-boots. Even so, dressed like a walking clothes-store, even so, the wind came through; even so, the cold crept up from the feet, up and up as the dead hours of the night watches dragged slowly past.

And still it grew colder.

On the fifth day the enemy found them. A Dornier 24 flying-boat came up over the southern horizon and, keeping just beyond gunfire range, proceeded to circle the convoy. Round and round, hour after hour, it flew; and the gunners, standing at action stations, watched it with angry eyes and cursed their impotence.

" If only we had a carrier!" moaned Padgett. "Even a Woolworth would do. If only we had a carrier!"

But there was no aircraft carrier with the convoy, not even one of those converted merchant ships known irreverently as ' Woolworths.' There was nothing—nothing but the outranged guns—and they were powerless to touch the German plane, flying so leisurely in wide circles and signalling to its submarine allies, signalling all the time.

When night fell they lost the Dornier, and in the night they altered course, trying to throw their pursuers off the scent. But when day came the Dornier found them again, and an hour later it was joined by six friends, Heinkel torpedo bombers. Then the alarm was really on; then the ships really awoke; then the air suddenly became full of glowing tracer and bursting steel, and the crackle, bark, and boom of the guns flung noise towards the sky as though to burst open that great steel door and drive on to the freedom of eternity.

Vernon sat on one side of the Bofors gun, watching through his sight a Heinkel coming in low across the line of ships.

Andrews was in the other seat, and Miller was on the platform, loading. Vernon could see the Heinkel crawling along the wire of his gun-sight, and he waited for Sergeant Willis to give the order to fire. It was a sitter: it was not doing more than a hundred knots. Surely it was in range? Why did not Willis give the order? What was he waiting for? Was he waiting to see the colour of the pilot's eyes? Now, now, now!

" Fire!" yelled Willis in Vernon's ear.

Vernon pressed his foot on the firing-pedal, and the gun began to rock on its pedestal, flinging out shells at the rate of two a second. It was a harsh, staccato song that the gun sang, but it was sweet music to the men on the platform.

Vernon could see the tracers curving away towards the Heinkel, and he could see that they were missing; Andrews was giving too much aim-off; you did not want so much with a plane coming in at that angle.

"Left, you idiot! Left!" he yelled; but he knew that he was wasting his breath, for the voice of the gun beat his voice aside, and no one heard him. But Andrews was bringing the gun over, bringing it on to the correct line; the tracers were creeping nearer to their target.

Now, thought Vernon, now we've got the bastard.

And then the gun jammed, and Willis was swearing at Miller. " You bloody, misbegotten fool! Don't you know how to load yet? "

Miller was struggling to free the shells in the auto-loader, but Willis thrust him aside.

" Gimme the unloading mask," he yelled. " You there, Payne! Don't stand gaping; gimme that mask. Hell! You'd think there was all day!"

But the action was over. Two Heinkels were in the sea, and the others were away, heading for base. And one ship lay crippled on the water, with a black column of smoke joining it to the grey ceiling of cloud.

The gunners cleaned the barrel, gathered up the empty shell-cases, and the convoy steamed on, leaving one ship to sink slowly into the oblivion of the Arctic Ocean. It was only a beginning.

That night they began to hear depth-charges. It sounded as though some one were beating on the plates of the ship with a hammer, beating in a rapid series of strokes. The gunners who were below looked at one another; all knew the meaning of those swift hammer-blows.

"Tin fish now," said Payne. "Pleasant outlook. How many more days to Murmansk?"

"Five or six probably," said Petty Officer Donker, rubbing the knob on his neck.

"God! Five or six days of this!"

"You get used to anything," said Donker, grinning slyly as more depth-charges drummed against the plates. "Even that."

Vernon found it impossible to sleep. He lay on his bunk fully clothed even down to his sea-boots, using his kapok life-jacket as a pillow. He hoped he did not show what a sickening fear there was in him, and he wondered whether the others were as afraid as he. Old Donker, for instance, with his weather-beaten face and knobbly hands—was he afraid? And Payne, the fat, balloon-like Payne—was he thinking, as Vernon was, of the icy sea beneath their feet? What chance was there of survival in that ? And suppose a torpedo struck just where this cabin was! It had been painful enough having the end of his thumb crushed; what would it be like to have one's belly ripped open, one's limbs torn to ragged tatters of flesh? The thought made him feel sick; this was what it was to be cursed with a vivid imagination. In such a situation complete lack of imagination was the greatest gift of all.

He looked from one to another of his fellow-gunners: Miller, the small, ugly Londoner, still sulking over the loading incident; Randall with his black hair and dark eyes that seemed always to be gazing inward at his own soul; Andrews, a boy not fully able to conceal his fear; Cowdrey, the short, bald, cheerful Cowdrey, still smiling; Padgett, who did his

daily quota of press-ups and could lift a Bofors barrel with
one hand; Willis with his ram-rod back and grim mouth; and
Warby, slow, willing, gentle Warby, who should have been
ploughing the land, and not the sea.

Vernon smiled as the last sentence formed in his brain;
that was from one of Housman's *Last Poems*. Vernon had
tried to be a poet, never with any real success. His poetry
was like the rest of his life, mediocre. What was it about
him, he wondered, what fundamental weakness had always
held him back, robbing him of the success he only attained
in dreams? Perhaps it was some lack of mental courage, or
perhaps mental laziness. He could build castles in the air, but
never one with solid bricks.

Lying on his bunk, gazing up at the dirty iron ceiling above
him, listening to the drumming of the depth-charges and the
occasional quiet slap of water against the side of the ship,
he let his mind drift back over his life, finding in it always,
not complete failure, but that partial failure which is so much
harder to bear.

He had started life with certain advantages in what Miller
would have called the " privileged class." His father had been
a solicitor in a small country town, not wealthy, but well
enough off in the world's goods to be able to send his son to
a minor public school and thence to Cambridge. It was at
Cambridge that he had conceived the ambition to be a poet,
and the acceptance of one or two verses by obscure, ephemeral
magazines which paid nothing for contributions and appeared
like daffodils in the spring, only to die with an equal haste,
fanned the flame of his ambition. The act was to be a dis-
service, for, scribbling his verses, he neglected his studies,
and after three years of university life he came down from
Cambridge without a degree and with the unwelcome
knowledge that to suppose he could ever hope to become a
poet of note was but to deceive himself.

It was at about this time that his father died—he had been
a widower for some years—leaving behind him only a sad
hash of debts and unwise investments. When this business

had been cleared up Vernon found himself practically penniless and without a job.

For four years he drifted from one underpaid teaching post to another; he seemed to be unable to think beyond the teaching profession, and though he cared little for such work, the long holidays appealed to his indolent nature. When the War started he was at a preparatory school not far from London run by a certain Mr Clement Tennyson, M.A. The War appeared to Vernon as a heaven-sent opportunity to escape; he volunteered at once, and said good-bye to Mr Tennyson and the pupils without regret. Perhaps in the Army he would at last find his right vocation, quickly gaining promotion, medals, and glory on some field of battle.

For eighteen months he lived in a wooden hut with a varying number of other men, manning an anti-aircraft gun in a locality which the enemy, for reasons best known to himself, studiously avoided. Vernon applied in turn for a transfer to the Commandos, the R.A.F., and the Navy, all without success. He put in for a commission, and was turned down on the grounds that he was not " officer type." He was bored, frustrated, and mentally stagnant. The granting of his application for a transfer to the newly formed Maritime Regiment came as a relief from torment.

Vernon's eyes were sore from the effect of the cold wind; his face burned, and when he passed his tongue over his lips he could taste the salt caked on them. He turned on his side and tried to sleep, but his cheek came into contact with the little red electric lamp clipped to his life-jacket. He swore softly.

In the night one of the tankers was torpedoed. It happened in Padgett's watch. The tanker was level with the *Golden Ray* in the next column to port. Padgett heard the explosion of the torpedo first, then another explosion as the petrol ignited, and at the same time a burst of flame soared up towards the sky.

" Jesus Christ! " cried Payne. " Jesus Christ! She's caught a packet."

There was a red glow lying on the water, and the red spout of flame mounting into the air took with it a black cloud of thick and filthy smoke. From the *Golden Ray* the gunners could hear the dull roaring of the flames, and they could see on the deck of the tanker tiny black figures of men running. There was something unreal about those figures; they were so small, so far away; one could hardly identify them with men whose flesh could feel the blistering touch of that furnace raging between the bridge and the poop. In a way they were like ants whose colony has been disturbed, running away from the scene of destruction. Across the forward cat-walk they scampered to cluster in the bows, crushed tightly against the rails. But the fire followed them, and one by one they dropped into the sea, trying always to avoid the flame. And even into the sea the fire went after them; it would not let them escape, but spread out over the surface of the water, groping for them with burning fingers. And so they died, roasted in an ice-cold sea.

But the tanker burned on, and the ships astern of her altered course and passed her by, passed her by and left her burning. And as they passed by, some on one side, some on the other, the red glow of her funeral-pyre fell upon those other ships, and it seemed that the life-blood of the tanker had splashed them all. So they pressed on, all of them driving onward into the night; but now there were only eighteen ships where there had been an even score.

" Oh, God," muttered Payne, " who's next on the list? "

On the seventh day it snowed—fine, hard snow that came beating up on the wings of the wind like a million tiny darts, pricking at the exposed flesh, and finding its way under scarves and Balaclavas, finding its way to necks and arms and backs, bringing everywhere an added chill and an added discomfort to those on watch. It found its way also into the mechanism of the guns and the racks of ammunition lying ready for the next emergency.

" One thing," remarked Andrews, " Jerry'll never find us in this lot."

But on the eighth day the weather cleared, and the enemy picked them up again. And this time he came with twenty aircraft, and they were Junkers 88's, which dive-bombed the ships and reduced the numbers of the merchantmen to sixteen. And in the night the submarines took up the attack and claimed another victim.

In the gunners' cabin the iron stove glowed red, and the glow extended half-way up the pipe. Yet the deadlight clamped over the port-hole six feet away was caked with ice an inch thick. Some of the gunners were sitting round the stove, their feet thrust out towards the warmth. They sat on boxes, for there were no chairs in the cabin and only long wooden forms in the mess; but sitting there or lying on hard bunks was paradise compared with being on watch.

" How many more days? " asked Andrews. His eyes were bloodshot from lack of sleep, his face haggard, dirty, and unshaven. He had not shaved for six days; for three days he had not washed. Nor had any of them; in the wash-place the temperature was away below freezing-point; soap froze to the wash-bowls; flannels became stiff as boards; ice formed on the water; and always, always the alarm-bells would start to ring. At any moment, day or night, they had to be ready to rush on deck, into the gale, into the blizzard, into the blown, freezing spray. They were weary as they had never been in all their lives, and they could sleep only in brief, nightmare snatches, waking with a start and a cry of " What was that? Did you hear that? " Sometimes they wondered how much a man can endure.

" How many more days? " asked Andrews. " Two? Three? "

" Two," said Payne. " Two at the most."

" How do you know? "

" I have information," said Payne. " Good authority."

" The galley," said Padgett derisively.

The strain of the last few days had had its effect even on

Payne; his bulk seemed to have shrunk, like a balloon that
has been half deflated. Yet his cheeks were puffed up more
than ever, swelling up like ramparts in front of his eyes. He
seemed too tired even to challenge the bombardier's gibe. He
swayed, pulled himself up with a jerk, yawned, and stood up.

"Think I'll turn in for a spell," he said. "Haven't been
any depth-charges for half an hour. Perhaps things are
quietening down."

He had one leg over the edge of his bunk when the alarm-
bells began to ring, loudly, imperiously, insistently.

"Oh, Lord!" he groaned. "What, again?"

Pulling on his Balaclavas and his duffel-coat as he went, he
joined the mad rush to the iron ladder that led to the deck.

Nine days had passed since the convoy had left Loch Ewe;
nine days of steadily increasing cold, of blizzard and biting
wind; days with the enemy at their heels and below and
around them the icy, pitiless sea; days of weariness and fear
and impotent anger. They had seen ships sunk, ships fiercely
burning, ships broken in two; they had seen men struggling
in the grip of the Arctic Ocean; they had seen men dragged
out of that ocean, dead men, slain by the cold in a few short
minutes. The smell of burnt cordite was perpetually in their
nostrils; they could taste its acrid flavour in their food and
in their drink; it was with them always.

Nine days had passed, and the sea was covered with ice—
soft, mushy ice which lay upon the surface of the water in
broken irregular shapes, like the tops of immensely overgrown
mushrooms. There was no wind, and it was as though a
strange hush had fallen on the world; the shrieking had died
away; the churning of water was muffled by the covering of
ice, and even the thump of the ship's engines seemed to have
become less in sympathy. The sky was covered with a vast
sheet of thick, grey cloud joining the sea all round the
horizon; there was no sun; there were no birds; only a great,
uncanny silence. It was a dead world, and the ships, stretching
in long lines across the ice, might have been dead also, for in

them was no apparent movement. Only an occasional plume of smoke drifting back from a grey funnel showed that their hearts still beat.

Vernon, stamping his feet in the Bofors gun-enclosure, heard the crunch of cinders under his leather soles, and the noise was like sacrilege. Willis had ordered the cinders to be brought up from the cabin stove and scattered round the gun so that the gunners should be able to obtain a foothold on the frozen iron; without that aid they would have slipped helplessly. Vernon stamped his feet and beat his right hand against his leg, trying to whip up some degree of circulation. In his left thumb there was no feeling; his left thumb, since he had crushed it, always succumbed first to the cold.

In the middle of the convoy he could see one of the corvettes refuelling from the auxiliary tanker. A long, flexible pipe lying over the stern of the tanker joined the two ships together, and out of the one flowed the oil that was essential to the animation of the other. He wondered what would happen if the tanker were to be sunk; would the escorts run out of fuel and become helpless? He supposed there must be some alternative. Charlie Blenkinship would know. Funny that Charlie should have come into his mind; but that was how it was; when you had nothing to do but think, one thing drifted into the brain and then another; there was no controlling them.

Charlie Blenkinship! How different from Harry Vernon! And yet they had been good pals at school and at Cambridge. The difference was that Charlie wooed success and won it; there was no hint of failure in Charlie's life, no taking the second best. You could not imagine Charlie as a gunner in the *Golden Ray*, grimed with soot, unshaven, smelling of cordite. Yet between himself in the *Golden Ray* and Charlie Blenkinship there was still a link, tenuous though it might be; for Charlie was now an officer in the Navy, though he had never been at sea, nor was ever likely to be. Nevertheless he knew where every convoy was, for he saw them moving on a great chart of the world. But to him they were simply numbered dots; and this convoy pushing its silent way through the ice, this convoy in which Harry Vernon was no more than an insignificant unit of man-power, would in his mind be K 12 or X 40, or whatever number it was. He would know if a ship were sunk; he might regret the fact; but it would not mean the same to him as it did to Vernon, who saw the column of black smoke billowing from the wreck, who saw the hull sinking lower and lower, and who felt the dull sickness of fear in his own stomach.

Vernon stamped his feet and forgot Charlie as easily as he had remembered him. He had drawn his Balaclava up over his nose, and, as always, his breath, passing through the wool, had frozen on the outside to form tiny icicles. Inside, the Balaclava was wet and clammy against his face.

Away to starboard the crew of a corvette were busy with picks and axes and shovels trying to clear the caked ice that was weighing down her bows. Vernon could see them clearly through the binoculars, but he could hear no sound of their labours, and this fact added to the eeriness of the whole unnatural scene. He looked down at the ice, and it seemed ridiculous to suppose that one could not walk across its surface from one ship to another; it was like a vast expanse of crazy paving. But, peering forward, he could see where the bows of the *Golden Ray* pushed the ice aside, and he knew that its appearance of solidity was no more than a snare, that beneath it was the Barents Sea, stretching downward in fathom after fathom of bitterly cold water. He began beating his hand again, and somewhere, beneath many layers of clothing, felt a tingle of irritation in the skin of his chest.

Half-way through the watch Ben Cowdrey appeared with three enamel mugs full of hot cocoa—that is, mugs as full and as hot as could be expected after the long and hazardous journey from the mess-room.

"Quiet, ain't it?" said Ben, hanging on to the gun-enclosure with one hand and passing across the mugs with the other, the index finger of which was curled through their handles. "No visitors to-day."

"Touch wood!" said Warby hastily. "You go an' talk like that, an' they'll be here in swarms."

"No, not to-day," grinned Ben. "They're giving us a rest." He glanced round the convoy. "Thinning out a bit. Oh, well! Soon be there now."

"You hope," said Warby.

Ben grinned and went below.

Vernon often wondered just what ship's cocoa was made of; it was not like any he had ever tasted in civilian life. It was thick and dark, and when you had mixed it there was always a kind of oily surface on the liquid. All the same, it was good stuff to drink when you were half frozen; it warmed you.

Suddenly the silence of the convoy was broken. The commodore's ship gave one long blast on its siren, and in turn each of the other ships followed suit. The hoarse, blaring sounds seemed to be shouting defiance at the ice.

"One to starboard, two to port," muttered Vernon. "Here we go again."

It was the signal to alter course, a manœuvre the apparent simplicity of which masked the need for accurate judgment. The leading ship in each column was the first to change direction, swinging over to starboard until it was moving away at an angle from those which followed it. The next ship continued on its old course until it came to the exact spot where the leading ship had turned; then it too swung away to starboard, following in the wake of the first. So each ship in turn altered its course, until, when all had done so, the convoy was lying spaced out just as before, but now it was moving on a new course.

So they moved on; so they moved on under a leaden sky. And the brief day faded into the long Arctic night, and there were no stars; only a small flame of hope that flickered stubbornly, refusing to die.

CHAPTER SEVEN

Promised Land

WHEN the *Golden Ray* sailed up the Kola inlet and the iron hills closed in upon her on either side Miller felt that he was nearing home. He felt that at last he was to touch the jewel that had attracted him for so many years, that had, indeed, constituted the sole object and purpose of his existence.

Miller should never have been born; that was an indisputable fact. His mother was a prostitute, and Miller was the result of a regrettable failure of technique. He was unwanted, neglected, ill-treated, ill-clothed, and underfed. His playground was the back-street of a filthy slum, and he grew up with a hatred of that society which, in his opinion, was responsible for all his sufferings. Occasionally he would travel up to the West End for the sole purpose of feeding his hatred. He would walk down Burlington Arcade, glancing into the windows of jewellers' shops, seeing fur-clad women buying bracelets that would have taken him five years of his life to earn. He would pause at the entrances of luxury hotels and watch Rolls-Royces driving up with livery-clad chauffeurs at the wheel. He would wander along Regent Street, looking at the expensive clothes, the silver-backed toilet-sets, the cut glass, the china-ware, the costly leather goods. And on all this wealth that was denied to him his hatred fed.

He was eighteen before this hatred became canalized, made to serve a purpose. Until then it had been simply an irrational, diffused emotion, a resentment that was incoherent and undirected, wasting itself and exhausting him. Then the Communist party found him.

His mother had died a year earlier, hastened into an early grave by occupational disease. He did not regret her passing, for she had never given him anything but hard knocks and blasphemous words. It would have been strange if he had

loved her, for love was not in their relationship. His father
he had never known; the fellow might have been an aristocrat
or a navvy; it was all one to Miller. Whoever he may have
been, he had sired a poor physical specimen; though that was
no proof that the stock was bad, for an unhealthy environ-
ment can ruin the best-bred stock in the world. Miller's
growth had been stunted from the first; rickets had warped
his limbs as a child, and a combination of factors had warped
his brain as a youth. To the Communists he was first-class
material.

The Communists brought to Miller what he had lacked—
an aim in life. Now, instead of spending his anger in futile
rages against the rich, he had a goal and a hope of reaching
it; it was the eventual overthrow of the present régime and
the substitution of Communism. Communism to Miller was
a simple creed without complications; it meant in effect taking
from the rich and giving to the poor—a grand share-out of all
wealth so that all should be equal. That to Miller, who had
nothing, seemed a highly desirable object, and if it entailed
the killing off of large numbers of worthless capitalists, why,
so much the better. Had they not ground the faces of the
poor for centuries? Had they not ground his, Miller's, face?
Why should they be shown pity in the day of judgment that
was surely to come?

To hasten the arrival of the great day Miller distributed
party leaflets, carrying them round the suburbs of London
and stuffing them through householders' letter-boxes,
thrusting them into the unwilling hands of passers-by, and
unobtrusively depositing them in waiting-rooms and cinema
foyers. In addition, he subscribed to the party funds, attended
meetings, and assisted with manual labour when it was
required. He would have liked to help also by speaking from
platform or soap-box, but after one or two attempts, which
ended only in ignominious drying-up, he came to the conclusion that among the meagre gifts bestowed upon him at
birth oratory had certainly not been one.

So Communism became Miller's life; and through the

telescope of Communism he saw a star, and the star was
Russia. The comrades spoke of Russia as the ancient Jews
must have spoken of the Promised Land; it was to them the
land flowing with the milk and honey of Marxism, ruled by a
demi-god named Joseph Stalin, in whom all the finest qualities
had united to produce a supreme being, a being so exalted
that it was unthinkable that he could do any wrong.

Miller, who had attended school as little as possible, and,
when there, had resisted every attempt to instil knowledge
into his brain, had only the vaguest of notions where this land
of Russia might be situated; but that made no difference.
There might be a hazy vagueness about it, but it was the
source from which all goodness flowed, and the aim of all
countries ought to be to model themselves on Russia.

When Miller joined the Communist party the civil war in
Spain was raging, and Miller, in the first flush of enthusiasm,
thought seriously of volunteering for service in the International Brigade. It was big George Denver who stopped
him. Denver was secretary of the party branch, a Goliath of
a man, with thick hair and a jowl that showed black two
hours after shaving. Denver put a hairy hand on Miller's arm.

" Don't be a fool, boy," he said. " Let the intellectuals do
that sort of nonsense if they like; let them die like ruddy
heroes if they want to; let them write their damn-silly poems
if that pleases 'em. But this is where the work's to be done—
here in London; don't forget that, boy. You stay here and
work; you'll find plenty to do—or we'll find it for you. And
if you want excitement you may find some of that here, too.
There's no need to go to Spain."

Secretly Miller was relieved. There had been reports of
bitter fighting in Spain, and he had no real desire to go to that
passionate country. So he settled down to work for the party
at home. And George Denver was right about the excitement.

There was one evening when the Blackshirts were having a
rally in an East End meeting-hall. Many people were showing
interest in Mosley's Fascists at that time, and the hall was
crowded. What the Blackshirts did not know was that among

the audience were about forty Communists who had come with the idea of breaking up the meeting. Miller was one of them.

At first the Communists did nothing; they had had their orders, and they knew when they were to act. Two speakers addressed the audience; they talked of the ideals of Fascism, citing Italy and Germany as two countries that had found salvation in a leader and a common purpose. That, they said, was what England needed; England lacked a driving force, lacked will-power; she was decadent and weak. But there was an answer: put Mosley in power; trust the Blackshirts.

The audience appeared apathetic; there was a little clapping, but no real enthusiasm. Then Roger Steinart began to speak, and a new atmosphere came over the meeting. Steinart was a tall man, who looked even taller by reason of his remarkable thinness. He wore black trousers supported by a leather belt and a black shirt with sleeves buttoned at the wrists. His hair also was black, plastered down with grease so that it shone under the electric light; his cheeks were sunken, his lips thin.

He made no gestures, but stood very straight, his arms at his sides, while the words flowed from him in a continuous stream. There was something magnetic about the man. Miller, against his will, found himself listening to Steinart, found himself moved, not so much by what the man said as by his manner of saying it. He had the audience with him; there was no doubt about that. There seemed to be a current flowing through them; they sat forward in their seats, watching Steinart, listening to the flow of words, held by mass hypnotism.

It was then that Dick Walters gave the signal. Forty Communists stood up and shouted: " Down with the Blackshirts! Down with Mosley! Down with Fascism!"

That was the start of the fighting; that was when Miller became afraid. He knew that the Reds were hopelessly outnumbered, and he wanted to get away. He began edging towards the door, pushing his way through the press of people, most of whom were neither Communists nor Fascists, but had simply come to listen.

Miller had almost reached the door when two Blackshirts seized him. Pushing his arms up behind his back, they forced him out into the street. Then they threw him down in the gutter and kicked him. Miller felt their boots crashing into his ribs, making him gasp for breath; and they went on kicking him, calling him a filthy swine of a Communist, a rotten Bolshie, a lousy Red. And all the time other Communists were being thrown out into the street.

After a time the two Blackshirts tired of kicking Miller and went back into the hall. Then the police arrived, and in the confusion Miller slipped away, bleeding from nose and mouth, with two teeth broken and with bitter hatred in his heart.

But Miller had his revenge. He knew one of the Fascists who had kicked him, and one night Miller followed him in the dark, and Miller had a bottle in his hand. And when there was no one to see him he hit the Fascist with the bottle so hard that the glass broke. And as the man fell Miller thrust the jagged end of the bottle in his face and left him.

Miller was twenty when he met Jessie Craddon. Jessie was a teacher, and was about five years older than Miller. Usually she wore a tweed skirt, a suede jacket, and stout, low-heeled shoes. Her hair was cut in a straight bob, she used no make-up, and she was an ardent Communist. Miller distrusted her at first, partly because she was clever and partly because she came from a class he had always looked upon as the enemy. Jessie went out of her way to win his regard. Within a month he believed he was in love with her.

Jessie began to instruct Miller in the theory of Communism. It was she who advised him to read the works of Karl Marx. But Miller preferred to hear her telling him about such things. To Miller only one thing was more difficult than reading, and that was writing. So he listened to Jessie's teaching, and while he marvelled at the power of her mind he thought about the body that pulsed with life under those thick, virginal clothes; and he wondered how he might possess it.

Yet, because of her intellectual ability and her class, Miller was never at ease with Jessie. In moments of self-revelation he imagined how he must appear when viewed through her eyes—he, a man of the slums; he, a prostitute's bastard. Sometimes, in an agony of self-pity, he would weep in the secrecy of his bedroom, cursing the misfortune that had made him as he was.

At other times he was more cheerful. After all, was not Communism the creed of equality? And was not Jessie Craddon a true Communist? Therefore she must believe in equality. She, of all people, would not hold his birth and upbringing against him. Indeed, for her there might be an attraction in a man so obviously misused by the capitalist, bourgeois society of England. So thought Miller in his more sanguine moments; and at such moments the world seemed a good world, and he would whistle between his broken teeth.

Miller felt he would always remember an evening in May in the year 1937; so much happened that evening; it might well have been that the events of just a few hours altered the whole subsequent course of his life. Had things turned out differently he might have been a different man; he might have been happy. Well, you could never tell at the time how you were going to be affected by events; you could never tell what a certain course of action would do to your life. That was the swine of it. If you could only see, if you could only judge the consequences, how differently you might act! But you were blind, and you could only grope blindly. That was the swine of it.

Miller and Jessie had been to an open-air meeting. It was a warm, pleasant evening, and Miller suggested that they should walk back to Jessie's lodgings. He had often taken her home before, and she agreed readily enough. They walked up one street and down another; and Jessie talked and Miller listened; but all the time he was thinking how wonderful it would be to have her in his arms, to have her always. The desire was so strong in him that he could feel his hands sweating, and his breath came sharply in little gasps. Yet he was afraid because, though she belonged to the party and worshipped the creed, she had nevertheless been born in far different circumstances from those in which Miller had been born. He was inferior, and he knew it. Suppose he took her in his arms and she repulsed him with disgust! Then it would all be over, all his bright dreams, all his hopes. So he hesitated; so, as Jessie talked, his desire battled with his fear, and he hardly knew what she was saying.

It was late; darkness had fallen on the streets, and where they walked the street lamps were oases of light with deserts of shadow in between. In one of these deserts Miller screwed up his courage and stopped walking.

" Jess," he said, " wait a bit."

She halted also and stood looking at him questioningly. He took her hand and pulled her into an alley which led off the street, a narrow alley made dark by the encroaching houses.

" Jess," he said, and his voice was hoarse, " you must listen to me; you got to listen to me."

He could tell by her voice that she was smiling in the darkness, and she did not attempt to draw her hand away.

" I'm listening, Fred," she answered.

" Jess, I don't know how to say this; I ain't no good at speeches; I never knew how to talk—not like you, Jess, not like you. Nobody never learnt me, an' that's gospel—true as I stand 'ere. I never 'ad a chance really—not a chance."

He was full of self-pity and near to tears. If she had laughed at him he would have lashed out like a child in a temper; he would have struck her, trying to hurt her for the way she had hurt him. But she did not laugh; she stood there, saying nothing, waiting for him to go on. He could see her only dimly, could not tell what expression was on her face, whether it was of pity or contempt or something else.

After a while he went on speaking, and his voice was still hoarse.

"I don't know what you'll think of what I'm going to say. Maybe you'll laugh; maybe you'll be angry. You're such a long way better than what I am—miles above me; that's the trouble."

"No, Fred," she whispered. "No."

But he went on vehemently. "Yes, you are, miles above. What am I? Something dragged out of the gutter! That's true. My mother was a whore; you may as well know that; somebody wouldn't be above telling you, anyway."

"We can't pick our parents, Fred."

"No; but it makes a difference, say what you like. Now, you, you're educated; you talk decent; you got brains. That's what makes it all so damned silly."

"I don't understand."

"Not but what," he continued, speaking hurriedly now, "not but what I mightn't better meself. I got brains, too, if I like to use them. I could learn; I could get on. I know blokes with less'n my start make good, work their way up an' get big money, stacks of it. P'r'aps I could too."

He seemed to have forgotten Communism, the Marxist theory, the creed. He felt her hand pressing his.

"Fred," she said, "Fred, this isn't what you stopped for. You could have said this as we walked. What did you really want to say?"

Suddenly the spirit seemed to go out of him; he felt deflated, hopeless.

"What's the use?" he said. "What's the use? But I got to say it. I got to tell you. Jess, I love you."

He expected her to start away, to call him a fool, to laugh at him in derision. She did none of these things. She said softly, "Fred, I love you as well. I thought you knew."

They stayed in the alley until they heard the sound of approaching footsteps. Then Jessie freed herself and said, "We must go. Mrs Porter will think I'm lost; it's late."

He kissed her once more, and they went out into the street and walked on. But now they walked hand in hand and talked no more of Marxism, but were silent, breathing the fresh night air, and each feeling that from amid the slums around them they had plucked a flower of rarest beauty.

It was ten minutes before Miller realized that they were being followed. Glancing back over his shoulder, he had seen three men, but at first he had suspected nothing. Then a feeling had come over him that all was not as innocent as it seemed. The street was very silent and empty, the hour late. He could hear the sound of his own and Jessie's footsteps jumping up from the pavement and echoing back off the drab houses across the way. There seemed to be no life in those houses; except for himself and Jessie and the three men thirty paces behind, the city might have been dead.

Miller stopped walking, holding Jessie back by the hand. The three men stopped also, huddled under a lamp-post, a silent, menacing group. Two were wearing caps; the third was bare-headed, and the lamplight falling upon him showed up his face, a face hideously, jaggedly scarred. Miller's breath came in a sharp, hard gasp.

"What is it, Fred?" Jessie asked. "What's wrong?"

He said, "Those men under the lamp-post—they're following us."

She looked back at the men. One of them was lighting cigarettes for the other two, and the smoke drifted up, writhing about the street-lamp, vanishing in the air.

"What makes you think that?" she asked.

"I've seen them before; they're Blackshirts."

"Even so——"

He said urgently, "Let's go on; let's get away from 'ere."

They began walking again, and the three men followed, keeping the same distance, not closing the gap, not letting it widen. Miller felt panicky; he could feel the sweat pricking out on his forehead. He wanted to break into a run, but he held himself in check by an effort of will. He would have welcomed the sight of a policeman, but the street was deserted.

He began to think furiously. Somehow he must shake off those three men. They were not following him for amusement;

there was something deadly purposeful in the way they came on, saying nothing to each other, hurrying only when he hurried, but always there.

" Jess," he said, and his voice trembled a little, though he tried to keep it level, " we'll take the next turning, and then run like hell for the next. We've got to give 'em the slip."

She understood. Some of his fear had communicated itself to her, and she did not argue. " All right," she said. " I'm ready."

Half a minute later they were in the turning and running. Fifty yards farther on was another turning; they raced into it and continued running. Two minutes later they were stopped by the wall of a building stretching across the road. They were in a cul-de-sac.

Miller began to swear, softly, fluently; but Jessie put a hand over his mouth.

" That's no use," she said. " And in any case we may have eluded them—that is, if they were really following us."

" They was following us all right," said Miller. " You don't need to 'ave no doubts about that. They was following us. One of 'em was a bastard I bashed a while ago. He'll 'ave it in for me. Blast 'em! 'Ere they come!"

The three men did not hurry; they knew there was no way of escape. They spread out across the street and advanced slowly. In their hands they carried short pieces of thick lead piping.

"They'll kill me," whimpered Miller. " Ain't there no way out? "

He looked round him desperately, and saw that he and Jessie were standing beside a pair of stout wooden doors, about nine feet high. He looked up at them, but they were too tall for him to climb. He could not reach the top with his hands, and there was no foothold. Then he heard Jessie speaking rapidly.

" Get on my back, Fred. It's you they're after; they won't touch me. Get on my back and climb over."

As she bent down the three men seemed to guess her

purpose, and they began to run. Fear gave Miller strength; he put one foot on Jessie's back, gave a leap, grabbed the top of the door, pulled himself up, swung over, and dropped on the other side.

He fell heavily, wrenching his ankle; but he picked himself up at once, for already he could hear some one else climbing the door. He could just discern by the dim, reflected light that he was in a builder's yard, and he began to pick his way between stacks of timber, piles of bricks, dumps of sand, wheelbarrows, hand-carts, and other paraphernalia. He had gone only a few yards when he heard a soft thud and realized that at least one pursuer was also in the yard. He bent low, making use of the ample cover, and knowing that if he moved silently the other man was unlikely to find him.

But suddenly a beam of light flickered across the yard and began to move about, sweeping over the blocks of concrete, porcelain sinks, an old tin bath. Miller whimpered again. The man had a torch.

Miller dodged round a stack of timber, and the torch-beam splashed over it and showed, leaning against a wall, a ladder. Renewed hope flooded Miller's heart, and he leapt for the ladder and started to climb. It was then that his pursuer saw him, and, giving a cry of rage, ran for the ladder also. But Miller was already astride the wall and feeling better. He waited there until the man was half-way up the ladder; then he thrust suddenly with his foot and sent the ladder toppling back into the yard. He heard a crash, a cry of pain; and then he dropped lightly down from the wall into the street behind and ran.

The following morning as Miller was going to work he felt a hand on his shoulder. Turning, he saw big George Denver.

" I want a word with you," Denver said; and his voice sounded strange to Miller; almost, one might have thought, menacing. Miller stopped.

" What is it, George? "

" Keep moving," Denver said. " We can talk as we go. You were at the meeting last night? "

" Yes," Miller said.

" Jessie Craddon was there too."

" Yes," Miller said again.

" You and Jessie," Denver said, " left together. You were seen going off together."

" Well? What of it? "

" Did you go home with Jessie? "

" I don't see what that's got to do with you," Miller said; but he spoke half-heartedly; he was frightened.

" I said, did you go home with her? "

Miller looked up at Denver's face and saw that it was grim, the mouth set in a hard line. Miller said, " No, I left her."

" Where? "

" I don't know—straight, I don't. Somewhere. What's it matter, anyway? Why are you so interested? There's no 'arm in walking 'ome with a girl."

" Not when she gets home. Jessie didn't."

Miller's stomach began turning to water; his lips trembled. " She didn't? Then what——"

" Jessie," Denver said slowly, " was found in a blind alley with her skull battered in."

Miller watched the hills sliding past as the *Golden Ray* steamed up the Tuloma river. Under their covering of snow, with dark pines thrusting up here and there, they looked like the pallid faces of old invalids, dotted with the growth of five-day beards. Between them the Tuloma flowed silently down to the Barents Sea. There were ice-floes on the river, and the air was cold and crisp, the sky a pale, washed-out blue. Somewhere, far, very far overhead, an aeroplane was drawing patterns upon the sky. Miller could scarcely see the plane, but he could hear the beat of its engine throbbing down through layer after layer of thin Arctic air, and he could see the white, swelling bandage of its vapour trail.

Ahead of the *Golden Ray* was the Harrison boat, astern of

her the surviving tanker; ahead and astern of those lay the
rest of the convoy, strung out in a long Indian file, and all
moving smoothly up the Tuloma towards Murmansk. And
from every ship men gazed with weary eyes upon the iron
hills, and were glad—glad to see the snow and the trees and
the little wavelets lapping against the shore; glad to see the
occasional wooden house and the wooden jetty reaching out
into the stream; glad to hear the fighter aircraft overhead;
glad to see the camouflaged emplacements of anti-aircraft
guns, and here and there a motor-lorry, and here and there a
pony sleigh; glad to see river craft, and warships lying snug
at anchor; glad above all else to know that they had left the
Barents Sea, the long groping through darkness, the incessant
thunder of depth-charges, the bitter lash of blown spray; glad
that the outward voyage was over.

At this moment Miller wished that Jessie could have been
with him to share his entry into the Promised Land. The
memory of Jessie was the only smudge on the bright shield of
his happiness. But it was only a tiny smudge, for the years
had heaped leaves of forgetfulness on that incident in the
cul-de-sac and the builder's yard, so that Miller no longer
saw Jessie clearly as a person with whom he had been in love,
but rather as a vague dream. Yet he knew that if the dream
had not been so rudely shattered his life might have been
very different; he might have been a better man—though
perhaps a worst Communist. It was paradoxical that Jessie,
devoted to the cause as she had been, should have been the
one to give him ideas that had nothing to do with Communism, equality, or the overthrow of the capitalist system.
But Jessie was dead, and without her there was nothing in
Miller's life but the party.

His faith had been shaken when Russia had made her pact
with Germany; he had been bewildered; there had appeared
to be no easy explanation of that move. Then Germany had
attacked on the eastern front and all was well; Miller found
that he was on the right side after all. Russia, the land of
beauty, of truth, of light, was fighting side by side with

Britain. The very thought of such an alignment warmed Miller's heart, made him less bitterly resentful of the life of drill and discipline that had been forced upon him. One had only to be patient; victory over Germany would surely come, and with it the great victory for Communism over all the western world.

Miller saw the last rays of the setting sun glint golden on the topmost ridges of the hills; then he heard the anchor-chain rattling out through the hawse-pipe, heard the anchor splash in the water and the chain continue rattling out, while the rust rose in a reddish cloud and the carpenter stood with his hand upon the winch. Then the anchor bit into the bed of the river, and the ship was held fast, swinging gently with her stern towards the sea. From the bridge rang down the signal, "Finished with engines," and for the first time since leaving Loch Ewe the mighty heart of the vessel was still and silent.

And Miller looked towards the land and felt that he had come home at last.

CHAPTER EIGHT

Murmansk

FOR seven days the *Golden Ray* lay at anchor in a small bay that seemed to have been scooped out of the surrounding rock. Some distance up-river was the port of Murmansk, and at night the crew could stand on deck and hear bombs bursting in the town and see the anti-aircraft barrage, the glitter of heavy shells and the streams of golden tracer that seemed to climb so lazily up the sky, where the white arms of search-lights waved to and fro as though in invitation.

On the first evening of their release from watches the gunners celebrated in their own fashion. For the first time for many days they took their trousers off. Then, clad in vests and pants, and with the stove aglow, they danced and capered to the tune of Ben Cowdrey's mouth-organ. Ben sat on his bunk, his back resting against the bulkhead, and played until his mouth was sore. And in the narrow gangway between the bunks the gunners capered and sang. With bearded faces and tousled hair, they looked in their long woollen underclothing like so many grotesque, overgrown gnomes; and the sight of one another set them laughing, and they laughed until the tears ran down their cheeks. They were all a little crazed, a little mad; for the tension had lifted and their spirits were bubbling over.

So they danced and so they sang, while the iron stove glowed red; and outside the long Arctic night closed upon the land with a grip of steel, and the rocks cracked within that grip, and the pine-trees shivered under an icy breath, and overhead the northern lights writhed in agony across the sky.

And Ben Cowdrey sat upon his bunk with his back against the bulkhead playing his mouth-organ, and the reedy notes shook themselves out of it and beat against the dripping iron above his head. The gunners sang and made poor jokes and laughed and sang again, and were suddenly, briefly happy. And Ben Cowdrey, playing his mouth-organ and beating time with his swinging feet, wondered what his old woman would think if she could see him now; his old woman far away in Stepney. And his workmates and his neighbours, the fellows at the local. They would never believe it was he; somebody like him, perhaps, but not really he, not Ben Cowdrey, the little tailor.

Certainly they would never believe that he was happier in this life than he had ever been. Yet he was—in many ways. Some of it was bad, of course; some of it was hellish. But on the whole he enjoyed this life; he liked the companionship of men; he liked the changing horizons, the boyish feeling of adventure, the excitement; he loved the smell of the sea and the kaleidoscope of life in foreign ports. The War was incidental, but it was the War that had given him these new horizons, that had dragged him out of the Savile Row work-room where he had for years plied his busy needle, living in a world of cloths and cottons, pins and chalk and

scissors. There, in that basement work-room, his vision of
the outside world had been limited to a small amount of area
railing glimpsed through the window, and the legs of passers-
by. Glancing up from his work, he would see the striped black
trousers of City men, the silk stockings of Society women,
the corduroys of artists, the tatters of out-of-works. There
he would labour on suits for the wealthy that might cost
twenty-five guineas, and when his own suit needed replacing
he would buy one off the peg for fifty shillings or maybe less.

Gladys and he had been happy, he supposed—in an
undemonstrative way. There had never been any great
passion between them; neither had been built for that. There
had been no children either. Both of them would have liked
a child, but they had not been unhappy. Really, it would
have been hard to find anyone more suited to his temperament
than Gladys; but there had always been one side of his
character that she could not understand, because it had no
reflection in her own. There was nothing adventurous about
Gladys; Cowdrey smiled at the thought. A home-lover, that
was what she was—all for safety first and staying in that state
of life in which it had pleased God to place her.

But to Ben the world had called; the wide world, the far
places, the strange, beautiful names: Pago Pago, Buenos
Aires, Shanghai, Vladivostock, Takoradi, Tierra del Fuego,
Madagascar, Zanzibar, Samarkand, Katmandu, Lhasa. How
often he would search through his old, dog-eared atlas,
muttering those names softly to himself and yearning for the
chance to travel! Often he would visit the offices of shipping
agents and go home with pockets stuffed full of brochures.
Sometimes he would buy a *Geographical Magazine* and turn
the pages again and again until they almost fell to pieces
under his touch.

But it all led nowhere; he stayed in his old job, sewing
tweeds and worsteds and flannels; yet dreaming always of
coral beaches, of snow-capped mountains, of tropical forests,
of ox-carts and the babel of foreign tongues. Then, when he
had thought that these things could never be more than a

dream, the War had drawn him forth from his shell and shown him the reality. He had been to Rio, to Buenos Aires, to Jamaica, to New York; now he was up on the northern rim of the world, and who knew where he would be six months hence?

So Ben played his mouth-organ, and his bald head gleamed and his eyes sparkled as he thought: This is the life; this is the life for me. God! I never want to go back to sewing suits; I never want to go back to that.

" To-morrow," said Vernon, " I shall wash myself all over. To-morrow night will be bath-night. It's about time; I begin to itch."

" You'll freeze," said Payne. " Maybe you'll catch cold and die."

" Then it will be in a good cause, and my lily-white soul will be wafted straight aloft."

" Other place more likely. Anyway, you'd better borrow a scraper off the bosun."

Andrews said, " I wonder how long we shall be anchored here."

" That," said Petty Officer Donker, who was paring his nails with a clasp-knife fully six inches long and an inch wide, " that, my son, depends on how many ships there are waiting to use the docks. We may be here a week."

" Shall we be able to go ashore in Murmansk? "

" Sure you will; why not? That's if you think it's worth your while."

" What sort of a place is it? " asked Payne.

Donker sucked in his breath with a loud, whistling noise. " It's bloody terrible," he said.

" What about the women? "

Petty Officer Donker stopped paring his nails and stared at Payne. " Women!" he said. " Women! I never see none —not to call women. 'Course," he went on, " there's some made in that shape, I don't deny. But you take my tip; you let that sort of thing alone till you get home. These lot are poxed up to the eyebrows."

"Ah, come off it," said Payne. "You hear that everywhere you go. 'Keep off the tarts in Cape Town,' they tell you; 'seventy per cent. have got V.D.' Then you go to Jamaica, and it's eighty per cent., and in B.A. it's ninety. Hell! you can't believe all that."

"You can believe what you like," said Donker. "I'm just giving you a friendly word of advice, that's all. And I'll tell you what happened last time we was here: the bombardier—the bombardier, mind you!—fell in with a prozzy and was out all one night. He came back covered with fleas—bastard great fleas all over him. We had a rare time, I can tell you; had to smother everything with flea-powder. But that wasn't the end of it; when we got back to Scotland they took him ashore with siff."

Miller broke in: "That's a rotten lie."

Donker waggled his knife at Miller. "Here, here! That's no way to talk. Why should I trouble to make up a tale like that? Anyway, you can check up if you want to; you don't have to take my word for it."

"It can't be true," said Miller. "Prostitution has been abolished in Russia. V.D.'s been wiped out."

Donker laughed. "Oh, my, my! You bin reading too much propaganda. It don't do to believe all that twaddle. You want to go ashore and take a look round; you may learn something. Personally, I mean to stay on board; I've had a bellyful of Murmansk, and I don't want no more."

Warby was the last to climb into his bunk, and, being the last, it fell to him to switch off the electric light. While at sea that light had never been put out; it had been dimmed with the aid of a piece of cloth, but it had always been left burning, night and day. Warby snapped it off, and only the glow of the stove showed through the darkness. Warby groped his way to his bunk, stubbed his toe, swore, and clambered in, thrusting his woollen-clad legs down between the rough blankets and drawing the fleece bed-cover up over his chin.

Already half the gunners were asleep; already a variety of snores and whistles came from the bunks—from Payne's especially, for it seemed that his soft bulk formed a natural reserve of wind to play upon the organ of his nose. Warby listened to these noises for a moment or two; then they faded out of his consciousness and he was asleep.

Only Miller and Randall were still awake, still awake and thinking. In Randall's mind the ghost of Lily danced on and on; always before sleeping he would think of her, and the sense of being an outcast, a man not as other men, would fall heavily upon him. Again and again he wondered: Have they found the body yet? Is there a warrant out for my arrest? Well, if they did not take him in Murmansk they would never have him; for his mind was made up: he was not going to survive the homeward journey. It would be so easy to end things; all he had to do was to step overboard one dark night; no one need see him go, there would be no alarm; he would just disappear. For a while he allowed himself the childish pleasure of imagining the sorrow of his shipmates when they realized that he was dead; but soon, in his weariness, he slept, as all the others were sleeping—all the others save only Miller.

Miller was twisting the words of Petty Officer Donker round his brain and tormenting himself. What did Donker know of Russia? Why did he tell those lies about prostitution? For they were lies; there was no prostitution in Russia. Why should there be? In a country with equal shares for all, where there were no rich and no poor, there was no need for it. Then why should Donker make up such lies?

Miller felt bitter against Donker; and, because the petty officer was so much senior to himself and there was no way in which Miller could hurt him, Miller had to bottle up his resentment; and that was something he did not like doing. These thoughts kept him awake for quite a time; but in the end weariness overcame him also, and with the others he slept.

Vernon waited until after tea before having his bath; and

since the bath itself was to be a somewhat speedy operation—
speed being necessitated by the far from temperate conditions
—he made his preparations in leisurely fashion, dragging
clean underclothing from the recesses of his kitbag and warming it in front of the stove. He had fetched a bucket of water
from the galley pump and had filled the kettle. Now it only
remained for the kettle to boil, and all would be ready. He
had the drill planned, and reckoned that, provided no unfore-
seen snags arose, he ought to be able to run through the whole
business in little more than five minutes. With the temperature in the wash-place as usual below freezing, that would be
quite long enough.

Vernon poured the hot water into a bucket, refilled the
kettle, and put it back on the stove. Then, taking soap,
flannel, and towel, he went into the wash-place and rapidly
stripped himself. It was cold, damned cold; but with great
energy and much puffing and blowing he began his bath,
standing on the duck-boards and swilling water from the
bucket over his body, soaping himself, and rubbing vigorously
with the flannel. He could feel an icy draught blowing down
from the deck-opening, but he consoled himself with the
thought that he would soon be back in warm clothes, in those
wonderful long and hairy underpants, the qualities of which
he had so much underrated in the old days.

He was working on his legs when the alarm-bells began
ringing, and almost simultaneously a wave of humanity burst
from the cabin and clattered past him, flinging him on one
side as though he had been straw, kicking his bucket of water
over, treading on his bare toes, and sending the air eddying
round his wet and shivering body in frosty whirlwinds.

"Come on!" said Padgett, rushing past him. "Air-raid!"

As the gun-crews clambered up the iron ladder and disappeared on deck Vernon cursed them, and his curses were
the only warm part of him. He cursed all air-raids also; he
cursed the Germans who made them and the Russians who
failed to prevent them. Most of all he cursed the alarm-bells,
which were still ringing. And while he cursed he found time

to pick up his towel and move himself into the deserted cabin.
There, standing in the ashes by the red-hot stove, he began
fiercely drying himself. Still only half-dry, he dragged on
his clean pants and vest, thrust himself into shirt, trousers,
socks, and boots, flung a coat over the lot, a steel helmet on
his head, gloves on hands, and with teeth chattering like
castanets followed the others.

He had just reached the top of the gun-ladder when the
order to stand down was given.

One by one the other gunners followed Vernon's example
and bathed as well as they could. Beards disappeared, and
the sound of scrubbing-brushes could be heard in the wash-
place as men laundered their underclothing. Lines strung
across the wash-place carried shirts, pants, and vests frozen
into rigid shapes, as though occupied by invisible men. Randall
went so far as to polish his greatcoat buttons. Time dragged.

Once a Russian soldier came down into the gunners'
quarters, conducted by a sailor. He wore a long sheepskin
coat, belted about the waist, and leather jack-boots; on his
head he wore a peaked cap that narrowed to a point at the
crown and bore on its front a red star. He had come aboard
from one of the launches that were continually visiting the
ship. He had a square, heavy face, with rather high cheek-
bones—a melancholy, badly shaved face.

Miller felt excitement throbbing in his brain when he saw
the Russian. Here, for the first time, he was seeing a son of
the Revolution, a Communist from the mother state of Communism. Miller wanted to shake the man's hand, to pat him
on the shoulder and call him brother, comrade. But with the
other fellows looking on he hesitated to do so; they would
not have understood.

" He wants cigarettes," said the sailor.

The Russian soldier nodded his head. " Seegret," he said;
" seegret." And he made the motions of putting a cigarette
to his lips and blowing out a cloud of smoke, as though he
were not sure that they would understand.

Miller dragged a packet from his pocket and offered it to the Russian; but the man shook his head, making negative motions with his hands.

The sailor laughed. " He wants to buy some," he explained. He turned to the Russian. "Fifty cigarette," he said slowly. " How many rouble? "

The Russian did not understand. " Seegret," he said.

The sailor asked, " Anybody got fifty fags he wants to sell? "

Payne took a tin out of his kitbag, and the sailor showed it to the Russian.

" Rouble," he said. " Rouble. How much rouble? "

The Russian held up both his hands, spreading the fingers.

The sailor looked disgusted. " No, no, no! That's no good. What, only ten roubles for fifty cigarettes? We can get one hundred roubles ashore; that's the proper price."

The Russian looked blank. Of this speech he understood just two words—rouble and cigarette.

" What do you mean? " asked Miller. " What do you mean by the proper price? "

The sailor answered condescendingly, as one who was in Russia for the second time and knew it all.

" Black-market price. English and Yankee cigarettes sell like hot cakes; you'll know why if you try some Russki ones. Any of the kids will give you a hundred roubles for fifty. This feller's trying to pull a fast one. But he isn't going to get away with that."

He began haggling with the Russian, trying to make him understand by means of a kind of pidgin-English spoken very loudly and slowly. The man had a wad of notes in his hand; he offered one, but the sailor pushed it away. " Not enough. *Niet dobra.* Not nearly enough."

Miller drew away. He was bewildered. What did it mean? Black market? In Russia? What could it mean?

On the fourth day in the anchorage two Messerschmitt Jaguars came without warning over the hills and dropped two sticks of bombs. Not a gun answered them; they were in and away almost before anyone could realize what was happening—away over the hills and streaking for Petsamo and the Finnish airfield from which they had come. Within a few minutes the pilots would be making their reports.

Randall and Vernon and Cowdrey were cleaning the Bofors gun when the attack came. They had the gun unloaded and the cleaning-rod rammed half-way down the barrel. They heard no sound at all until the planes skimmed over the hills; then it was too late to do anything. They saw the bombs dropping in the bay, raising great spouts of water; then the ship seemed to give a leap and shake itself like a dog, and that was all. After a little while they continued cleaning the gun, and the ripples died gradually away.

For seven days the *Golden Ray* lay at anchor; then she pulled in her hook and moved up-river to Murmansk docks, where, for the first time since she had left Immingham, she made fast to the land.

" So this," said Sergeant Willis, leaning over the rail on the shoreward side, " is Russia." After a minute or two he dropped his cigarette-end into the narrow strip of water lying between ship and quay, and added, " What a shambles! "

The quay was a picture of disorder: packing-cases stood piled one on top of another; pieces of machinery lay rusting in the open; a stack of motor-tyres reached to a height of fifteen feet, left just where they had been unloaded; behind them were bales of hay; and on all these, on cranes, railway-trucks, ships, barrels, hawsers, bollards, gangways, on the peaked caps of sentries, the fur hats of stevedores, and the astrakhan hats of Government officials, on men and women, English, Russian, and American, even on the miserable hound searching without apparent hope for something to keep body and soul together, the interminable, silent snow drifted down out of an opaque sky.

" So this," said Sergeant Willis again, " is Russia."

And Petty Officer Donker spat into that same strip of water

into which the sergeant's cigarette had fallen, and answered, " Russia! "

On Miller the snow fell also, and he scarcely noticed it. He too was gazing at the cluttered quay, at the trucks with their strange, outlandish lettering, at the men and women with their quilted clothing and felt boots. He too was breathing the word " Russia," but in how different a fashion! In Miller's mouth it became a word of magic; even as a man might murmur in wonder and only half-belief, " Eldorado! " so Miller breathed " Russia! "

Yet, in a way, he felt as though something were missing; there should have been some visible, outward sign that this was truly the land of Communism, the genuine Utopia. Miller did not know quite what he had expected to find—certainly not banners of welcome; yet surely something different from this, something different from these silent people moving in the enveloping snow. He had expected some impact, something that he could no more define than a child can define the hoped-for joys of to-morrow. But here there was no electric surge of fulfilment; nothing but the silent people and the silent snow. Suddenly Miller was afraid, and what made it worse was that he could not tell whence his fear had sprung.

" Murmansk," said Vernon to Cowdrey and Payne, who were standing beside him, " is within the Arctic Circle— in Lapland, as a matter of fact. You will notice that many of these people have flat, Mongoloid features; that is because——"

" All right," said Payne; " we don't want a lecture. This is Russia."

" Certainly," said Vernon. " Oh, most certainly it is Russia. God help it! "

The tanks were taken off by a British ship equipped with heavy-lift derricks. The ship came alongside the *Golden Ray* and picked up the tanks as though they had been so many toys.

" Thank God for that," said Vernon, as he watched thirty

tons of steel and engineering skill twisting in mid-air. " Now
we shall be able to move along the deck without for ever
tripping over wires."

" See that," Petty Officer Donker said; " not a crane ashore
that's strong enough to lift a tank; we even have to provide
a ship with jumbos to do the job." He sniffed contemptu-
ously. " Anyway, I don't suppose they've got any trucks on
that tinpot railway what'd take a tank." He pointed to the
ship into whose holds the tanks were disappearing. " That's
the *Empire Nightingale*; she'll take that lot to Archangel when
the White Sea thaws out enough for the ice-breakers to get
through. What price serving in her, eh? Oh, my, my; I don't
envy them their job. Oh, my, my!"

And Petty Officer Donker shuffled away to see how the
working-party was getting on with the twelve-pounder, shaking his fur-capped head as he did so.

Vernon was just turning to make his way back to the
gunners' quarters when a hand smacked him on the shoulder
and a thick, hearty voice cried, " Well, Harry, you old devil!
Fancy meeting you here! "

Vernon knew that voice, and he knew the florid, ugly face
that went with it.

" Smithy!" he cried, grasping the hand that had thumped
his shoulder. " Smithy! How did you get here? "

" By the standard methods," replied Lance-Bombardier
Panton-Smith. " As a matter of fact, our ship was next to
yours on the starboard side—the *Merryweather*—and not a
bad packet on the whole."

" When did you join her? "

" We left Southport the day after you. Remember that
Friday night? What a booze-up! Remember that tart—what
was her name? Rita or Nita, or something of that sort. Lord!
it was time to get away."

" Where's your ship now? "

Panton-Smith jerked a thumb over his shoulder. " Two
berths farther up. We moved in a couple of days ago. Looks
as if it'll take the Russkis two weeks to unload us."

" How did you know I was on this ship? "

" I didn't. Hadn't the foggiest idea where you were until I got to the top of the gangway and saw you. No, old man; the fact is I'm delivering mail."

" Mail? In Murmansk? "

Panton-Smith grinned. " Not for you. One only—wrongly delivered to our ship in Loch Ewe too late for transfer. You've got a gunner of the name of Randall, haven't you? "

" Sid Randall? Yes."

" That's the boy. Is he aboard? "

" Sure to be; probably in the cabin. Come on; I'll show you the way."

Randall was lying on his bunk reading a book.

Vernon said, " There's a letter for you, Randy."

The book dropped from Randall's fingers, and his eyes went wide, terror peeping out of them.

Panton-Smith was feeling in his pocket. " Why, don't look so scared, lad," he said. " It's not a summons—only a letter. You're lucky; we don't all get letters in this godforsaken hole."

His fingers found the letter, and he drew it out. The envelope was mauve, rather crumpled, rather worn at the edges. He handed it to Randall. " There you are—and a love-letter, or else I'm greatly mistaken."

He turned to Vernon. " How are you off for fags, Harry? Our bastard of a steward has run out of supplies."

" I can let you have some," Vernon said. " Couple of hundred, anyway."

" You're a pal," said Panton-Smith. " It'll save my life."

He sat down on one of the boxes by the stove, stretching his feet out towards the warmth and turning his back on Randall. " Talking of Southport," he said, " do you remember Betty? "

Vernon puckered his forehead. " Betty? Betty? "

" Betty Peters—that bit old Jock was trotting around." Panton-Smith drew imaginary lines in mid-air with the cigarette Vernon had given him.

Vernon nodded. "I remember."

"You'll laugh," said Panton-Smith. "Jock thought he'd shaken her off when he got posted to Shoeburyness; but dash me if she didn't follow him there—and she's in the family way."

"He'll have to marry her."

Panton-Smith laughed. "Not Jockie—not without committing bigamy."

Randall had drawn back into his bunk. Payne and Warby and Andrews were in the cabin, but they were gathered round the stove with Vernon and Panton-Smith. Randall wished he could have found some private cell where he could have hidden with his letter; but there was nowhere—no privacy at all; not even a curtain that he could draw across his bunk. He lay there, holding the letter in his hand and waiting for the address on it to stop dancing before his eyes, waiting for courage to flow back into his heart.

The address was written in block capitals; there was his Army number, then his rank, name, and initials: Gunner Randall, S.M.O. He pushed a trembling finger in under the flap and ripped the envelope clumsily open. The letter was folded twice, and Randall's nostrils caught the faint odour of cheap perfume.

He began reading: "Darling Sid, When are you coming home? I'm that lonely without you—— "

Randall closed his eyes, holding on to sanity, holding on to self-control.

Panton-Smith was saying, "What do you mean—you shot it down? Let me tell you that Heinkel was ours; no doubt about it."

"Yours," said Payne. "Like hell it was! Why, we could see our tracer going into it."

Randall opened his eyes and looked at the date on the letter. It was six months old—an echo sounding out of the past. He looked again at the envelope, and saw that it had been to New York and other places; it had followed him across the world.

" Darling Sid, When are you coming home? I'm that lonely without you—— " It was childish handwriting, done with a thick nib on ruled notepaper. It was blotchy, characterless; and it had belonged to Lily as completely as the tiny mole on her left breast. Randall drew in his breath with a sharp stab of pain as the memory came to him.

" Sergeant Fordwent," Panton-Smith was saying, " Sergeant Fordwent was on that tanker. Poor devils! They hadn't a snowball's chance in hell. Wonder what it feels like to be burnt alive? "

" Darling Sid, When are you coming home? I'm that lonely without you—— "

Randall crumpled the letter in his hand and bit his lip until the blood came.

CHAPTER NINE

Wondrous Life

MOVE over, Harry," Warby said. " I want to make a bit of toast."

Vernon shifted the box on which he was sitting to one side, and Warby raked the ash out of the bottom of the stove, so that red-hot cinders fell down into the opening.

" Nothing like a bit of toast," said Warby, "a bit of toast and cheese to keep the cold out. You can't beat that."

He held the bread close to the stove, using a knife as toasting-fork, and Vernon watched the steam drifting out of the bread.

" Bit doughy," said Warby. " Damned cook don't know how to make decent bread. Now, when I was on the *Reina del*—— "

" All right! All right! " interrupted Payne. We've had about enough of the *Reina del*; give it a rest."

Warby looked aggrieved, but made no answer. He could

never forget the six months he had spent on board the *Reina del Pacifico* and the wonderful food that had been served in that graceful liner. She was the standard by which he judged other ships, and much of his conversation began with the words "Now, when I was on the *Reina del*——" He was surprised to find that his shipmates might become tired of such an opening gambit.

Before Warby had asked him to move Vernon had been half asleep; half asleep and dreaming of the past. In that way he was able for a while to forget his surroundings—all the filth and discomfort, even the ache in his thumb which would never leave him. This was how it was, he mused: you lived in two worlds—one the world that was around you; the world of guns and night-watches, of drinking and seasickness, of bawdy talk and stinking blankets, of long boredom and sudden terror, of aching, longing, and hoping; the world of Warby and bread toasted on a knife, of old Donker with the knob on his neck, of young Randall with misery in his eyes; the world that your shipmates saw, experienced, and shared with you. But there was another world which none of the others shared because it was yours alone—the world of memory. And it was this that gave you strength to endure; this that fed the lamp of hope. In a way the world of memory was the real world, and this solid present the dream; a nightmare interlude that must eventually fade and drift away into those hazy regions over which kindly time will always cast its mantle of warm colours, smoothing out the peaks of pain, filling in the valleys of despondency.

He realized that Payne was speaking to him. "What's that? I'm sorry; I didn't hear you. What did you say?"

"I said, why haven't you got a commission?"

"Why should I have one?"

"I d'know," said Payne. "You talk like a ruddy officer. You've had education—public school, university—all that bilge. I'd have thought you'd have been an officer. Did you try for a commission?"

"As a matter of fact, yes. They turned me down."

"They did!" cried Payne incredulously. "Why?"

"Well," said Vernon, "you know how they test you: a couple of quacks look in your ears, one on either side of you. If they can see each other they give you a commission; if not, you've had it. I carried too much wood up top."

Payne laughed. "That might explain a lot. I didn't know the method."

Payne's question had set the train of recollection going again in Vernon's mind. Certainly he had tried for a commission; he remembered clearly the day when he had gone for his interview with the selection board. It had been such a vile day in every possible respect that he was not likely to forget it.

It was an Austin utility van, and there were six prospective officers in the back. One of the others was Panton-Smith. It was mid-winter; there was six inches of snow on the roads, and a journey of a hundred and fifty miles ahead of them. The interview was to take place at Oakham—none of them knew exactly why, but they did not question the necessity. All they knew was that they had been roused abominably early, that breakfast had been a cold failure, and that they were frozen, cramped, and completely fed up.

They had travelled about ninety miles when the driver lost control of the van, and it skidded into a snow-filled ditch. It took them half an hour, using the time-honoured ingredients of brute strength and ignorance, to put the vehicle once again on the road; and by then they were more fed up than ever. At the next public house they unanimously insisted on stopping for a livener. Perhaps they had too many liveners; perhaps it was that which robbed Panton-Smith and him of their commissions. What did it matter? Perhaps in any case they would have made poor officers.

Vernon's recollections of the rest of the proceedings were vague, as though a haze had settled over them. He remembered a bare, cold room in which they waited. He remembered being marched into another room—"Quick march! Right turn! Left turn! Halt!"—it was like being a defaulter. He

remembered an officer with a face like a toad and assorted
gold upon his shoulder-straps—possibly a brigadier; possibly
even a general; Vernon was unable to tell. The officer was
sitting at a table, and there were other officers on each side
of him. Vernon stood facing them across the table, and they
began shooting questions at him.

" What school did you go to?" " Were you at university?"
" Which one? " " College? " " What games did you play? "
" Have you ever been convicted? " " Why do you wish for
a commission? " " How old are you? " " Were you in the
O.T.C.? " " What was your civilian occupation? " " Do you
drive a car? "

Then the officer with the face like a toad puffed himself
up and asked a question which, to Vernon's mind, in its rather
alcoholic state, appeared altogether funny. It was: " Have
you ever fired your gun in anger? "

Looking back on the event, there seemed nothing particularly amusing in the question; yet at the time it had been so,
irresistibly so. Perhaps it was the toad-like face of the officer;
perhaps the way he rattled out the question like a burst of
machine-gun fire. Whatever it was, Vernon found himself
unable to control his laughter. He supposed that was why he
failed to get a commission.

And because of that failure he had lost Gillian. What was
it she had said? In a moment he would remember. Yes,
now he had it. " We may as well face it, Harry; you haven't
got success in you; you've never really succeeded at anything,
have you? I can't marry a failure. We'd better call it off."

He had been cut up at the time; but he had got over it.
You got over most things. There had been other women—
plenty of them. In a way, it was better not to have one in
particular; when you were tied up with a girl it was worrying,
both for her and you. Everything was so uncertain; you
could never tell what might happen to you; it was best not to
have any ties.

All the same, he had been in love with Gillian—damnably
so. There could never be anyone else quite like Gillian.

Warby belched and turned his toast. Payne walked to the port and looked out.

"It's snowing again," he said. "There's a couple more ships moved up-river. They're lying at anchor over there. There's a tug taking a string of barges across the river. You'd wonder what there is over there; it looks dead—just dead."

Warby was thinking about the *Reina del Pacifico;* the *Reina,* with her twin funnels, her 18,000 tons, and her speed of nearly twenty knots. Payne might sneer, but the *Reina del* was a fine ship, really fine. And the food! you would not have found better food in a first-class hotel. Snug little cabin, too, handy for the gun and connected to the galley by a working alleyway, so that you never had to carry meals across the open deck. That was how things ought to be. And the galley-boy bringing sausages and bacon and eggs for you to cook in the night in case you got hungry on watch. Bread made by a real baker, too; not by an unwilling cook with other things on his mind. Why, on some cargo ships you were still eating shore bread when you had been at sea for two or three weeks, bread as dry as dog-biscuits and almost as hard. There had been nothing like that on the *Reina del.*

Warby began to scrape the toast where he had burnt it.

Petty Officer Donker and Sergeant Willis were playing draughts on the mess-room table.

After long deliberation Donker moved a piece, and promptly lost two others. Leading-seaman Agnew, who was following the game, drew in his breath sharply. "You shouldn't have gone and done that."

Donker said stiffly, "When I want your advice, killick, I'll ask for same. Meanwhile you can keep your trap shut."

"All right," said Agnew. "Don't get shirty."

"I'm not shirty," said Donker. "I'm just telling you. I'm playing this game, not you."

He began to roll a cigarette, studying the draught-board as he did so. He appeared to be in no hurry to move again, and Willis did not attempt to hasten him. Donker went on with a tale he had been recounting; it was the tale of a convoy early in the War.

"Cut to pieces," Donker said; "cut to pieces—that's what we were. Seventeen ships sunk out of about forty. Every night those blessed U-boats would come and knock somebody off. Seemed like you had nothing but ships doing down all round you. And there was no proper rescue ship in those days; corvettes used to pick up a lot of the survivors; but there ain't too much room in a corvette for the crew, let alone a pack of survivors."

Donker lit his cigarette and wheezed smoke into his lungs. The smoke came up as he went on speaking, drifting out of his mouth as though coming from some smouldering fire deep inside him.

"We was at the tail of the convoy, and when things got real bad our skipper asked for permission to help pick up survivors. It didn't seem so bad after that; we had something to do to take our minds off things. What a sight! What a sight it was! All those poor devils floating about in the dark with their life-lights on; we'd never have seen 'em else. They looked," said Donker, and paused, trying to think exactly what they had looked like, "they looked like a carpet of blessed glow-worms stretching away across the sea." He seemed pleased with the simile, and repeated it. "A carpet of glow-worms. Ah, but there wasn't much glow inside of 'em—not in that water—not in the North Atlantic in the middle of the night. Oh, my, my!

"Funny thing, too! When we drifted up slow as possible to avoid running any of 'em down some of the silly bastards started swimming away; thought we was a blessed derelict. Then we let nets down over the side, and a lot of us went down to help 'em up. It was a tough job; they were half frozen, proper numb with the cold, and they couldn't help themselves hardly. We got 'em in, though; we got 'em in and steamed on. All told, we collected nearly a hundred."

Donker moved a draughtsman and sat back with a look of triumph.

" We was pretty full up after that. You couldn't hardly move in the quarters. And you could never tell what those fellers were going to do; it took some of 'em funny, you know. There was one man wanted to kill our captain because he thought his own skipper had been pushed out of the way. We couldn't persuade him different. Nutty, I reckon. Then there was some couldn't keep still; used to walk about on deck all the time; never seemed to sleep. And some just used to lean on the rails and stare out across the convoy; and if you spoke to 'em, like as not they'd start crying just like kids. Some was kids—not twenty, some of 'em. One boy couldn't stop shivering, even when he was in the warm; and there was another did nothing but moan about some silk stockings he'd lost. ' My Judy won't arf carry on,' he used to say. ' Special order, they was. She won't arf let into me!' Not pleased at all that he'd been saved; all he could think about was those blessed silk stockings. I told him a whole skin was better than fifty pairs of stockings; but he couldn't see it. ' She'll be mad at me,' he'd say. ' She won't arf be mad!' "

Donker moved another piece, and promptly lost it.

" Why, you damned silly old bastard!" Agnew exclaimed.

" Here, here!" said Donker. " Not so much of the old!"

" Did you get through all right? " asked Payne, who had wandered into the mess-room. " You didn't get bumped with that lot on board? "

" No," said Donker, " we didn't get bumped then; but we did on the next trip, and then we was alone. It was like this: we'd left the convoy off Halifax and turned south, having some cargo for Valparaiso and meaning to go through the Panama Canal. But we never got that far, because in the middle of the Caribbean Sea a dirty big submarine came up and put four torpedoes into us. Four! You wouldn't have thought they'd have wasted all that lot on one poor old tramp steamer. It was only to be expected that she'd sink pretty quick with them in her guts; but we got two boats away; crowded they was and all.

" The submarine came up alongside us soon after that, and

the commander asked us some questions. He was a young chap, not more than twenty-five I'd guess, and a lot of the crew didn't look more than eighteen or so. He spoke with a thick accent, but pretty good English; asked us if there was anything we wanted. Well, of course, what we really wanted was a bit of dry land, and he couldn't give us that. What he did give us was some chocolate and brandy—both French— and a few fags. Then he told us the latest bearing and sheered off. He wasn't a bad feller as Huns go.

"As I say, we was pretty crowded at first; but we soon thinned out. There was one kid in our boat what had had his right arm blown off close to the shoulder. It was an untidy job, all jagged and messy, with the end of bone sticking out. We did our best for him; we tied it up as best we could; but we weren't none of us doctors. He kept moaning; he never left off moaning. Well, I expect it hurt. It wasn't the only thing, you see; he'd had a great piece ripped out of his left buttock, and because of that he couldn't lie on his left side. But owing to his arm being off he couldn't lie on his right side either. No wonder he moaned.

"You wouldn't hardly have thought a man in that condition could have lasted any time; but he took four days to die, and moaning all the time, except when the pain took him real bad, and then he'd shriek. Some of the men wanted to throw him overboard to the sharks; he got on their nerves; but Cap'n Pown'll wouldn't hear of that, and he was master in that boat just like he'd been master in the ship. He wouldn't have it—not at any price.

"There was a nigger—one of the greasers—got a bit mad at the end of the twentieth day—lack of water and sun and that. He picked up a hammer and was going to do for some- body, and he didn't care who. The Old Man just looked at him and said, quiet as you like, 'Drop it!' That's all he said, and the nigger dropped the hammer. He dropped himself overboard two minutes later, and we was well shot of him.

"Huff you!" said Donker, rubbing the knob on his neck as

though he were polishing a door-knob. " Huff you! You could 'a took me there."

Willis swore. " That's what comes of listening to your talk. Well, what happened to you? "

" Nothing much," said Donker. " We just drifted on and on. Somehow or other the sail had got lost, so we just drifted. We lost touch with the other boat the first night, and never heard of it again. The heat was the worst thing; there wasn't no shade and precious little water. Sometimes we used to hang over the side and soak ourselves, but there was sharks and barracuda, which didn't make it a safe occupation. Besides, the Old Man wouldn't allow us too much of that. Proper discipline he kept; proper rationing of food and water, and proper routine. That's what held us together, I reckon. All the same, we'd had about enough of it when we was spotted by a seaplane. There was five of us left then out of twenty-one. Funny thing, we was only twenty miles off one of the Leeward Islands; that night we was ashore."

" I bet it got your weight down," said Agnew.

" Ay," said Donker, " it did that. What's more it taught me always to keep my teeth either in my mouth or in my pocket. That time I left 'em in the cabin. It's a job eating biscuit with no teeth."

" How long were you in the boat? " asked Willis.

" Forty days and forty nights, just like Moses in the mountain."

" That's a long time."

" People have been in boats longer. There was a Chinaman lived on a raft for a hundred and thirty days, and then drifted ashore little the worse."

" What did he live on? "

" Flying-fish and rain-water chiefly, I believe."

" Chinese are different," Payne said. " They haven't got the same sort of minds as we have. A white man would have gone mad."

" You don't know. Depends on the man."

" A ship I was in ran across a strange piece of business

in the Sargasso Sea," remarked Rogerson. He was a small, studious-looking sailor, who seemed out of place in naval uniform—rather like a serious-minded reveller in fancy dress. "You know what the Sargasso is like—all that floating weed. We were steaming along the edge of it, and the weed wasn't so thick—just chunks about two or three feet across, looking like overgrown bath-sponges, and drifting silently past. And then we saw something that wasn't a chunk of weed at all, though at first we couldn't tell what it was. Then when we got nearer we could see it was a raft, and the Old Man gave orders to heave to and investigate.

"We were sailing alone, you understand; and when the screw stopped churning and we just drifted up to the raft we seemed more alone than ever. I don't know what it is about the Sargasso, but it always makes me think of a dead world. There it is, all that weed, drifting there—Gulf weed, so I've heard, carried out there from the Gulf of Mexico; more and more coming out and dying. It's like an immense graveyard; and there's the heat and the stillness—not a breath of wind; it seems unnatural, somehow.

"Well, there it was—this raft—a ship's raft like we carry. And there was nobody on it."

"Nothing very strange in that," said Payne. "It'd have been stranger if you'd found a dozen men waiting to be picked up."

"Wait a bit, though," Rogerson said. "There wasn't anybody on the raft; but there was something. It was wedged between two of the slats, and it was black and skinny; but you could see easily enough what it was; it was a human hand. There was nothing else on the raft—nothing at all; just that hand, broken off at the wrist and wedged between the slats."

"No rings on the fingers?" asked Payne.

Rogerson frowned. "You can laugh," he said; "but none of us felt much like laughing at the time. There's a lot you can build up from a hand and a raft if you have the imagination; a lot that isn't very pleasant."

"That's true," said Agnew. "You don't know how many men there were on that raft to start with, and you don't know how long they lasted or how long it was before they gave up hope. You don't know how that hand came to be torn off. There may have been some bloody work on that little island. But nobody'll know now; nobody'll ever know. What did you do?"

"We left it there," Rogerson said. "We left it just as it was. It seemed a long while before it vanished out of sight. Maybe it's still there, still floating about in the Sargasso with that hand wedged between the slats."

Donker knocked the ash off his cigarette and studied the draught-board. "Wonder whose hand it was," he said.

A Russian interpreter had come down into the mess-room. He was a young man with very thick black hair and black eyes. His English was remarkably good. He picked up a book that was lying on the table.

"I see you read Dostoevski."

Vernon nodded. "I have just finished it."

The interpreter was an earnest young man who appeared to take himself and life very seriously. Vernon had invited him to come down into the gunners' mess for a cup of coffee and a cigarette.

He murmured the name of the book, *The Brothers Karamazov*, and put it down again. "What did you think of it?" he asked.

"Frankly, I don't know that I quite understand it. It was heavy going in parts, especially at the start; but it held me later on. It held me as a nightmare would. That was how it impressed me—as a nightmare. I felt the power of the writing, but I did not altogether understand."

"But is that not true of all books that have any value? One does not fully understand them at once—perhaps never. And to understand Dostoevski I think it is necessary to be a Russian."

"Your writers are inclined to obscurity."

" English writers too. I am often puzzled by Dickens."

" Dickens! Then you read him? "

" Oh, yes."

" But why are you puzzled? Dickens is quite straightforward."

" To an Englishman, perhaps; for a Russian he is not so easy to understand."

Vernon made coffee and handed a mug to the Russian, who sipped slowly.

" Dostoevski suffered; he suffered deeply; that suffering found expression in his books. You have read *Letters from the Underworld*? "

" No."

" Ah, you should. There you will find the agony of his soul —a great soul, but a tortured one. You know that he spent five years in a penal settlement in Siberia, and that once he was about to be shot, but was reprieved at the last minute? "

" Yes, I have read about that."

" Such experiences affect a man's character and have a bearing on his work. Turgenev could not have written as Dostoevski did."

The interpreter sipped his coffee; his eyes were dark and brooding.

" Ah," he said, " if only Tolstoy were alive to-day, how much he would have to write about—the struggle of our people against the forces of evil! If only he had seen the epic of Stalingrad! You have heard the latest news from there? "

" No," said Vernon, " we don't get much news."

The interpreter spoke as though he were quoting a news item which he had learnt by heart.

" Our troops are moving in for the final, crushing blow. The German armies attacking the city are trapped. It is reported that they have lost more than three hundred thousand men, including twenty generals. The Red Army has captured seven hundred aircraft, fifteen hundred tanks, six thousand guns, and sixty thousand motor vehicles. It will be difficult for the Nazis to replace such losses."

"They made a mistake," said Vernon; "they made a mistake in attacking Stalingrad; it couldn't have been as important as that; the cost was out of proportion. But I don't think Germany is beaten yet."

"It will not be long," said the interpreter. "It will all be over very soon."

"It can't be over too soon for me. I wish it would end before we have to go back."

The interpreter looked sharply at Vernon. "It is, then, so bad out there beyond the river-mouth?"

"Bad enough. It's no pleasure-trip."

"I have heard so. It is not easy for you. I expect you are glad when you meet our warships and our aircraft half-way."

Vernon stared. "Do you mind saying that again?"

"I said, you are glad to see the warships we send to meet your convoys."

Vernon laughed. "Somebody's been telling you fairy-stories. The only warships out there are British and German ones—apart from an odd Pole or Norwegian."

The Russian stiffened, and his face darkened. "That cannot be true," he said. "You forget our North Fleet."

Vernon did not pursue the subject; it seemed hardly worth a quarrel; but it showed where propaganda led you. The Arctic convoys would be in a poor way if they had to rely on Russian escorts. And as for Russian aircraft, why, you never saw any of them until you were practically in Kola Bay.

He began speaking of other things; but he could see that the interpreter was offended, resenting the slight upon the Russian naval forces. Soon the man got to his feet, thanked Vernon formally for the coffee and cigarettes, and took his leave.

Payne guffawed. "Well, what d'you think of that? North Fleet! You know what it is—half a dozen motor-boats which only go down the river when there's an air-raid on Murmansk. Meet us half-way! Oh, dear, what next?"

Vernon let the book fall from his hands and lay on his

back, staring at the bunk above his own. From the deck he could hear the intermittent clatter of steam winches, and from closer at hand the sound of Warby scraping burnt toast. Always Warby seemed to be making toast; always the winches clattered overhead; and always the stove poured soot into the fuggy atmosphere of the cabin. Everywhere there was soot; blankets were no longer white, but a dirty grey; clothes carried their load of grime; dirt was ingrained into the skin and seemed to be there permanently, never again to be got out. On everything in the cabin, on bunks, on books, on shelves, on men, soot had laid its grimy finger, smearing them all, as though in anticipation, with the mark of the grave.

Vernon picked up his book and began to read again. He read:

> What wondrous life is this I lead!
> Ripe apples drop about my head;
> The luscious clusters of the vine
> Upon my mouth do crush their wine;
> The nectarine, and curious peach,
> Into my hands themselves do reach;
> Stumbling on melons, as I pass,
> Ensnared with flowers, I fall on grass. . . .

Vernon took his eyes away from the words of Andrew Marvell, and saw the bulkhead covered with moisture like great drops of filthy sweat; he passed his fingers through his hair and felt the grittiness of coal-dust; he saw a pair of sea-boot stockings hanging from Payne's bunk and smelling of Payne's feet; and he heard the heavy thud of some piece of cargo bumping against the side of the hatch as it was drawn up from the hold.

"What a bloody life!" he muttered.

"It's the first ten years that's the worst," said Warby.

CHAPTER TEN

Tinsel

THEY were the first slaves that Andrews had seen. The interpreter called them political prisoners, saboteurs, enemies of the people; but whatever name you gave them they were still slaves. They came shuffling down to the ships under an armed guard, trudging wearily through the churned snow; they came in a long, drab column, ragged, dirty, without hope and without joy, waiting for the old turnkey, Death, to release them. They were hungry, tired, and silent; they were men turned into animals, dumb beasts of burden. And they were like a blight falling upon the *Golden Ray*, a dark dew of misery.

Andrews watched them coming up the gangway; he watched them taking off the hatch-covers; he watched them clambering down into the hold; and he thought of zombies—the living dead. They had the same drawn, earthy faces, the same expressionless eyes, the same slow, robot-like movements. The dock crane lowered a net into the hold, and they filled the net, awkwardly, inexpertly. Then the crane lifted the net from the hold, and they began filling another. So it went on; and on the snowbound, icy deck a Russian soldier lounged with slung rifle—the servant of a vast political machine.

" There," said Andrews to Miller; " there's Communism for you. They look happy, don't they? This is the bright Utopia you're always preaching about."

" There's prisoners in England," Miller said. " They break stones on Dartmoor. This is more sense; this is useful work."

But after dinner Miller had something to think about, something to turn over in his mind, trying to find an answer.

Andrews called to him to come up on deck, and he went, wondering what Andrews wanted. Up the iron ladder they went and out into the open.

" This way," Andrews said, drawing Miller towards the

forward end of the poop, from which they could look down upon the main deck. " See that? "

Miller looked in the direction in which Andrews was pointing and saw the Russians at work on number four hold. But that was not all he saw. A large packing-case had been dumped on the deck, and behind this screen Miller noticed that a man was hiding. He was crouched upon his haunches, picking something from a bucket with his bare hands, and stuffing this something into his mouth. He ate as a man will who has long been starving, regardless of what it is he eats, so long as it may serve to fill the aching hollows of his stomach. Yet the man was fearful; frequently he would glance over his shoulder to see whether he was observed; then he would go on eating.

" You see what it is he's making a meal of? " said Andrews.

" What? " asked Miller.

" Our swill," said Andrews. " That's our gash-bucket he's tucking into; there's tea-leaves and all sorts of filth in there. Shouldn't reckon the poor devil is overfed, would you? "

Miller said nothing, because he could think of nothing to say. He watched the man eating, and thought that he had never seen a human being swallow food so ravenously. He put Miller in mind of a stray mongrel dog foraging among dustbins; and he had the same furtive, frightened air.

" The guard's seen him," Andrews said. " What happens now? "

The guard saw the prisoner, and the prisoner saw the guard at the same moment. The prisoner straightened up from the bucket and backed against the packing-case. In his right hand he still held a chop-bone; down his black, stubbly chin saliva had dribbled. He backed against the case, staring at the guard; and his hand, still clutching the bone, came up involuntarily, as though to shield his meagre body. Miller and Andrews could hear no word, either from the prisoner or from the guard, for the steam winches were clattering and the air was full of overpowering noise; they could only look down and watch what was taking place.

Suddenly the guard kicked the prisoner; he kicked him in
the lower part of the stomach; and as the man doubled up in
pain the guard struck him on the side of the head with the
butt of his rifle. The prisoner staggered back, and the guard
struck him a second time. Blood began to trickle down from
the man's ear.

The guard's lips were moving, but what he said was
inaudible to the two watchers above; it was like a drama
enacted in dumb show. But the prisoner heard and began
moving towards the hatch. As he went the guard kicked him
again; he kicked him persistently until the wretched fellow
disappeared over the coaming. And as he went down into the
hold Miller saw that he still clutched the bone in his right
hand.

But it was not only prisoners who worked on the ship;
there were free men as well. And there were women too,
toiling side by side with the men and doing the same hard,
manual work.

Miller went ashore alone. He could not bear to have
anyone with him when he made his first contact with the soil
of Russia—that blessed soil from which had sprung Lenin
and Stalin and all the other leaders of the Revolution. For
Miller this was a great moment, a moment of fulfilment, of
realization; the moment he had waited for so long.

When the sentry at the entrance to the dock stopped him
for his pass Miller felt that he would have liked to embrace
the man. But he restrained his feelings and handed over his
pass and his Army pay-book. The sentry examined them with
great care and handed them back. Then he said, " Seegret,
comrade? Please, seegret? "

Miller gave him a cigarette; the sentry took it with a word
of thanks, and Miller passed on out of the dock. But in
Miller's heart again was a tiny voice of unease; for surely in
this mother state of Communism there should have been no
need for a soldier of the people's Army to beg a cigarette
from the foreigner stepping ashore in his country?

But other blows were to fall upon the ramparts of Miller's faith; and immediately he was to discover that that black market of which the sailor on the *Golden Ray* had spoken did in fact exist. For he had not walked twenty yards away from the dock before he was surrounded by a crowd of urchins, all shouting in shrill, treble voices and all thrusting towards him wads of rouble notes—fives, tens, fifties, and hundreds.

"Here, comrade! Here, rouble! Rouble, see! Seegret, choclit! Rouble; rouble!"

Miller was bewildered and unhappy. It was unbelievable that Russian children, young and tender children, should be the agents of black marketeers; that they should besiege foreigners coming off capitalist ships and importune them thus for the sale of cigarettes and chocolate. Yet he had to believe the evidence of his own eyes, however painful that evidence might be, and however degrading it might seem to the land of his heart's desire.

The children flocked about him, fur hats pulled down over their ears, their quilted clothing greasy and ragged, their noses dirty, and in their hands hundreds and hundreds of roubles which they were eager to exchange for a few cigarettes or a handful of chocolate.

"Rouble, comrade! Rouble for seegret, choclit!"

"No," said Miller. "No cigarettes; no chocolate!"

Not at any price would he sell such articles to these children of Russia; it would have seemed a betrayal of his faith. He walked on faster, trying to shake the children off.

"No cigarettes; no chocolate! None, none, none!"

The hardiest spirits—those least easily dissuaded—followed him for a long way, pleading, urging; but eventually even they trailed off, dropping disconsolately behind and stuffing their dirty roubles into still dirtier pockets.

Miller walked on alone into the town of Murmansk.

What he had expected to find he would himself have had difficulty in describing. Streets paved with gold? They were paved with iron-hard snow. Brave new architecture? There were log cabins and square, concrete buildings, already cracked, peeling, crumbling away, having about them a down-at-heel and out-at-elbows appearance. Shop-windows full of the products of Communist industry? Half the shops were boarded up with rough planks; in some were a few shoddy articles. Happy, smiling people? Here was no laughter upon the air; here were faces etched with all the signs of misery.

Miller did not know what it was he had expected; yet he knew that it was not this. He told himself over and over again that this was the land he had always wanted to see, ever since the party had claimed him; that this was Russia. But, looking round him, he saw only that it was bleak and cold and dilapidated—and he did not know what to do.

Suddenly there seemed to be no aim nor object in his being ashore; for he knew no one and no one knew him. He felt lonely and depressed. But he walked on, and, passing a shop, he almost ran into an old woman. She had a shawl draped over her head and shoulders, and Miller, looking into her face, thought that he had never seen one so incredibly wrinkled. The old woman gazed at Miller, but there was no emotion in her gaze, only an infinite resignation, and with a muttered word she moved to one side and passed by him, clutching beneath her shawl half a loaf of black bread.

Miller had never seen the old woman before, and he would never see her again. He did not know whence she came nor whither she was going; he did not know where she had been born, how she lived, nor where she would die; he did not know whether she had sons or daughters, husband or friends; he knew only that her face was wrinkled, that it had about it the colour of earth, as though it were changing slowly but perceptibly back to dust, that there was a shawl over her head, and that she carried in her hand a piece of coarse bread. For a brief moment he had seen the old woman; for a brief moment she had walked across the path of his life and was gone out of it for ever; yet in that moment, had he known it, he might have beheld gazing up at him from her dull eyes the true, undying soul of that Russia he had come to find.

On one street corner Miller saw a sailor of the Russian

North Fleet, reeling drunk, being sick in the road. Miller walked on.

Sometimes a motor-lorry would grind past, scarcely making an impression on the hard-packed snow. Now and then a pony sleigh would slip by, and once Miller saw a girl on skis. Then he passed a group of Army women, dressed in sheep-skin coats, leather jack-boots, and fur hats with the red star set in the front. They took no notice of Miller, and he felt somehow like an outcast.

Here and there about the streets were loud-speakers hung on posts; sometimes music came from them, sometimes speech; but Miller saw no one stopping to listen. In one place he saw a large war-map posted up on a board; but it showed only the Russian front, and there was no indication that fighting was going on anywhere else, nor that Russia possessed any allies.

Miller felt miserable; there seemed to be nothing to do and nothing to see. Moreover, he was cold. Then he saw Warby and Ben Cowdrey about to enter a building.

" Hi! " he shouted. " Hi, there! "

The other two stopped and looked back. " Oh, it's you," Cowdrey said. " Where are you off to? "

" Just looking round," said Miller. " What's this place? "

" The International Club," said Cowdrey. " They're giving a film show to-night. Why don't you come? "

" Pictures! " said Miller in disgust. " No, thanks! Not for me! None of that tripe! "

He turned and walked away, the other two watching him.

" There's something queer about that blighter," Cowdrey said; " something damned queer. Well, let's go in and see what the Russkis have got for us."

Miller walked on. He had no idea where he was going, but he walked on, leaving the big concrete buildings behind, following the road out to where the log houses thinned. He walked over a level crossing, and suddenly saw the river on his left hand, and ships. And still he walked on over the rough, icy road; and still his heart was heavy because this was not what he had hoped to find.

It was quite dark when he turned back, and a breeze had sprung up, drifting in from the frozen wastes of tundra, bringing the frigid touch of the terrible northern winter. Miller slapped his gloved hands as he walked and stamped his feet hard on the crusted road. He began to wish he was back on board, for the cold slid down upon him and his lips were numb.

It was a night of many stars shining with a peculiar added brightness, as though the snow and the wind had polished them into a greater luminosity. There was the Great Bear keeping watch over its own land; there was the Little Bear with the Pole Star in its tail; there were Cassiopeia and Perseus, Camelopardalis and Draco. And other stars without number stood in the vast distances of the night; distances so great that in comparison the Earth was but a dust-mote upon the face of the sun. What, then, of Miller walking upon the Earth? How infinitesimally small a portion of the universe was he! Yet to himself the rest was as nothing. He was the centre, the hub around which all revolved. Worlds and planets, stars and constellations, galaxies and nebulae—all these meant less to Miller than the one grain of doubt nagging at his little mind.

He recrossed the railway and climbed up the slope towards the town. The houses came darkly out of the gloom, and he went on, slipping now and then on the icy ground and steadying himself with outflung arms. Amid the silence of the night and the silence of the dark houses from which no light shone he felt like a lost child, terribly alone. And with this sense of loneliness came a touch of fear; he was fearful of the night, the darkness, and the cold. The sighing wind, that was like the hand of Death feeling beneath his coat and clutching at his face, frightened him also. And he knew that he had lost his way.

After a time he feared that he had gone too far and was coming out on the other side of the town; so he turned and went back, wandering amid the houses and not finding the road down to the dock where the *Golden Ray* lay moored. He was off the main streets, and there were only low log houses around him. Then suddenly a wedge of light shone upon the snow in front of him, and he saw that a door had opened. From within the house he heard a gust of laughter and the strum of a guitar; then the door closed again, and Miller could discern the dark outline of a man standing against the wall of the cabin. He thought of asking the stranger to direct him on his way, but the utter impossibility of making himself understood to a Russian made him hesitate; and as he hesitated he heard the man begin to whistle softly.

Miller felt envious of the stranger, because he would soon be going back into warmth and light and companionship, while he, Miller, must still grope along, trying to find a lost path. Then the man turned, fumbling at his buttons; and as he turned he saw Miller.

" Hullo! " he said. " Who are you? "

At the sound of English words Miller's self-confidence came flooding back, and he answered with much of his usual perkiness.

" If it comes to that, who are you? "

" Oh, you're English, then," said the man. " Are you coming inside? "

" Inside? " Miller repeated. " What's inside? "

" Come and see; it's open house, and a good time will be had by all—that's if you've got any roubles. Have you? "

" Yes," said Miller, " I've got some."

" All right, then. Come in if you're coming. It's perishin' out here."

He opened the door, and Miller, blinking in the sudden glow of light, followed him inside. He found himself then in a large, plain room, in which were a number of men and women gathered round a glowing, pot-bellied stove. On one side of the room was a table on which stood a samovar, several glasses, and two or three bottles of vodka. The guitar was being played by a tall, black-haired man with the badge of the Merchant Navy in his lapel, and the other men also appeared to be seamen.

The air was thick with tobacco-smoke and fumes from the stove; it was a hot, choking atmosphere that caught at Miller's throat and made his eyes water. His face too, after being exposed to the cold wind, felt stiff; and when he opened his mouth the skin stretched taut across his teeth like a band of perished rubber.

The man who had invited him in—a square, thick man, wearing a blue serge suit and blue roll-neck pullover—slapped him on the shoulder.

" Come on, mate," he said; " come and get warm."

It was then that Miller saw the fat woman. She was seated on the far side of the stove, almost in shadow, and she seemed to flow over the chair on which she sat like a great hill of flesh. Her hair was black, coarse as the mane of a horse, and cut in a straight fringe; it fell on either side of her enormous, heavy face like the frame enclosing a hideous caricature of womanhood. Her eyes were like small currants thrust in the folds of an immense suet dumpling; her teeth were an old, rotten fence, gapped and decaying; on her upper lip was a palpable moustache. She breathed in quick, gasping breaths, and as she breathed her massive bosom rose and fell, like the waves that rise and fall against the side of a ship.

" Mother Carey," said Miller's guide. " You'll have to pay her. This is her house."

" How much? " asked Miller.

" Don't give her more than a hundred roubles. That's plenty. She'll take all you like to give her; but a hundred roubles is enough."

The man with the guitar was playing *Jealousy*. Now and then he missed a note; now and then he played a wrong one; he slurred the rhythm, and his head drooped as though he were half asleep. But he lifted his head to wink through the haze of smoke. None of the others gave more than a glance at Miller as he walked across the room to where Mother

Carey sat, overwhelming her chair with abundant flesh.

Standing in front of her, he could see the dirt that seemed to be flowing down from her hair like a creeping tide, and he could see the moisture glistening on her skin. She was like a female Buddha at whose throne he had come to worship, and she stared at him with her little, shining eyes without speaking for so long that he fidgeted beneath the impact of her gaze. Then she nodded slowly and held out her hand, palm uppermost.

Miller took two fifty-rouble notes from his pocket—it was half the Russian money he possessed—and placed them on the old woman's hand. She accepted them without thanks and thrust them away in some recess of her clothing. Then she called to one of the girls, "Anya! Anya!" adding some words which Miller could not understand.

The girl thus addressed was short and plump. She had a broad face, a wide, flat nose, and rough skin. Her hair was plaited and pinned in two coils, one on either side of her head. She took Miller's arm and led him to an old sofa covered with plush cloth that had once been red, but now was almost black with dirt. At one end of the sofa a sailor sat with his feet thrust out before him, his head lolling forward, his eyes closed. His snoring could be heard above the chatter and the music of the guitar.

Anya signed to Miller to take off his coat and cap; and he did so, hanging them on the back of the sofa. Then she went to the table, poured out a glass of vodka, and brought it to him, sitting down beside him on the sofa.

Miller drank some of the pale liquid, and a stream of warmth seemed to flow to the extremities of his body. He drank again, and the room closed in on him, warm, pleasant, exciting. Anya was leaning against him, and Miller found himself wedged between her and the arm of the sofa.

"Please—seegret," she said.

As he put down his glass of vodka and felt for the packet Miller could not help thinking how strange it was that every one should ask him for cigarettes. Cigarette, comrade!

Cigarette, cigarette! Always it was cigarettes! He handed the packet to Anya, and she took one. As he lit it for her she smiled lazily at him through the haze of smoke, then, taking the cigarette from her mouth, leaned suddenly forward and kissed him on the lips.

In Miller was the sense of being trapped. He felt at the same time attracted and repelled. Something inside him was urging him to stand up, to leave the house and go away— somewhere—anywhere. In that way he might retain some shreds of his illusions, some tattered remnants of his faith. But there was no strength in his limbs; it was as though his bones were softening, melting down into powerless jelly. And the girl pressed upon him, warm and sensual, drawing him into the net of her sheer animal attraction.

He drained his glass of vodka, and Anya refilled it. He drank again, and the noises of the room seemed to come to him from an infinite distance, like the sound of waves falling on a far-off shore. A woman had the guitar now and was fingering out a sad, slow tune, singing in a husky voice, almost like a man's. Heat flowed out of the stove, and Mother Carey sat motionless and watchful on her chair.

Miller lit a cigarette for himself, and drew smoke down into his lungs, letting it drift out again through nose and mouth, letting it drift up towards the blackened ceiling of the room. He was hot now, beginning to sweat under his heavy clothing. With slow, fumbling fingers he began to undo the buttons of his khaki battle-blouse. Anya noticed the tape by which his identity-discs were slung from his neck, and she pulled up the brown stamped discs from inside his vest. Holding them in her hand, she looked at them, frowning in puzzlement. Then she traced the inscription with her finger—Miller's Army number, his name and initials, and, underneath, his religion, C.E. It could with as much reason have been R.C., or Pres., or Meth.—with as much reason or as little, for religion meant nothing to him. Nevertheless for Army purposes his religion was Church of England; whether he believed or whether he did not made no difference to the authorities.

Anya put the discs back inside his vest, tickling him playfully as she did so. Again Miller felt that strange mixture of attraction and repulsion; he saw the girl's bony, Asiatic features close to his own; he saw that she had little pockmarks under the eyes and that one of her front teeth had been broken off, leaving a jagged stump. And above all the other scents in the room—the tobacco-smoke, the vodka, the fumes from the stove—he could smell the warm, animal odour of her body.

He began to feel drowsy. It was the effect of the heat and the vodka. He wanted to close his eyes and drift away into unconsciousness, into the world of sleep and dreams. But Anya was standing beckoning him to get up and follow. So he followed her—across the room and through a doorway covered by a heavy curtain—having no will to resist, no will of his own at all.

When Miller left the brothel the sky was full of light; but it was all man-made: searchlights wavered to and fro; glowing tracers and flaming onions, dark red against the night, climbed towards the stars; while parachute flares drifted slowly down towards the bombers' target. Overhead Miller could hear the steady, rhythmic drone of aeroplane engines, and occasionally splinters of anti-aircraft shells would fall with a slight hiss into the snow beside him.

But he took no notice. He might have gone to a shelter if he had known where there was one; but he did not, and so he walked on, trying to find his way back to the docks and the *Golden Ray*. He had lost all his roubles; he had lost about two pounds in English money also—Anya had wheedled it from him—and he had lost his cigarettes and his lighter. But for these things he cared nothing; they were replaceable. He could earn more money; he could buy more cigarettes. What he mourned was the loss of something that could never be replaced—that vision he had cherished for so long. That was why his heart was heavy, why his eyes burned. He looked into the future and saw nothing. Life had lost all meaning. He was like a man who has followed a star, only to find in the end that it is tinsel.

Miller realized now that the Russia of his vision did not exist, had never existed but in his own imagination; and that realization was bitterness to him. Now he had nothing to cling to; he was lost, adrift, rudderless. In the anguish of his spirit he could have wept.

He heard the whistle of the falling bomb, and in the same instant fell flat upon the ground with his face in the snow. He could feel the ground shudder beneath him with the force of the explosion, and it seemed as though his ear-drums were being sucked out of his head. Then lumps of snow and pieces of earth fell on him. Then there was nothing more; and after a time he got to his feet and went on.

He saw a wooden house blazing, flames thrusting up through the roof. He saw men and women running, heard them shouting; but they were nothing to him—nothing at all.

Away beyond the town he saw a chandelier of incendiaries fall upon one of the hills. There in the snow they sparkled, and it was as though a cluster of stars had fallen upon the earth. They were beautiful, but Miller had no eyes for beauty. He could hear the bomber droning in for another run across the town, and he wondered whether this time a bomb would have his number on it. But the bombs fell half a mile away, and the plane droned off into the night, heading for Petsamo. Then the guns became silent, the searchlights ceased to play upon the sky, and only the flicker of red flame remained as a sign of what had occurred.

" Seegret? " asked the sentry at the dock. " Seegret, comrade? "

Miller did not answer. He took his pass back from the man's hand and walked towards the gangway of the *Golden Ray*. As he climbed up to the deck he felt infinitely weary, as though all the spirit had been drained out of his body. In the cabin the dim bulb was alight, and he saw all the other gunners were in their bunks. He began to undress, and Payne, who slept in the bunk below his own, awoke and gazed sleepily at him.

" Hullo!" said Payne. " Had a good time? "

He was asleep again before Miller could think of an answer.

Weary as he was, Miller did not sleep at once. He lay on his back, staring up into the gloom, and his soul ached. He had seen the land of his dreams, and he never wished to see it again. He had been ashore in Russia for the first and last time.

Suddenly he thought of Jessie; and, thinking of her, his lips trembled and his eyes filled with tears. He turned over and bit into the life-jacket that he used as a pillow, stifling his agony in the soft folds of kapok.

CHAPTER ELEVEN

On Russian Soil

VERNON, Payne, Andrews, and Lance-Bombardier Panton-Smith were sitting round a small table in a room on the first floor of the Arctica Hotel. The room was large and warm, and contained many tables at which sat many men—some English, some American, some Russian. They talked earnestly in low voices; there was a little laughter, but not much; life in Murmansk was not a very laughable affair.

Vernon, Payne, Andrews, and Panton-Smith were drinking tea and vodka. The tea was hot and sweet, but without milk; it was served in glass tumblers. There was a small glass of vodka and a large glass of tea to wash it down. In the way of solid refreshment there were sweet, sickly-tasting cakes filled with a kind of cream that hung greasily about the mouth.

Panton-Smith finished off his glass of vodka and said, " I prefer whisky. What's this stuff made of, anyway? "

" Plain alcohol, I should think," said Payne. " Not much colour about it. I agree with you; whisky's better."

"I'd rather have beer," said Andrews.

"Ah," said Payne, "now you're talking. I could just do with a dirty big pint. And I wish I was in the Trip to Jerusalem drinking it."

"Are you from Nottingham?" asked Panton-Smith.

Payne nodded vigorously. "That's right."

"Do you know the Flying Horse?"

"Oh, yes; but I didn't used to go there."

"I was on a gun-site in Nottingham for six months," said Panton-Smith. "That was a couple of years back." His eyes became dreamy. "There was a girl called Elsie; I met her in the Flying Horse. We had some good times. Lord, yes! What a game it is, eh?" He sipped his tea. "What a game! What a game! Elsie! Oh, Lord!"

Outside it had begun to snow again. Vernon gazed out of the window of the Arctica Hotel and saw the snow like an immense dotted curtain falling upon the silent town. He looked down into the street and saw a Ford lorry driving past. The back of the lorry was open, and Vernon could see five figures sitting with their backs to the cab and their legs stretched out; he could not tell whether they were the figures of men or of women, but as the lorry turned a corner he saw them roll to one side and then straighten again. Then they were out of sight and snow was already filling up the marks of the lorry's wheels.

"Freddie's ship caught a near miss last night," said Panton-Smith. "Damaged a propeller. Looks as if she's going to miss the next convoy."

. "Nice for Freddie," Vernon said. "Another month in this hole!"

"It's a bastard right enough; but I can't say I'm looking forward to the journey home."

Payne wiped cream off his moustache. "Oh, no need to worry over that. Jerry don't trouble with the empties. Have a fag."

Panton-Smith took one of the cigarettes and fished up a lighter. "Don't count on that," he said. "A ship is worth a torpedo whether she's full or empty. I won't sleep sound till I see the Orkneys."

Vernon took one of Payne's cigarettes and lit it from Panton-Smith's lighter. " Did you hear about the accident in our ship, Smithy? "

Panton-Smith shook his head. " Accident? No. What was that? "

" Stevedore killed. Bit messy, one way and another. I saw it."

" How did it happen? "

" Damned fool of a crane-driver caught a slingful of boiler-plates under the lip of the hatch as he was drawing them up out of the hold. The sling broke, and down went the plates. One of the stevedores happened to be in the way, and the plates fell on him—couple of tons of iron, I suppose. You wouldn't have known it was a man when they lifted the plates off—just a mass of pulp—blood spattered all over the place—very messy."

" What did they do? "

" Picked up the bits and went on as if nothing had happened."

" Well, he won't be caught again."

" No."

Panton-Smith turned to Payne. " Ever go to Trent Bridge? The cricket-ground, I mean."

Payne had been lifting a glass of vodka to his lips. He paused with the glass in mid-air, just as though Panton-Smith's question had frozen him. Then he answered slowly, " Yes—yes, I did." And after that he put his glass down again without drinking, and was silent.

Panton-Smith began telling some interminable story of a Test Match he had once seen; but Payne was not listening; he was back at Trent Bridge under the hot sun, hitching up his trousers and casting a glance round the field before starting on that smooth, accelerating run to the wicket that he had modelled on the great Harold Larwood. He was seventeen, already playing for Nottinghamshire second eleven, and

people were beginning to notice him, even beginning to speak
of him as a possible successor to Larwood and Voce. Not
without reason; he had the build for a fast bowler—plenty of
height—six feet three inches of it, and muscle too. " Strong
as a horse, our Ted," his father used to say. " Bit stronger,
mebbe!" But it was not only height and strength he had;
those attributes alone did not make a bowler. No, he had
more than that; he had skill—the ability to move the ball—in
the air and off the pitch, and the ability to keep a length.

Much of that he owed to old Tom Watson. Tom's
cricketing days had long been past, but he still had an eye for
a promising youngster, and Ted Payne caught that eye.

" Come on, boy," Tom had said. " You do as I tell you,
and you won't go far wrong. Trust old Tom. He may be
gettin' stiff in the joints, but he still knows a thing or two."

And that was no idle boast. Tom did know a thing or two
when the subject was cricket. Young Payne listened and
learned.

" Length," Tom used to say; " length first. Pace and tricks
afterwards; but length first, me boy."

So he had curbed the exuberance of youth which would
have sent his pupil in a tearaway run to the wicket, to hurl
the ball as hard as he could somewhere, anywhere, in the
general direction of the batsman.

" Softly," Tom used to say; " softly does it, boy. Length
first; length first. Other things'll come."

And they had come.

" Remember," Tom said, " remember you got fingers. They
ain't just there to keep the ball from falling out of your hand;
they're there to put the 'fluence on it—the 'fluence! Ah!"

So Tom taught him how to put the " 'fluence " on the ball;
taught him how to bowl the out-swinger and the break-back;
how to make them sit up and how to make them float; how to
vary his length by those imperceptible degrees which caught
the batsman off his guard. All these things the old bowler
patiently taught him.

" But it's the one that moves away that's the best," Tom

would always say. " The one that moves away is worth ten of
the one that moves in. Make the ball leave the bat, and you
have 'em groping. Then, snick! and it's in slip's hands. Make
'em move away, boy; make 'em move away."

Old Tom remembered players of earlier generations—Hirst,
Armstrong, Jessop, Fry, Sid Barnes, Bardsley, Trumper, Hill,
Tunnicliffe, the brothers Foster and Ashton; he remembered
the Graces, Johnnie Briggs, Peel, and Spofforth, the Demon.
To listen to Tom was like browsing through old, dog-eared
numbers of *Wisden's Almanack*. He would talk about the
great fast bowlers—Lockwood, Richardson, Kortright, Fielder,
Gregory—of Bill Hitch, with his startling leap at the wicket.
" But Korty was the best of the lot, boy! Korty could make
'em fly! Why, bless me, I've known batsmen—and good
batsmen too—shaking at the knees because they had to go in
and face Korty on a lively wicket. Not but what they had
some reason to be scared; I was scared meself; but then I
never did reckon to bat."

Tom himself had bowled to Hayward and Ranjitsinhji, to
Hobbs, MacLaren, Johnny Tyldesley, and a host of others;
but he admitted that he had never been more than a county
man—a good stock bowler who could keep one end going
without too much expense. But as a coach he was in the top
class. Ted Payne listened and learned, and it was not long
before the county scouts cast an eye on him; and not long
after that he was given a trial; and soon he was in the second
eleven and signing professional forms.

He was twenty when he got his first chance in the county
side. It was a home match, and his father took three days off
work, so that he could come and watch. Young Jackie, his
brother, was there too; and, of course, old Tom. People
talked about the happiest day of their lives, and perhaps few
of them were really sure which was the day; but Payne knew;
he knew there could never be another day as wonderful as
that first day of his first match for Nottinghamshire. It was
like a fairy-tale: there were the two batsmen—he could see
them now—one tall and dark, the other short and fair, one an

amateur, the other a professional; they had put on 140 runs, and looked like occupying the centre for the rest of the day. Then his captain tossed the ball to Payne, and he, with his first delivery, his first ball for the county, before his own crowd, before his father and Jackie and old Tom, broke the partnership. He would always remember the sheer, mad delight of that moment as the off stump went cart-wheeling out of the ground, and the great roar that went up from the stands. There would never be anything like it again for him.

They had his photograph in the evening papers, and there were headlines: " Young Bowler takes Wicket with First Ball!" " Payne Another Larwood!" " Startling Debut!" He gloated over the accounts, and went about for days with a head much larger than it ought to have been. He already had his career mapped out. He was going to play for England; he would tour Australia, South Africa, the West Indies; he would help England to win the Ashes. It was all going to be wonderful.

Then something happened; he began to put on weight. At first he was not worried; it was nothing—just the natural increase of maturity—added muscle. But soon he had gained a stone and was beginning to feel it. He was unable to get the same pace in his run-up to the wicket as he had done; it took fewer overs to tire him; his wind was not so good. And still his weight increased; and there was no question now about its being muscle; anyone could see the fat on him.

He was alarmed. If this went on there was not likely to be any future for him as a fast bowler—no future in cricket at all. He consulted a doctor, and the doctor put him on a diet. It was tough going, but he stuck to it, and his weight began to fall. But he was always hungry—hungry and weak— so weak, in fact, that he had to cut his run-up by half.

He had dropped out of the county side long before this. Soon he was dropped from the second eleven also. At the end of the summer his professional contract was not renewed. His cricketing career was finished.

So he gave up the diet and let the flesh come, trying to

forget that headline which had read: "Payne Another Larwood!" But it was not so easy to forget: it would have been better if he had never had the hopes, if he had never got as far as he had. To fall away after touching the edge of success was the galling thing. He felt humiliated; he hated to look into old Tom's eyes, to read the disappointment in them.

"It ain't your fault, boy," Tom said. "You can't help being made that way. Don't take it so hard."

But he had to take it hard, because over and above his own disillusionment was the feeling that he had let Tom down. Tom had worked on him, given him all he had to give; Tom had had faith in him and had hoped to make of him an England bowler and take vicariously those triumphs it had been beyond his skill to grasp in any other way. Now that hope was dead, and Tom was too old to take another pupil.

There were some dead matches on the table in front of Payne. He began arranging them in the form of wickets— three long ones and a short piece across for bails.

"Yes," he said musingly, "I went to Trent Bridge."

Panton-Smith and the other two looked at him, grinning.

"Hullo," said Vernon, "are you still in those regions? You've been day-dreaming. We're off cricket now."

Payne said, "I used to play for Notts."

The other three laughed. "You really have been day-dreaming," said Panton-Smith.

Payne was not worried by their laughter; he had not expected them to believe him. He knew what people saw when they looked at him—a great, balloon-like carcase, a mountain of flesh; they never paused to think that he might once have been lean and athletic. If only he could have stayed like that! How different life might have been! But the fat would come; there had been no denying it. It was, he supposed, something to do with glands. He sighed and lit another cigarette.

"It's stopped snowing," Vernon said. "Should we go?"

Bombardier Padgett went ashore with the killick, Leading-seaman Agnew. They went to the International Club. It had been the killick's idea.

"There'll be a film show," he had said. "It'll probably be lousy, but you've got to do something."

Padgett went because he was sick of being on board ship; he wanted to stretch his legs; he felt cramped, cooped up, like a dog that has been too long confined to its kennel. Padgett would have liked to have more space for movement. He did his press-ups regularly, his muscle-building exercises, his deep breathing; but what he missed was the daily run; there was no chance of that on board the *Golden Ray*; instead he had to substitute a brisk walk on ten feet of iron deck. Backward and forward, backward and forward; one, two, three, four, five—five hundred to the mile; backward and forward, backward and forward—leaning against the roll of the ship, counting to himself—two hundred, three hundred, four hundred—five hundred to the mile.

"Mustn't go soft," he told himself. "Got to keep fit. Got to keep at it. Mustn't go soft."

It was his greatest worry—the fear of going soft.

Leading-seaman Agnew was a Liverpudlian. He was a man who delighted in gloom, taking always the most pessimistic view of everything and always expecting the worst to happen. From his appearance one might have supposed that he had at one time or another received a blow in the chest so powerful that it had forced that part of his anatomy into permanent concavity, while producing at the same time a balancing convexity in the region of his shoulder-blades.

He had first seen the light in a miserable house in Scotland Road, and it had been a feeble light, almost exhausted by having had to thrust its way through heavy clouds, many layers of smoke and fog, and a small, grimy window. Most of the regulation ailments of childhood had aimed their blows at his unfortunate body, and both his father and mother had looked upon it as their right and their duty to cuff his ears whenever those large and misshapen articles chanced to come within striking distance. As soon as he was old enough he had joined the Navy, and had left the bosom of his family with the liveliest feelings of pleasure, glad to be at last free of that oppressive growth.

Agnew was forty-five years old, and spoke with that adenoidal snuffle which is the birthright of all born under the ægis of the Liver birds. He was a man much learned in the ways of sin, and tough as a piece of horse-hide.

When Padgett and Agnew arrived at the International Club there was in progress what Agnew described later as a small "frackus." It was taking place in the passageway near the cloakroom, and the trouble was being caused by two merchant seamen—an American and an Englishman—both drunk and quarrelsome. What the argument was about Padgett and Agnew were never able to discover; but a Russian policeman had been called in, and the seamen were threatening him with word and gesture. Meanwhile the interpreter—a tall, thin, worried man—was trying to pacify both sides. It was obvious that the policeman was rapidly losing patience; he began to pull his revolver from its holster.

The American swayed forward. "Pull that gun," he said, "and you're a dead guy. Jest pull it—that's all!"

The interpreter was almost dancing with nervousness. "Now, now," he pleaded, "don't be foolish; please don't be foolish. Nobody is going to shoot. This isn't Chicago; this is Russia; this is a civilized country."

If there was one kind of person that Padgett despised it was the man who drank and could not hold his drink. Padgett himself was an abstainer, but he did not object to other people drinking if they wished to do so. What he did object to was their making beasts of themselves and becoming public nuisances.

The policeman was still tugging at his revolver; he had it half out of the holster, and the two seamen appeared about to jump on him. The interpreter was still fussing round as ineffectually as a broody hen. Then Padgett intervened. It was necessary, he explained afterwards, for the good of international relations and for the Anglo-American good name. He grasped the American with one hand and the Englishman with the other and marched them to the door. Then, one after the other, he flung them out into the snow.

"You can come back," said Padgett, "when you've cooled off."

The two Russians had come to the doorway. Seeing the drunken seamen sprawling in the snow, they burst suddenly into laughter, and the tension was broken. The interpreter shook Padgett's hand. "Thank you," he said. "You are very strong. The way you carry those two out, it is funny; I have to laugh."

The seamen had got to their feet; the cold air appeared to have sobered them. For a moment they seemed to have thoughts of continuing the argument; but the sight of Padgett obviously willing to oblige made them change their minds. They brushed the snow off their clothes and walked a little unsteadily away.

The interpreter said, "Silly boys. Too much vodka. Very silly." He felt Padgett's arm. "Big muscles, no? Very big muscles; very useful. Now we will go inside."

Padgett and Agnew gave their coats to the girl in the cloakroom and received metal tags in exchange. Then they wandered into a large room, on the walls of which hung massive pictures of Stalin, Churchill, and Roosevelt, together with the national flags of the three allies and maps of the battle-fronts. In big lettering were extracts from some of the speeches of each of the three leaders. It was all very much the *entente cordiale* in the International Club at least. There was no hint in there of differences between the allies—those peevish demands from Stalin for a second front, those tart replies of Churchill, and Roosevelt's conciliatory efforts. There were the pictures smiling down from distempered walls: Stalin, Churchill, Roosevelt—three big, friendly brothers.

The film was as bad as Agnew had predicted. It was a Russian film, and a woman interpreter, seated on a high stool, made valiant efforts to keep pace with the incomprehensible noises that came from the screen. The audience of seamen was patently bored, and only once was it roused from that boredom to spontaneous laughter. That was when two men kissed one another on the screen; at this there was laughter and whistling.

The interpreter rounded on them at once, crying scornfully. "Don't be so narrow-minded; it is an old Russian custom." Then she added, "You are nothing but a lot of wolfs in sheepskins."

At this the laughter broke out afresh so loudly that the film sounds were swamped. In Agnew's opinion it was no loss.

Randall did not go ashore. Sometimes he tried to read; but his brain, always wandering back to the one absorbing subject, refused to assimilate what his eyes reported, and at length he gave up in despair. He would not play cards or ludo with the other gunners; would not join with them in any games or discussion. He felt he was not as they were, and he kept himself apart. He did what duties were required of him thoroughly and willingly; but beyond that he did not go.

The others thought him strange, a man who did not fit in— perhaps a little wrong in the head. But after a time they accepted him as he was and did not seek to pry into his private affairs. Randall, behind the tall fence of his aloofness, was grateful to them.

To pass the time and to make himself less conspicuous while keeping himself apart he began to make slippers and sandals from old rope which he obtained from the bosun. This rope he would unravel, plait the strands, then shape and sew the plaited lengths with sail-maker's twine. He became reasonably skilful in the use of palm and needle, and the products of his skill bore quite a professional appearance. Soon he had made quite a number of sandals and slippers. He did not know what he would do with them; he did not look beyond the journey home, because his future did not extend beyond that. But he went on sewing because it occupied his hands and there was nothing else to do.

Sergeant Willis did not go ashore for reasons which he might have found difficulty in defining. They had to do with his character as a soldier of the King. Russians were Communists; they had killed their own royal family; they denied God. All this seemed culpable to Willis.

He knew that Miller was also a Communist; it was a fact that had caused him no little worry. He had sometimes heard Miller preaching Communism, and that had appeared to him perilously close to sedition. Yet Russia was Communist, and Russia was an ally; so where were you? There was here some confusion. To a man like Willis, who liked all things to be clearly marked in black and white, without blur or haziness, this fact presented some difficulty.

He was glad to see that none of the other gunners took Miller's lectures seriously; indeed, they ragged him without mercy. Yet it was wrong that the man should be allowed to speak as he did; though, how could you stop him? He never suggested straight out the overthrow of the monarchy; he was too wary for that, and Willis would have come down on him hard if he had done so. But was not that process inherent in the Communist programme?

And what of the soldier's oath of allegiance? But did these conscripts like Miller take the oath? Willis believed not.

To Sergeant Willis the oath he had freely given was binding; it was something he would not think of breaking. He was a King's man, and always would be. Damn Communism and damn Republicanism; damn every other kind of 'ism' if it came to that! 'Isms' were dangerous things, not to be trusted. Look at the state the world was in now, and it was all due to these confounded 'isms'—Nazism, Fascism, totalitarianism—all a lot of foreign twaddle. Willis knew what was what: fear God and serve the King; that was what; stick to that creed, and you would never go far wrong.

Willis had a simple faith; it never occurred to him to doubt the existence of God, nor the essential rightness of God, nor the warlike character of this Almighty Being. God liked a smart parade; that was why church parades were part of the Army curriculum; He liked polished brasses and shining boots, blancoed webbing and the brisk word of command; He liked men who marched smartly with hobnailed boots striking out a rhythm—left, right, left, right, left, right, left. Willis was not in the habit of painting pictures in his mind; but if he had painted God it would probably have been as some very high-ranking Army officer. God was warlike, but He was just; He fought always upon the side of right—the British side.

Yet these damned Communists, these Russians, contended that there was no God, and had executed their king. And they were our allies. It was, of course, a question of expediency; one enemy at a time. They were our allies for the moment, but there was no need to fraternize. Sergeant Willis did not go ashore.

And Petty Officer Donker also stayed on board ship, sometimes hovering about his guns and rockets, his paravanes and smoke-floats, his P.A.C.'s and his small-arms; sometimes spitting morosely into the icy waters of the Tuloma; sometimes sitting by the mess-room stove and slicing his corns with a cut-throat razor; sometimes rolling cigarettes; sometimes swearing at the carpenter, with whom he was at loggerheads; sometimes carving exquisite little models of fully rigged sailing-ships; and always, always, fingering the lump upon his neck.

For long hours Donker and Willis would sit playing draughts or double patience with cards that had become soft, almost fluffy, at the edges from constant use. Sometimes as much as a shilling would change hands in one of these gambling sessions.

So, on board and ashore, the hours drifted away. There had been a hundred and ten air-raids on Murmansk since the arrival of the convoy, and more than once incendiaries had fallen on the deck of the *Golden Ray*, to be thrown quickly overboard. At times high-explosive bombs had fallen uncomfortably close; at times the gunners had wondered whether this was to be the end—their ship sunk at the quayside. But at last the holds were empty; at last the *Golden Ray* loosed her grip on the bollards and slipped out into mid-stream. Then she moved down-river to a small timber jetty which thrust its wooden arm out into the current. Here a few hundred tons of fertilizer were loaded—powdery, dusty material that penetrated to the cabins and cast a film over everything. Then the hatches were battened down, and the ship, riding high in the water with her light cargo, moved to the convoy anchorage and dug her iron talon into the bed of the river.

"And now," said Vernon, "now for England, home, and beauty."

"If we get there," said Payne.

Padgett slapped him on the shoulder. "Don't you worry about that, boy. Jerry don't trouble with the empties."

"That's what you think," said Payne. "That's what they tell you on the Atlantic run, but it don't stop you from being bumped on the way to Yankee-land. You want to tell it to the U-boat captains; maybe they haven't heard."

"We'll get through," said Vernon. "I've got a date."

"Wonder where the *Tirpitz* is," said Warby; "and them two battle-wagons—the *Scharnhorst* and the *Gneisenau*—they're somewhere in Norway, an't they? Nice people to meet, they'd be."

Padgett said, "You're just looking for ruddy trouble. Anyway, who's afraid of the big bad *Tirpitz* so long as we've got old Donkey and his four-inch cannon?"

They were on the gun-platform, preparing everything for the voyage home; the Bofors was oiled and greased, the shells clean and clipped up ready for use. Vernon rested his gloved hand on the low steel wall that surrounded the platform and gazed up-river to the escort anchorage. There, swinging at their cables, were cruisers, destroyers, corvettes, and armed trawlers—escorts that had come up with outbound convoys,

and now, after a brief respite, a brief refuelling, a brief
replenishment with depth-charges and ammunition, they
would be ready to take another convoy home.

Sometimes Vernon envied the men in the escort vessels. It
must be so much easier to keep up morale in ships that had
been built for fighting, ships that were made for attack, and
not just passive, waiting for the enemy to strike. And again,
looking at them from the freighter's decks, it always appeared
so much safer on board a corvette or a destroyer; one never
considered the possibility of their being torpedoed or struck
by bombs. It was always the slow, bulky merchant ships that
sat up and asked to be hit.

Vernon realized that this was merely a point of view, and
a biased one at that. Possibly the crews of the escort vessels
were just as envious of the merchant seamen and the D.E.M.S.
gunners, feeling that it was the latter who had the cushy jobs.
Corvettes and destroyers, it might be pointed out, were just
as liable to be torpedoed as freighters; it might be claimed
that they were less comfortable to live in, rolling and pitching
like nobody's business; that their crews enjoyed less time in
port, and that discipline was stricter. All these things might
well be true, but to Vernon, standing on the deck of a crawling
merchant ship, the corvette and the destroyer always looked
like places of safety.

" Picking out the escort? " asked Padgett. " What'll you
have—two corvettes and a destroyer, or an armed trawler and
a cruiser? "

" Fifty of them wouldn't be too many."

" You're right!" agreed Payne. " You're damn right! I
wish it was a hundred; I wish it was two hundred; I wish
to God we was sailing up the Clyde."

CHAPTER TWELVE
Lame Duck Lagging

SPRING seemed suddenly to have come to the north. The sun shone, the hills glittered, and the Tuloma, flowing silently down towards the sea, was a moving mirror, reflecting the pale blue of a sky that held only one vagrant, feathery cloud. The air was fresh and cold; it was like air that had never yet been used; air that perhaps would flow down towards the regions of temperate climate, and on towards the tropics and the equator, gradually becoming staler and more enervating, gradually losing that fierce, exhilarating quality, just as a stream that starts in the mountains as fresh, limpid water, cold and transparent, becomes at last the turgid, commercial river, carrying seaward the filth of towns, and bearing upon its surface the scum and flotsam of civilization.

And yet it was not truly spring. February was not yet over, and there was much bitter weather to come. But here, into the heart of winter, had arrived a promise of the better days that must surely come at last. This day was a messenger bringing a golden vision of things to come; and on this day the convoy left the shelter of its anchorage and moved out towards the grey terror of the Barents Sea.

Eighteen merchant ships slipped down the Tuloma—some carrying timber, but most, like the *Golden Ray*, practically without cargo and riding high in the water, so that they appeared strangely top-heavy, their propellers almost breaking the surface as they turned over. With them went twenty warships, and two of these were armed trawlers. Again there was no aircraft carrier; again they would be helpless to reach out beyond the range of their guns; again there would be no ' umbrella.'

And this time they were to travel slowly, for a lame duck was coming with them, and in convoy the lame duck lames every other ship. The speed of a convoy is no more than the speed of its slowest member, and though some of the ships might have been capable of twelve or even fourteen knots, all were to travel at five, for that was the speed of the lame duck, a tanker that had been bombed and half disabled as it lay at anchor in the Tuloma. It had been patched up as well as possible with the limited resources available, and now it was to limp home to a dry-dock in Liverpool or Glasgow. And limping with it would limp seventeen other ships, and seventeen other crews would look across at the lame duck and curse it for laming them all, holding them all upon the bitter sea for extra days of danger.

But the crew of the lame duck would think only about their own patched-up engines; going about their work with one ear always alert for a break in their rhythm—the break that might be the presage of disaster, of helpless drifting on a deadly ocean.

Vernon knew that feeling. He had sailed in a ship cursed with unreliable engines—a diesel ship that was continually breaking down and falling behind. Then she would lie drifting helplessly, while the convoy steamed on, moving nearer and nearer to the rim of the horizon, sliding over that rim; at length only a faint smoke-cloud to be seen above the edge of the sea; then nothing. The crippled ship would lie, heaving gently upon the swell, and there would be only the creak of timbers where before there had been the steady beat of the engines. There she would lie, waiting for a torpedo, and the engineers would work feverishly upon the sick engines, and the rest of the crew would wait, able to do nothing, sweating it out.

Then, at last, the engines would come to life again—a little uncertain at first, but gathering confidence. Then the ship would vibrate and they would be on their way, trying to catch up with the vanished convoy, hoping that they would not break down again, and listening, always listening, for that cough, that sudden choking of the sick man labouring below decks.

No, thought Vernon, it was no fun being a lame duck.

Night came quickly, dropping its black curtain over the receding land; and with the night came the aurora borealis, glowing in green and purple upon the sea and ships. At the head of the port column steamed the *Golden Ray*; astern of her the s.s. *Merryweather,* with Panton-Smith on board.

" I'll keep an eye on you, Harry," Panton-Smith had said before they parted. " I'll be looking across at you."

And much help that'll be, thought Vernon, gazing back at the dark shape of the *Merryweather.* Much help his watching will be to us.

All the same, he felt somehow the companionship of Panton-Smith across the gulf that lay between the two vessels. "Are you on watch now, Smithy? Are you asleep in your bunk? You are there somewhere in that shadow moving along behind us. You are facing the same dangers as we. Sweet dreams, Smithy—and may we meet in England."

Cold it was on watch on the tall gun-platform, and there, exposed to the wind, four hours crept away on feet of lead. Vernon stamped his icy feet and thought of Jamaica basking in the lap of the Caribbean Sea. A year ago he had been there, disembarked from an east-bound ship, waiting for a west-bound one requiring gun and gunners.

For five weeks he and the rest of the gun-team had revelled in sunshine and the easy-going life of Port Royal. Three or four times a week they would travel across the bay to Kingston—Kingston with its open-air cinemas, its saloons, its shops, its squalid slums, and its light-hearted way of living. Then in the evening, with the soft breeze ruffling the water, with stars hanging overhead, and other stars shimmering below in the bay, they would return to Port Royal and sleep under the mosquito-nets of the barrack-room.

Vernon remembered the black women who came with baskets of fruit balanced upon their heads—oranges, tangerines, bananas, bread-fruit, pawpaws—luscious fruits at a farthing apiece. He remembered, too, the swimming-pool, with its warm, limpid water and the wire fence that kept out sharks and barracudas; he remembered the tiny green lizards rustling among the dead leaves under the citrus-trees, and the sun beating fiercely down upon the concrete fives court, where they played until the sweat poured from them. He had only to close his eyes and he could see again the white buildings glinting in the sun; he could see the Blue Mountains thick with tropical vegetation; he could see the surf creaming up on the long, white beaches; he could see the palm-trees and the black children fishing from the jetty's end—and over it all the blessed, blessed shimmer of heat.

Oh, God, he thought, to feel the warmth of the sun again! Oh, God, let me not die here; not here in the Arctic! Let me feel the warmth of the sun again before I die.

And the hours of the watch dragged by upon their leaden feet, and the cold slid down from the Pole, and the northern lights flickered and Miller cursed. Miller's hands were cold and his feet were cold; his whole body was cold and his heart seemed dead. So he stood, almost hidden beneath Balaclavas and duffel-coat, his shoulders hunched, his hands thrust into his pockets; so he stood, cursing softly and fluently, cursing the cold, cursing the wind, cursing the War; cursing everything that came into his mind to curse.

And as Miller cursed and Vernon dreamed and Warby thought of home the convoy moved northward at five knots, and each hour brought it nearer the ice.

When morning came there was no sun, only a cold grey light filtering through the unbroken roof of cloud. The wind had fallen and the sea was calm, scarcely a ripple disturbing its surface. From their tall platform the gunners looked towards the horizon, the almost indistinguishable meeting of sky and sea; and in whichever direction they looked they could see nothing but the ships of the convoy and their escorts: nothing else broke the surface of the water; nothing flew in the air; they were alone and unmolested. Yet, such was the awesome character of those desolate regions, this calm seemed but the presage of fearful things to come, so that each one went about his business with a sense of foreboding, and men spoke quietly, as though always listening;

and their eyes moved restlessly, as though in search of a warning—some sign upon the waters or in the sky. But the day passed and no sign came, and as night closed upon the convoy, shutting it into its little, moving world, a light breeze sprang up astern and moved forward with them—a ghostly, nocturnal companion, bearing with it scuds of fine, pricking snow.

To-morrow, thought Payne, feeling the raw bite of cold in the middle of his back, to-morrow and the day after and the day after that—and we shall still be up here on the roof of the world. Five knots! Oh, God, what a bloody speed! A whole day and you shift less than a hundred and fifty miles. And zig-zagging at that. Jerry must find us; we're so slow; he must find us. Five knots! Why a man could walk as fast. Five knots! If I ran along the deck from bows to stern I'd be going back faster than the blasted ship was taking me forward.

Payne swung his arms for warmth, and moved round the confined circle of the gun-platform, his heavy leather sea-boots crunching on the cinders.

Just like a damned great elephant, thought Ben Cowdrey. What a weight to carry about! Ought to keep him warm, though.

Ben was suffering from wind-sores; his lips were cracked, and sometimes the cracks bled; it hurt him to smoke. He had tried smearing butter on them, but the butter was salt, and the salt had gone into the cracks. Cowdrey did not complain, but he longed for warmer weather. He remembered tropical nights when he had gone on watch clad in no more than a shirt and denims; he remembered cursing the heat in the Red Sea. Yet how could anyone ever curse the heat? It seemed unthinkable. After this he would never again complain of heat.

" Ben," said Bombardier Padgett, " slip down and see if the stove is all right."

" O.K., bom."

Cowdrey eased himself away from the gun and climbed

over the steel protecting wall, only too glad to snatch a few minutes below and a chance to thaw his frozen limbs.

"Don't go to sleep down there," said Padgett.

"Bombardier! As if I would! Go to sleep! Oh, dear me!"

"All right, all right. Get cracking."

Ben disappeared down the ladder, and the elephantine shape of Payne came drifting round the gun.

"Quiet," observed Payne. "Real quiet, ain't it? "

"You're right."

"I bet there's something brewing. Oh, Lord!. I bet we're due to cop a packet."

"You think too much," said Padgett. "Personally, I like it quiet. When it's quiet you know there's nothing happening."

Payne pushed his Balaclava helmet up over his mouth, so that when he answered his voice came thick and muffled through the wool. "Yes, I know that, but all the same, you can't help thinking that something is going to happen. P'raps it's the northern lights; p'raps it's the ice and snow; whatever it is, there's something queer about these regions: it's too far north, that's what it is—too near the Pole. I'd rather do twenty Atlantic crossings than one of these Russian trips. Beats me why they want to send all this stuff to the Russkis; you'd think we could use it ourselves—and we wouldn't lose half of it at the bottom of the Arctic Ocean neither."

"When you get to be Commander-in-Chief you'd better see about it," said Padgett.

"That I will," said Payne, stamping his feet. "That I will."

Cowdrey had replenished the stove, had taken a few quick draws at the stump of a cigarette which he had found in his duffel-coat pocket, and, not being able to think of a valid reason for staying below any longer, had clambered once again up the iron ladder to the cold discomfort of the deck. Stumbling out into the open, he was just in time to see a vivid spearhead of flame shoot up from the level of the sea away on the port beam. Seconds later came the rumble of an explosion.

Cowdrey stood with his hand on the ladder to the gun-platform, suddenly immobilized, his heart jumping, as he watched the flame growing bigger and bigger, lighting up the sky as if it were the sun rising.

It's one of the escorts, he thought. It couldn't be anything else out there. We're in the outside column; there aren't any more merchant ships on our port. It must be a corvette or a destroyer; might even be a trawler.

The flame was still growing, blood-red against the darkness of the night; but after the single initial explosion no sound had reached Cowdrey's ears. The flame grew silently, a gigantic, semicircular glow reflected in the water and throwing into relief the raft hanging on the after rigging of the *Golden Ray*.

Then the alarm-bells began to ring, and Cowdrey, waking from his stupor, grasped the ladder and climbed up on to the gun-platform. He heard Payne's excited voice.

" I told you it was too damned quiet; I told you something was brewing. I bet that sub was lying in wait. God, what a fire! That'll melt the ice on her decks."

There were other gunners climbing out of the bowels of the ship, men roughly torn from sleep, not yet knowing what had happened, dragging on duffel-coats and helmets, shivering as the cold struck suddenly into their bones. Willis was the first to reach the gun-platform; nobody ever beat him to the jump; Ben used to say the sergeant slept with his eyes open.

He spoke to Padgett—quietly, unexcitedly. " What happened? "

" One of the escorts," Padgett said. " Must have been torpedoed—no warning—nothing at all—just the flame suddenly leaping up."

Five minutes had passed since Cowdrey had come out on deck, and the flame on the port beam was still growing. The end came with startling rapidity; the flame burst upward and outward, carrying with it billowing masses of black smoke that cast grotesque shadows upon the fire. Then the rumble of the explosion—the final, shattering explosion—came rolling across the sea.

"The magazine," said Padgett; "the magazine's gone up."

In the morning there was a gap in the defences; a destroyer was missing. The convoy moved onward to the music of depth-charges, and sleep became a rarity.

But the day and the night passed without further incident, and so they moved on into the third day. They were steaming along the edge of an ice-field when five German heavy destroyers came up over the southern horizon, and the defending warships moved out to meet them. And while the battle raged outside the ships of the convoy took refuge behind the glassy ramparts of the ice-field, thrusting their way through where no thin-plated destroyer could follow—through into an ice-surrounded lake of clear water. On that lake they stayed for three hours, steaming round and round, like ducks upon a pond, until it should be safe to break out and continue their journey.

Many of the British destroyers were old and small; some were ex-Americans obtained in the Bermuda exchange, and easily distinguishable by their four funnels; but, old and small as they were, they drove off the German ships. Then the convoy came out of its retreat and proceeded on its way.

On the fourth day a Focke-Wulf Kurier found them and began to fly round the convoy without coming within range of the guns. The gunners, standing to action stations, watched it, cursing their own impotence. For an hour it circled them—a cold, slow hour of watching and waiting; while the ships slid almost imperceptibly through the icy sea and the plane held them effortlessly within its sight, as though mocking their futile efforts to escape.

Warby shook his fist at it in sudden rage. "You bastard! Come closer, you rotten bastard, and we'll show you! Come closer, d'you hear? Come closer!"

The others looked at Warby in surprise. It was so unlike the slow, phlegmatic countryman. There was a sense of shock also, a feeling that if Warby could act like this anything might happen; others might break down under the strain. They looked at him, but said nothing, and Warby stopped shaking his fist and fell silent, a little ashamed of himself. They were all silent.

The Focke-Wulf had been with them for almost two hours. But for the shape, it might have been a Catalina or a Sunderland keeping watch for submarines. But the shape gave it menace, and it was a menace they could not shake off. They could only watch and plough on at their five knots, which was so pitiful a speed. And the Focke-Wulf, circling easily under the grey cloud-covering, now at the head of the convoy, now at the rear, was like a vulture waiting for a death.

It's like a nightmare, thought Vernon. You run as fast as you can, and you make no headway at all.

At eight bells the galley-boy made his way aft and called up to the gunners the information that dinner was ready. The galley-boy was wearing a duffel-coat which at some time or other he had scrounged from a naval rating. When he threw his head back to call to the gunners on their high platform the hood of the coat fell back and left his head bare. He had a pale, pimply face and bad teeth; he was shivering, partly from cold, partly from nervousness; he was sixteen years old, and he had been six months at sea.

" It's scouse," he shouted, " an' spotted Dick for afters. Can you come and get it? "

They were all hungry, and the thought of hot food was attractive. Sergeant Willis rang through to the bridge and asked for permission to send the men down for dinner, one watch at a time. Permission was given, and he sent Vernon, Miller, and Warby down first, because they had been on deck the longest. The remaining six stamped their feet, beat their hands, and watched the Focke-Wulf.

" Round and round and round," Payne grumbled. " It's enough to make you dizzy."

Vernon had taken exactly one mouthful of food when the alarm-bells began ringing. A minute later he and Miller and Warby were again on the gun-platform, and the gun was beating out its restless tune as twenty Heinkel 111's came in on a low-level torpedo attack.

They shot down one Heinkel; they had that satisfaction. They saw the pilot climb out of the wreckage before it sank, and they saw him drift past, kept afloat by his life-jacket in the icy water. They saw his white face silhouetted against the dark sea; and now, robbed of his lethal weapon, his black aircraft, he seemed suddenly very helpless, very much alone—a piece of useless human flotsam caught upon the tide of war.

He floated past in his life-jacket, his body wrapped about by the cruel waters of the Arctic Ocean, and his white face gazed up impotently at the grey ships he had come to sink. And from those ships men gazed back at him—watching without pity, since pity had been killed in them. They watched the white face with hate in their hearts, and as they watched an Oerlikon gun suddenly chattered and the face dissolved in pulp. And the convoy steamed on.

But the s.s. *Merryweather* did not steam on with the other ships; the s.s. *Merryweather* would never steam on again. And Panton-Smith would keep an eye on the *Golden Ray* no more; for Panton-Smith was dead.

The convoy fought fiercely for its life; it fought the Heinkels off with a bright spray of scarlet fire and bursting steel until they turned and ran for home. But in the night the U-boats pressed home their attack, and on the following day a dozen Junkers 88's dive-bombed the ships. And still they fought, spending their nerves, their last reserves of strength, for the one purpose of clinging to that life which all had many a time cursed as futile. And at five knots the ships steamed on, crawling, like flies upon a globe, across the frozen roof of the world.

" At this rate," Payne said, " we shall be home at Christmas."

" Which Christmas? " asked Andrews.

" Who cares! " said Padgett. " It would be good to sleep! Think of all the people who're snug in bed at this minute; just think of it! And here we are freezing to death; and not an egg-cupful of sleep for four days. How much longer is it going to last? "

That was what they all wondered. How much longer? How much longer could they endure it? How much longer would they be there to endure it? Ah, that was the great question that lurked behind each man's weary eyes. By day and by night the ships were being picked off. When would it be their turn?

The lame duck was still with them, and there were many who looked across at that tanker grinding through the seas on her patched-up engines with the thought that if she were gone it might be better for the others. For without the lame duck they would be able to increase speed—perhaps to double it; and so much less time would they have to live under the threat of bomb and torpedo. So every morning they looked across to the starboard column just to see if the tanker was still there; and always she was, ploughing on and holding them all down to their five knots. No one would have admitted that he wanted the tanker to be sunk; they did not go as far as that; but many a man watched the log-line trailing slackly from the taffrail of his own ship and turning lazily, lazily over as it registered the slow miles; and many a man thought: Lord, if it's got to be any ship, why not the lame duck? But life is sweet, and the lame duck did not want to die.

So they moved on into the sixth day—weary, unshaven, haggard men standing to the guns; men whose faces had become graved with deep lines in which the grime lay unheeded; men whose eyes were red and aching from the everlasting wind; whose lips were salt with the taste of spray; whose feet and hands and bodies were permanently cold; men almost sleeping as they stood, yet whom the enemy would never allow to rest; men who wondered each day how much longer they could carry on, and yet, between brief snatches of sleep, did carry on, enduring because they must, because there was no retreat, no place to hide, no choice but to persevere.

On the sixth day the sun shone briefly, but there was little warmth in its rays. It shone on the ice clinging to the bows

of the *Golden Ray*, the ice coating the forecastle head, the
ice blown in freezing spray upon masts and derricks, rafts and
boats, the ice blocking up the scuppers and making treacher-
ous every alleyway and cat-walk, the ice lying like a glassy lid
upon the hatches, the ice on bollard and winch, on davit and
pulley, on bulwark and handrail, on ventilator and shell-
locker—the ice everywhere. The sun shone upon it, and found
rich colours inside the substance of it, drawing them out for
all to see; but the sun did not melt the ice: from all that
shining, glacial surface it brought forth no single drop of
water, no slightest suggestion of moisture. There was glitter
and sparkle and colour; but there was no warmth: the ice
was master.

And along the path of the sun came the bombers, and the
guns swung to meet them, spitting out their venom. Flame
and steel and high-explosive came up like a curtain, and the
Junkers and Heinkels broke upon that curtain and scattered
over the sky, coming in to attack in ones and twos, some from
one side, some from another, so that the gunners hardly knew
which way to turn. On the Bofors platform of the *Golden
Ray* empty shell-cases were rolling about, and the gun-barrel
was burning hot. Randall trod on a shell-case and fell with
a clip of shells in his hands. Willis swore at him, and he
struggled up, handing the shells to Miller on the loading-
platform.

For Miller the action was all noise; he could see nothing
but the clips of shells that were handed up to him and the
auto-loader which sucked them in like a mincing-machine.
When shells were slow in coming up Miller yelled for more,
standing with legs wide apart, braced against the rocking of
the gun and swaying of the ship which combined in an
attempt to throw him from his perch. Miller did not dare to
look up at the planes which he could hear roaring overhead,
nor at the ship to starboard which had been hit and was
pouring out black smoke. Miller knew that if he once took
his eye off the shells and the auto-loader the gun would jam,

and there would be hell to pay. So he kept his head down, ramming in clip after clip, too busy to feel afraid.

The small splinter of cannon-shell which hit Miller had ricocheted off the gun-mounting. It seemed to Miller as though a hammer had struck him in the stomach and torn its way in through clothing and skin and flesh. He doubled up, and the clip of shells which he had been about to load fell from his hands and went clattering to the deck. Miller shrieked with pain and fell also. The deck seemed to fly up towards him, to crash into his face; he felt the blinding shock of impact, and then all the pain and confusion dissolved in oblivion.

Miller did not know that Randall had leapt to take his place on the gun; the pause in its action was scarcely more than momentary; then it was rocking on its pedestal again, the barrel going in and out, recoil and recuperation, the shells flying up, up, up, the tracer painting its golden arc across the sky. But Miller knew nothing of this, for he was lying unconscious at the back of the platform, where they had dragged him. He did not know that a minute later the action was over and the bombers gone; nor was he aware of Padgett picking him up like a roll of carpet and carrying him down to the cabin, taking off his coat and life-jacket, and laying him gently on one of the lower bunks. It was only later that Miller came back to the agony of consciousness, only then that he felt the steel imbedded in his stomach, the pain shuddering up through his stunted body in sweating waves of horror.

He saw Willis looking down at him; at least he thought it was Willis; but he could not be sure because the face was blurred, seeming to expand and contract, to advance and retreat, to waver confusingly.

" How are you feeling? " Willis asked.

Miller did not answer; he could not answer; his throat was parched, his tongue dry, like old leather.

Willis appeared to understand. " Not so grand, eh? You had tough luck."

Miller lost sight of him then. But he was back a moment later with a sponge soaked in water. He raised Miller's head and sponged his lips and brow, handling him gently, as one would handle a child. Coming from Willis, such gentleness was unexpected and surprising. Miller lay back again, and his head throbbed; brilliant lights seemed to flash up behind his eyeballs and fade out again. From a long way off, it seemed, he heard Willis speaking.

"You got one in the guts. The steward bandaged it up. You'll be all right till they take you off. You'll be all right. No need to worry."

Miller did not understand. What was the sergeant talking about? What did he mean by that talk of taking him off? How could he be taken off. They were at sea—miles from land. What was Willis gassing about?

Willis said, "The Old Man is going to send a signal to one of the destroyers asking them to take you off. You'll be all right then—proper sick bay—proper M.O. You'll be all right then; you'll be all right."

All right! thought Miller. All right! Oh, Jesus Christ!

He lay with the pain grinding at him, and the sweat stood out on his forehead. He lay in a tiny world of pain—isolated, cut off from all human contact—a world holding only two things: himself and the pain.

On the bridge of the *Golden Ray* the second mate was signalling with an Aldis lamp to one of the destroyers. "We have a wounded gunner. Can you take him off?"

The question came flashing back, slowly spelt out: "How bad is he?"

The second mate swore, nettled by the implied condescension to Merchant Navy speed in the slow rate of signalling. "What do they think this is?—a bloody kindergarten?"

It had been his early ambition to become a naval officer. Obstacles had stood in the way, chief among them a family lack of money. The Merchant Navy had been a second best, and his disappointment took the form of trying at every opportunity to demonstrate its superiority over the other

service. The signals rating on the bridge of the destroyer was
surprised at the speed with which the answer to his question
flickered back.

" He is very bad. Wound in stomach. Medical attention
essential."

The second mate smiled with satisfaction as the reply came
across from the destroyer at full naval speed. But the signal
itself gave him little satisfaction. It read: " Regret cannot
take your rating now. Will do so when heat is off."

" Heat! " snorted Captain Pownall, when the signal was
repeated to him. " Some heat! "

But he knew as well as the second mate did what heat it
was—the heat of submarine attack. Until things quietened
down the destroyer could not risk drawing alongside, could
not risk many lives in the hope of saving one.

Captain Pownall himself took this information to Sergeant
Willis, lowering his creaking body down the iron ladder to
the gunners' quarters.

" Where is he—your wounded man? "

Willis pointed to the bunk where Miller lay, and the
captain, hat under arm, the scabs on his head and face
showing dark against the pallor of his skin, bent down and
looked at Miller. He did not speak, but he laid his hand on
Miller's forehead and stood thus, silent for a long minute.
And the gunners, watching him, were silent too, so that there
was no sound in the cabin but the beat of the engines, the
creak of straining timbers, and the occasional rattle of a plate
or mug moving with the roll of the ship. Then the captain
straightened himself, and the others saw that Miller was
asleep.

Captain Pownall spoke to Willis. " We hope to have him
taken aboard the destroyer later. At present they are
busy—too busy. He'll be all right once he's aboard the
destroyer."

He bent his way through the cabin doorway, rammed his
hat fiercely on his bald head, and climbed back to the deck.
And immediately, as though to demonstrate how busy the

destroyers were, a salvo of depth-charges exploded on the port beam, drumming loudly on the sides of the *Golden Ray*. The vessel shuddered, and Miller awoke from his brief sleep, and, awaking, felt the pain in his stomach and cried out in agony, " God! Oh, my God!" not realizing how strange it was that he should call upon a deity in whom he professed not to believe.

When the aircraft alarm sounded Miller was left alone. He lay gazing at the bunk above him and waiting for the waves of pain to beat up through his body. Somewhere, far away it seemed, he could hear the sound of gunfire and the whine of dive-bombers. He knew that again the ships were fighting their way through; he knew that at any moment the *Golden Ray* might be struck by a bomb; but he was past caring; he could not bring his mind to bear upon anything but the agony within him; that was everything; there was nothing else.

It was almost dark when the gunners came down again. They had seen another ship sunk; the bomb had gone down her funnel and blown the middle out of her. She had sunk in less than a minute, and only one boat had got away.

But the lame duck was still with them.

On the bridge of the *Golden Ray* the third mate was taking a signal from the destroyer. " Too dark to remove your rating now. Will have him to-morrow."

" ' To-morrow and to-morrow and to-morrow,' " he muttered to himself, and tried to remember what play the words came from. Was it *Macbeth* or was it *Hamlet*? Or perhaps *Othello*? It worried him that he could not remember, and the words kept nagging him, breaking in upon his thoughts. Other lines came into his mind; he felt sure they were from the same speech. " And all our yesterdays have lighted fools the way to dusty death." The third mate smiled grimly. " Dusty death " was not a visitation he feared just then. He would have been grateful for the promise of such an end. " I would fain die a dry death—— " That was from Shakespeare too—Gonzalo in *The Tempest*. He was sure of that one because he had acted Gonzalo in his last year at school. God! he thought. We have come a long way since then.

He turned to the apprentice standing beside him on the wing of the bridge.

"Go and tell the sergeant his wounded man will be taken off in the morning."

CHAPTER THIRTEEN

Tempest

THE wind came out of the north. It was a bitter wind, scudding down from the polar ice-cap. As the night wore on it grew steadily in strength, lashing the sea into heaving protest. When Padgett, Payne, and Cowdrey went on watch at midnight it was blowing half a gale; when they crawled thankfully below decks four hours later a full gale was spending its fury on the convoy, and the seas were rising.

Vernon and Warby, deprived now of the company of Miller, huddled in the lee of the gun and braced themselves against the roll of the ship. The wind was like a living thing, a wild, howling virago. It shrieked through the rigging with a high-pitched wail that filled the darkness with fearful sound. To make themselves heard Vernon and Warby had to shout to each other at a foot distance, and the wind tore their words away and scattered them in the wastes of the night.

Sometimes snow came with the wind, beating across the decks in a blinding blizzard that stung like the lash of a whip. Spray and spindrift were flung over the ship in a continuous cascade of moisture that froze on bridge and mast and gun and davit; froze, too, on duffel-coat and Balaclava, casing all it could find in a sheath of ice.

Vernon peered into the darkness, trying to make out the shape of other ships; but he could see nothing. Nothing was visible but the white crests of waves sliding past. He wondered whether the officer of the watch could see anything, or whether he was trusting to prayer or luck. Suppose the following ship were to ram the stern of the *Golden Ray*! Suppose she drifted away to starboard and crashed into the next column! In such a night a ship might be invisible two yards away.

All day it had been the Germans who had harried them; now in the black womb of night was born this other danger. Storm could be as lethal as bomb or torpedo, and if they should be blown too far off course there were rocks that could rend as surely as any mine. Oh, God, thought Vernon, was it not enough that they had been attacked again and again, that they were weary to the point of exhaustion? Was it not enough that they had the incessant cold to endure, the cold biting into the marrow of their bones, tearing at the skin of their faces, seeking for any opening through which to strike and flay? Was not all this enough, but now they must have the storm to batter their bodies and threaten their lives?

To stop the gun from swinging they lashed the barrel to an upright. In such conditions it was not likely to be needed in a hurry. Indeed, in such conditions it would have been almost impossible to use it, far less to fire with any degree of accuracy. Anti-aircraft gunnery was difficult enough with solid ground beneath the gun; a gun mounted on a madly bucking ship would have required supermen to handle it effectively. With the possible exception of Bombardier Padgett, none of the gunners had any illusions that he fitted the rôle of superman.

The previous watch had tied the cover on the Bofors gun, but soon the gale loosened it. Vernon and Warby were forced to lash it more securely, fumbling with numb fingers at ropes they could scarcely see. The wind snatched at the canvas, lifting it and slapping it back upon the gun with a report like thunder. It was a wild, hectic night, and the *Golden Ray* struggled, shuddering, through a torrent of darkness, groping her sightless way from wave to wave while the sea poured across her decks.

" What price being on one of them trawlers or corvettes!" shouted Warby.

Vernon yelled back, "This is bad enough for me." He could not worry about trawlers or corvettes. He had doubts even about the *Golden Ray*. He would have had doubts of any ship in such a sea.

But the gale had not attained its full strength. By the time daylight had crept up over the horizon it was a yelling, tearing shattering demon, and the convoy was broken—scattered over a sea that was nothing but great foam-capped mountains and deep white-streaked valleys. There was no question of maintaining formation; it was a sufficient battle simply to stay afloat. The human enemy was forgotten. Here was an enemy more powerful, more terrifying—the primeval foe of all mariners—the tempest.

It was a strange sight, viewed from the deck of the *Golden Ray*. From horizon to horizon ships lay struggling in the grasp of the storm, some on one course, some on another, tossed here and there, raked by creaming seas, shuddering and groaning. At times it seemed that the trawlers were gone, sunk beneath the towering waves; but always they rose again upon the crest, riding it out as well as any of the ships.

" Brought up to it," growled Petty Officer Donker. "Trawlers take some sinking. Tough little baskets, they are. Want to be to get through this lot, though. I've seen some weather, but this beats anything. Oh, my, my! Look at them bloody seas! You wouldn't think water could pile itself up that height. Look out! Here we go again! Oh, my, my!"

Half-way through the morning a particularly heavy sea broke over the side of the *Golden Ray* and stove in the two starboard lifeboats. An hour later one of the starboard rafts was carried away. Life-lines had been rigged across the decks, but in spite of this a fireman making his way aft to the crew's quarters at the noon watch change was caught by a sea and carried overboard. He was not seen again.

Below decks was chaos. In the gunners' mess-room plates

and mugs careered hither and thither; a drawer opened and a cascade of cutlery fell out; a tin of jam crashed to the floor, and a pack of playing-cards, floating down from the shelf on which they had been stowed, settled upon the sticky mass like autumn leaves caught in a bog; and from the stove hot cinders shot out upon the hearth, sometimes accompanied by a burst of flame darting out like a serpent's tongue.

The noise was scarcely less than that on deck. Every timber, every plate, every rivet in the ship, seemed to be groaning in protest. Every moment she seemed to be threatening to crack in two under the terrible strain that was being put upon her. Sometimes, mounting a wave, she seemed to be standing upon her stern, her bows pointing to the sky; then she would tilt upon the crest, hesitate a moment, and dive, shuddering, into the trough beyond. At such times her propeller would be flung clear of the water, and, finding suddenly no resistance, would thresh wildly, the engines racing and sending vibrations through the length and breadth of the ship.

So it went on, hour after hour. The *Golden Ray* nosed her way through the seas, rolling, pitching, tossing, trembling, creaking, groaning—a hell above decks and below, and the one slender link that bound her crew to life. For all knew well that if the *Golden Ray* foundered there was no hope— no hope in all that raging ferment of waters; no boat could live in it, and a man on a raft would not be able to cling to life for two minutes.

And always the cruel, bitter wind was driving them south, driving them towards the jagged coast of Norway. The wind had scattered the convoy—scattered it as a child with one puff may scatter the seeds of a dandelion. They could not stand before the storm; they could only bow their heads and wait for its fury to abate.

And as the storm raged, as the *Golden Ray* rolled and trembled, Miller lay on his bed of pain and groaned in agony. There was no longer a question of taking him off: the chance of that had gone; not until the sea had calmed would it be possible for a destroyer to come alongside; and no one knew when that would be.

So Miller lay and groaned, his face ashen, while every roll, every vibration, of the ship sent fresh waves of agony shooting through his body. The gunners took it in turns to hold him, trying to shield him against the movement; but, try as they might, they could not protect him completely. Sometimes he coughed; sometimes blood welled up like froth upon his lips; sometimes he cried out, and his cries joined with the clatter of plates, the rattle of the engine that drove the rudder-chains, the clank of an insecure derrick-boom, and the crash of waves against the hull.

There was little sleep for anyone; and they wanted sleep so much. They were haggard, their eyes sore from the wind, and their limbs and muscles aching from the constant strain of walking, standing, sitting, or lying; for there was no real rest in any of these positions. They had forgotten what it was like to sleep in comfort. They had been only a week at sea, and it seemed as though they had been wandering in this world of blizzard and storm, of bomb and torpedo, this world of hate and terror, of cold and discomfort, for years without number. They could not see the end of it; the old world had faded into the semblance of a dream, far away and unreal; only this was real—this world of ice-capped waves, of blown snow demons, and the northern lights. Of this there was no end.

Even to fetch the meals was a hazard. Leaping from ladder to hatch, from hatch to deck, they watched the seas warily, judging the moment when it was safe to move, clinging to the life-line with one hand, carrying the food-containers in the other, and feeling their feet slipping on the wet ice.

The galley itself was awash. The seas had burst in, and now, as the ship rolled, water swilled backward and forward along the floor, carrying with it a mess of dead cinders, coal-dust, and scum. The cook, standing with his gum-boots ankle-deep in icy water, was in a flaming temper. He swore at the galley-boy; he made the maximum of clatter with saucepans and kettles; he almost threw the food at those who poked their heads in at the galley door. It was all spiced with curses and flavoured with ash from the cigarette which seemed glued permanently to his upper lip.

The cook had not shaved for a week; nor, to judge by his appearance, had he washed. His hands were black with soot, his check trousers smeared with grease, and the white jersey, which was his concession to the temperature, showed evidence of every meal that he had prepared since donning it. Added to this, he had recently been in heated argument with one of the firemen, who had saved him a certain amount in dentist's bills by removing two teeth without the aid of anaesthetic. He had then followed up this painful and wholly unnecessary operation by closing one of the cook's eyes. The cook, there-fore, was neither feeling nor looking his best, and his temper, sour at all times, was now worse than vinegar.

Not that the gunners worried about the cook's gall; they had other things to worry about, and one of these was how to move from quarters to galley and back again without being washed overboard. Sometimes it became a choice between food and life; when two hands were needed on the life-line the food was abandoned. Few of them considered it worth eating, anyway; toast and cheese, toast and jam—this was the staple diet. As Vernon remarked, "You've got to toast the bread; it's the only way of getting it properly cooked."

So the stove was kept stoked up, and the kettle, wired to the pipe, shot boiling water from its spout whenever the ship heeled over to starboard, scalding the hands of those toasters who were not quick enough on the retreat. To keep the stove going they had to fetch coal from the stokehold amidships. It was worse than fetching meals, for the heavy bucket filled with coal was a difficult burden to carry across the heaving, slippery deck, washed by high-running seas.

Once when Vernon went for coal the third engineer took him along the 'tunnel,' a narrow passage, about six feet in height, through which the propeller-shaft ran from the engine-room to the stern. Vernon followed the third engineer down the hundred-odd feet of tunnel with the massive shaft revolving very close to him on the right.

" Six bearings," said the third engineer, pointing along the shaft, " and damned important ones too. Come along; let's go to the end."

At the end of the tunnel the shaft disappeared through the stern of the ship. Here was a constant trickle of water seeping in, and Vernon could hear the massive blades of the propeller churning the ocean outside. When the stern lifted and the propeller came out of the water there was a fearful racket as the engines raced.

" That's bad for them," said the third engineer.

A ladder led up out of the tunnel at the after end, and, as far as Vernon could discover, that and the path by which they had come from the engine-room were the only ways out of the tunnel. The realization that they were standing at the bottom of the ship, that they were possibly thirty-five feet below deck-level, and that anything might happen made him suddenly uneasy.

" I'd better be getting back," he said.

" Just as you like," said the third engineer. " I've got another three hours down here."

Vernon was glad to be on deck again, away from the confining walls of the engine-room, with the iron ladders leading up, up, far away above you. He thought of the men working down there during submarine attacks, hearing the depth-charges and unable to do anything except work on. He thought of them wondering if the ship would suddenly split open and icy water come gushing in. What chance had they? What possible chance?

God, he thought, I'd rather be on the guns!

Night fell, and the gale had not abated. The seas, if anything, were more violent than ever, and there had been no opportunity for the convoy to regroup. Overhead a thick cover of lead-grey cloud shut out the sun by day and the stars by night; the cloud-cover was so low and so metallic in appearance that when the *Golden Ray* soared high upon the crest of a wave Vernon almost expected her mast-heads to scrape the ceiling.

Leading-seaman Agnew was gloomy. " This wind's driving us off course—driving us south. We'll end up on the Norwegian rocks if we ain't careful. What with no sun and no stars, I bet nobody knows where we are. Dead reckoning ain't much use in this drift. We're lost—that's what we are—lost."

He seemed to draw some kind of gloomy satisfaction from this—as though it were a state of affairs which he had foretold and was now seeing come to pass. " Well," he seemed to be hinting, " they got us into this mess; now let 'em try and get us out." One might almost have supposed that nothing would please him more than to see the *Golden Ray* wrecked on the coast of Norway, and that if this failed to happen he would be disappointed.

When he came down from the afternoon watch he had more news to impart with his usual lugubrious gusto.

" The D.G.'s had it. About fifty feet of cable's been ripped away from the port side. Bloody good if we come up against magnetic mines now!"

"How did it happen? " asked Willis.

"Happen! Easy enough! A sea came over and washed some loose ironwork bang against the cable—there's some force in those seas, I can tell you. It cut the cable in two places and carried a damned great chunk overboard. Made the sparks fly and all. Now we've got no D.G. Healthy, that is!"

Nobody disbelieved Agnew. The de-gaussing cable was not built into the *Golden Ray*, but lay, for the most part, just above the scuppers. A heavy sea armed with metallic debris could easily have carried some of it away, thus breaking the electric circuit which served to neutralize the ship's magnetic field, and exposing her to the menace of magnetic mines.

" Oh, well," said Willis, " the engineers will soon mend it."

" No, they won't," said Agnew. " They've had a shot; but

they can't manage it. Haven't got the right cable or something. It'll have to be left till we get back—that's if we get back. Well, boys, don't forget your life-jackets. We'll be lucky if we get through this lot."

Which thought appeared to cheer him considerably, for he immediately began humming the tune of *Lilli Marlene*, a little off key, while he made himself a mug of cocoa. He even sang a few of the words, but in the region of " underneath the lamplight " found himself suddenly out of his depth, and reverted to humming. He sipped cocoa with a sound like that of dirty water making its final escape from a bath. Then he looked slowly round the mess-room and asked, " Do any of youse bastards believe in a life hereafter? "

Nobody answered him; nobody appeared interested in this sudden entry into the realms of theology. Agnew began slicing a plug of tobacco and stuffing the shreds into his pipe.

" You'll soon find out," he said.

Miller had begun to wander in his mind, muttering and mumbling, appearing to see things at which he stared with wild eyes. Sometimes he lifted his hands as though in an attempt to ward off evil shapes. At times there was fear in his eyes, at times anger and hatred; at times their expression turned to something gentler; at times they filled with tears.

Often Miller would talk with every appearance of rationality. " No, George, it wasn't my fault, I tell you! Don't blame me, George! You can't blame me; you can't! George, George! You do understand, don't you? "

Miller's tone would change. He would begin to talk wheedlingly. " You know me, George; you know me—Fred Miller. You know I wouldn't do a thing like that—not me, George —not me."

Then his voice would rise in a note of alarm. " George, don't look at me like that. Keep away, George; keep away!"

At other times Miller would speak more softly, so that it was impossible to hear his words except by listening very closely. It was at these times that his expression softened and his face appeared less mean. There was nothing noble about Miller. Yet at such times his battered features seemed to acquire a vague trace of nobility.

"Yes, Jess, I'll do that; I'll do anything you say, Jess. Help me, Jess. I need you. You're the only one can save me."

Then again his voice would rise with that note of alarm. "No, Jess, don't leave me. I can't do without you. I can't; I can't." The alarm was subtly different now. "Jess, I can't see you. Where are you, Jess? Come back to me. I want you. Please come back to me. Oh, Jess, Jess, I can't see you."

He would finish in a sob of despair.

Sometimes he would try to sing. It was a pitiable effort. He would sing snatches of bawdy songs—Army verses set to Salvation Army hymn tunes—and occasionally a bar or two of *The Red Flag*. Then he would start to cough, and his body would be racked by paroxysms. Blood would come, staining his thin lips. And after a while he would be silent, staring with unseeing eyes at the bunk above him.

At midnight on the third night of the gale Miller awoke from sleep or coma and spoke in his normal tone—quietly and sanely.

"Hullo, Harry," he said, looking up at Vernon, who was sitting by him. "You're a good pal, really. I take back all I ever said about you. You're a pal."

He paused, wrinkling his forehead, as though trying to collect his wits. Then he went on almost in a whisper: "I want you to do something for me. You will, won't you?"

Vernon nodded.

"That's right. I knew you would; you're a pal. I want you to see that Jessie has my things—all of them. You'll do that?"

"Jessie who?"

Miller did not appear to understand. "That's right. Give them all to Jessie; she's got to have them—all to Jessie."

His voice trailed away, and he seemed to be sleeping again. But after a moment he opened his eyes. "You'll do that, Harry?"

" Yes," said Vernon, " I'll do that."

" Thanks," said Miller. " Tell her—with Fred's love. Just that; she'll understand—with love from Fred."

When he closed his eyes again he was smiling. He smiled in his sleep, and the iron in his stomach seemed to have lost the power to hurt him.

Half-way through the middle watch a light came on in one of the rafts hanging on the after rigging. Willis guessed what had happened: the light was of a type which would float in water, bulb uppermost, and in that position it automatically switched itself on. It was tied to the raft by a length of cord, and normally was stowed with the bulb downward. The rolling and tossing of the ship must have shifted this one, so that it had turned the other way up and come alight.

In the murky blackness of the storm it showed up bright and clear—a beacon marking the position of the ship. With all around it the smooth, unbroken darkness, there was something almost obscene about that one shining light; it was like a beggar's sore exposed to view or the white scale of a leper. The immediate reaction was to try to cover it, to hide it at all costs.

Willis cupped his hands and shouted to Randall. " Do you think you can climb on to the raft and put that light out? "

Randall said, " I don't mind trying."

That was true enough. He was in that state of mind in which he would have tried anything. He was past caring.

He clambered down from the Bofors platform, climbed upon the rail that surrounded the four-inch-gun deck, reached up towards the rigging, and was just able to grasp the bottom of the raft with his hands. He was on the starboard side, and he waited for the ship to roll to port, then, with a great heave, pulled himself up and got one leg on the raft. Another heave, and he was lying crab-wise upon its slatted surface, clinging tightly as the ship heeled over again upon her starboard side.

The wind tore at Randall's clothing, shrieking in his ears, so that he heard no other sound—neither the shouted instruc-

tions of Sergeant Willis nor the vibration of the ship's engines
—heard only the high, shrill screaming of the gale. He found
that the rescue-light had become wedged in an upright
position between two slats, but it came away easily enough in
his hand. He reversed it, and the light faded away, losing
itself in the darkness. He hung the lamp up by its cord, so
that it was unable to light again, and, having done so, he lay
for a time motionless upon the raft, clinging to it as the ship
rolled, first one way, then the other.

Looking down as the ship heeled over to starboard, Randall
could see the white glint of water rushing past in a frothing
ocean of foam. It was only a few feet below him as he hung
there, and it was like a torrent tumbling into some dark,
infinite cavern—a cavern of oblivion. Randall decided to let
himself slip into that oblivion. There was no future for him;
he had forfeited his future and might as well make an end of
things at once. He had simply to loose his grip, let himself
drop like a plummet, and allow the cold waters to close over
his head.

Yet he still clung to the raft. The hood of his duffel-coat
had fallen back, and fine spindrift, blowing like white smoke
off the crests of the waves, penetrated the thick Balaclava
helmet that he was wearing. It was as though the icy breath
of death were already upon his neck.

He thought, Now I will leave go—now, as she heels over.
It will be a swift end. I shall disappear, and they will all think
it was an accident.

He began to kick his feet free, imperceptibly loosening the
grip of his fingers.

Now, he thought, now! In a moment it will all be over.
And then he felt Willis's hand upon his arm and heard Willis's
voice shouting in his ear. " Are you all right? Can't you get
down? "

"Yes," he said. " Yes; I'm coming."

And he followed Willis back to the deck, and climbed after
him up the rocking Bofors ladder.

"What the hell!" shouted Willis. " What the hell were

you doing? Couldn't you hear me yelling? You must've been
hanging there for ten minutes or more. Did you go to sleep? "

" I was thinking," Randall said.

" My God," said Willis, " what a place to sit and think! "

By morning the storm had abated considerably and the seas
were going down. And as relative calm settled on the waters
the convoy began to reassemble its scattered members, the
destroyers, like sheep-dogs, searching far and wide, and
drawing in strayed sheep from this horizon and from that.
And as the destroyers searched, collecting a ship here
and a ship there, the others steamed round and round in a
wide circle, waiting for the strays to join them—waiting
impatiently, with watchful eyes upon the sky and watchful
eyes upon the sea.

And as the convoy lay waiting for the lost ones to return a
destroyer drew close to the *Golden Ray*, and a voice shouted
through the loud-hailer. It seemed like the voice of the
destroyer—metallic, yet cultured—a naval voice—a voice of
unemotional efficiency—a voice to drive away doubts and
fears. " Ahoy, *Golden Ray*! Ahoy! I am coming alongside
to take off your wounded rating. Is everything ready? "

It was Captain Pownall himself who answered, speaking
through a megaphone.

" You are too late—too late. He died last night."

Miller was buried at sea, sewn up in a hammock, with an
iron grating at his feet to make him sink. They laid him on
a board, and the captain read a brief service. Then the board
was tilted on the bulwark, and Miller slid silently down into
the ocean.

None of the gunners had really liked Miller; yet they all
felt the loss of him. There was a blank in the mess and an
empty bunk, and these were unpleasant reminders—reminders
of man's mortality—reminders of the slenderness of that
thread by which each one of them clung to life.

" He hardly made a splash," Andrews said. " He just went
down—straight down."

"He was small," said Payne; "no more than a scrap of a lad. He didn't need much space."

Andrews seemed unable to take his mind off the picture of Miller, no more than an oblong bundle in a canvas covering, sliding silently down into the water.

"Hardly a splash. Straight down he went. I wonder what it's like down there. Cold and dark. I wonder what lives down there. Horrible things; slimy things. It's awful—going down, down, down, and never coming up no more. It's——"

Willis broke in savagely. "Forget it! Forget it, I tell you! Ben, for Christ's sake play that bloody mouth-organ!"

By nightfall all the stragglers had been found and drawn again into the fold—all except the lame duck. Somewhere, some time, in that terrible gale, the lame duck, struggling along on her crippled engines, had ceased to struggle. Some time, somewhere, she had foundered, sinking without trace beneath that cruel sea. So, when the convoy formed again into its ranks and steamed on towards the setting sun, the lame duck was no longer with them, and would never be with them again.

And now the others experienced a feeling akin to guilt, because they had secretly wished the lame duck to die. Now that she was dead, her death hung about their necks like the Ancient Mariner's albatross, and they wished her alive again, so that the sense of guilt might fall from them. But she was dead—dead and gone for ever.

So they steamed on as the sun sank and the daylight faded —on into the night. And the sky was like a perforated hood with light shining through the holes; and soon the aurora sprang up in the north and cast its eerie glow over them all. And as they moved on beneath the aurora and the myriad stars they thought of the lame duck and of others which were no longer with them, and they wondered who would be the next.

Then the fog came upon them—a grey, opaque blanket, chill and clammy, folding the ships within its dripping arms and hiding them, one from another. Soon visibility was down to a few yards, and out of the fog came the sound of ships' sirens braying their warning, as all moved nervously forward, crying out at brief intervals, and seeing nothing but the grey blanket above them and all around, and the grey water below.

Captain Pownall was on the bridge of the *Golden Ray* with the second mate. Both of them were peering into the gloom; both were listening for the sirens, trying to judge the direction from which the sound came, trying to gauge the distance. But the fog confused sound, altered directions, played tricks with hearing; and they could not tell with certainty where any other ship was. They knew only that within the radius of a few miles there were nearly forty vessels—merchantmen and men-of-war—with any one of which they might collide.

There was a look-out in the bows watching for danger ahead. It was a cold post, and he shivered, wishing himself back in Swansea, where he had been born. His eyes smarted with the strain of gazing into a blank wall. What was that creeping out of the gloom? Was it the shape of another ship? Was it a shadow? Was it only the child of his own imagination?

He shivered again and stared ahead—wondering—wondering.

On the Bofors platform Andrews cried suddenly, "Look, sarge! Look down there! It's a periscope—a periscope!"

Willis looked where Andrews was pointing, and saw a little column of churned-up water, like a fountain playing. It rose and fell, rose and fell; and it kept pace with them, moving along beside the ship, level with the stern of the *Golden Ray*.

"It's a periscope," Andrews cried again. "What do we do?"

"Don't be a fool," Willis said harshly. "It's a fog-buoy."

Andrews felt silly. Now that Willis had told him he could see that it was a fog-buoy—one of those T-shaped wooden floats that ships towed in fog to make a spurt of water and warn following ships to keep their distance. But it ought not to have been where it was; it ought to have been ahead of the

Golden Ray. They must be getting uncomfortably close to the ship in front.

Willis picked up the telephone and rang through to the bridge. "There's a fog-buoy running beside us, sir. It's about level with the gun-deck."

The voice of the second mate answered him. "Thank you, sergeant. I wondered where it had got to. Keep your eyes skinned for that tanker astern of us. We don't want a boot in the arse."

He rang off, and Willis watched the fog-buoy gradually drawing ahead. He stamped his feet and looked for the tanker following them, listening for the voice of her siren, and, when it came, not able to say for certain whether it was hers or that of some other vessel wandering off its course.

At the moment of peril he had no time to warn the bridge, for the blare of the tanker's siren and the outline of her towering stem looming out of the fog came simultaneously.

Willis, Andrews, and Randall were like men observing some inevitable tragedy; they were like the audience at a Greek play—powerless to prevent what must occur. So they stood quite still, watching the bows of the tanker moving steadily closer to the stern of their own ship. They knew that nothing they could do would prevent this calamity. They knew there was no way of suddenly stopping the momentum of thousands of tons of steel and timber; it was a force that could drive a brutal wedge into the *Golden Ray* and sink her with as much effect as any torpedo.

"God!" Andrews muttered. "Oh, God!"

There was a look-out in the bows of the tanker. He was waving his arms and shouting madly. But he too was powerless; and suddenly he was still and silent like the gunners, waiting for the crash that could end all their lives.

But at the last moment the tanker swung her head to starboard; there was a sullen, grinding noise as she slid past, and a great scar appeared on the surface of her paint, a scar stretching from bows to stern on her port side. Then she was gone—swallowed up in the enveloping fog.

" By God!" said Andrews, his voice trembling. "That was close!"

" Too close," Willis muttered. " Damn this fog! Damn this bloody fog!"

He rang through to the bridge again. " It was the tanker, sir. She's gone now."

It was the returning gale that drove away the last tattered remnants of the fog. Soon the convoy was once more ploughing through the mountains and valleys of a raging sea, shivering under the lash of a freezing wind, assailed by driving blizzards which turned the ships into pale ghosts, and torn out of its symmetrical pattern of ranks and columns.

But calm followed the gale, and a Focke-Wulf found them —a Focke-Wulf coming up out of the south with almost the first light of day and playing the old game of encirclement.

The convoy was battered and weary; the gunners' eyes were red from lack of sleep; but there was a bitterness in their hearts born of the memory of dead comrades, and when the Heinkels came—summoned by the Focke-Wulf—they found the grey ships ready and waiting. And from those slow grey ships such a curtain of flame and steel flew upward that the Heinkels would not come in low, but dropped their bombs from 5000 feet and raced for home, with the red flame of tracer and the deadly glitter of shell-bursts following them as they went.

And the convoy steamed on without further scathe— driving westward to the lodestone of Iceland.

When the Catalina met them the men in the *Golden Ray* raised a cheer.

" It's a Cat! A good old Cat! Oh, what a sight for sore eyes!"

It was good to see a Catalina again. The Catalina was like a hand reaching out across the water to help them home. For days the only aircraft they had seen had been German; and there was something evil about the very shape of a German plane. Now here was the friendly old Catalina, winking a greeting and keeping an eye open for U-boats; and it did their hearts good to see it.

When they sighted the coast of Iceland they had been at sea for thirteen days. Here they saw a bleak, rugged land, with bare mountains rising almost directly from the shore and showing the veins of horizontal strata, as though they had been built up gradually, layer upon layer. For a day they stayed within sight of those mountains, feeling a false sense of security with the proximity of land; but on the fifteenth day they were moving steadily southward over a gently heaving sea, and Iceland had disappeared astern.

They were moving out of the Arctic, and their hearts were glad. The ice began slowly to relinquish its grip, falling from mast and derrick with sudden clatter, dripping away down grating and scupper, powerless to stand against the warm air creeping up from the south.

From all of them the dark cloud of the north was beginning to lift, and their spirits were soaring with it. They no longer believed that they would not reach home.

And then Seaman-gunner Higgins went mad.

CHAPTER FOURTEEN

Bar the Shouting

SEAMAN-GUNNER Alf Higgins was twenty—a thin, narrow-shouldered boy with pinched features and hair like straw. When he was no more than nineteen he found himself bound for the Far East in a tramp steamer that had run down the slipway into the Tyne thirty years earlier, and was now nothing but a clanking crate of iron held together by rust and faith and blasphemy.

They had put in at Takoradi and were steaming south with Cape Town as the next port of call when the torpedo struck them. The ship sank in less than five minutes, and only one boat got away. Higgins was in that boat with fifteen others. The rest of the crew were lucky; they died at once.

Higgins lost count of the days that the boat drifted in the Atlantic. He was wearing only a singlet and underpants; by day he was scorched by the fierce tropical sun; at night he shivered with cold.

Two of the men were wounded; they were the first to die. The others were strong then, and were able to roll the bodies overboard. They rationed the water and erected a sail, keeping watch upon the horizon for signs of rescue or the thin haze of land. When the water was finished they began to despair.

Higgins watched them die—one by one. He saw how each man died in a different way, according to his individual character. Some died quietly, as though resigned to the end, slipping out of life as quietly as a child drifting into sleep; others died in fear, dreading a journey into the unknown; some, unable to endure the agony any longer, flung themselves overboard, where the sharks were waiting; and some drank sea-water and were for a while appeased, until the salt flame roared up to burn the tongue and mouth and throat with a searing fire of torment.

Higgins, a boy of nineteen, watched all this happen as the boat drifted on over the shimmering sea, and the days and nights trailed away on a belt of endless agony. At last he was left with only two companions. When they no longer moved he concluded that they were dead. He had no hope that within a short while he would not be as they. He lay between them in the bottom of the boat, waiting for the end.

That was how his rescuers found him—lying in an open boat between two dead men. At first they feared that he was dead also, but with the resilience of youth he recovered quickly. He was put ashore in Freetown; two months later he was back in England; a month after that he was at sea again, bound for Russia in the s.s. *Golden Ray*. The doctors had passed him as fit for sea; and as far as his body was concerned, no doubt he was. They had ignored the scar upon his mind.

It was strange that Higgins should have gone mad now, when the tension had slackened, when the sea had calmed, and the cold had released its grip. One might have supposed that his hold on sanity would have broken earlier, when the attacks were taking place, when ships were being sunk, when the gale was battering them, and Miller muttering away his life. But the ways of the mind are strange, the balance a razor-edge; and it was now, with Scotland almost in sight, that Higgins chose to tilt the balance.

He began by emptying a dish of stew over Petty Officer Donker's spiky head.

It was fortunate for Donker that the stew was nearly cold; otherwise he might have been badly burnt. As it was, his first reaction was one of bewilderment. The thing had happened so suddenly and with so little warning that for a moment he could not understand why his face should be running with grease or why the dish should be sitting on his head like a helmet.

The others seated at the mess-room table were surprised, but not unpleasantly so. It was amusing to see old Donker sitting there with the dish on his head and chunks of meat and vegetables rolling down on to his shoulders and lap. They did not at once realize that this was more than a grotesquely far-fetched joke. Then they saw Higgins's eyes, and they knew that there was nothing funny about the business; that it was indeed deadly serious.

Higgins began to scream. " I'll show you who's captain in this ship. You can't get the better of me. I'll show you."

He snatched up a table-knife and made a lunge at Donker. The petty officer gave a yell of pain and fell backwards off the form, clutching at his arm. Higgins seemed about to spring on him and deliver another blow, but Agnew moved more quickly. Seizing the boy's arm, he began twisting it, trying to make him drop the knife. But Higgins's body had drawn strength from madness, and, wrenching himself free, he flung the knife at the prostrate petty officer. The knife hit Donker flat; it struck him in the chest and fell harmlessly to deck.

By this time the other gunners had recovered from their amazement, and three of them had seized Higgins. But again he shook off the hands laid upon him, and, leaping over the mess-table, was away before they could stop him.

" The lad's crazy! " shouted Willis. " Grab him! There's no telling what he may do! "

They could hear Higgins clattering up the ladder to the deck, and they ran after him, hindering one another in the doorway, pouring out of the mess-room, and streaming up the ladder in pursuit. Padgett was the first of them to reach the deck, and he was just in time to see Higgins leap on to the taffrail, as though about to fling himself into the sea.

" Hi! " yelled Padgett. " Come back! Come back, Higgie! "

The shout arrested Higgins. He turned and looked back at Padgett and the others crowding out on to the poop, steadying himself with one hand upon a stanchion.

" Keep back! " he screamed. " Keep back, all of you! You'd mutiny, would you? You'd try and kill your captain! Well, you won't. You won't get me. "

Padgett signalled to the others to keep back; he knew that a single unwary movement might send Higgins to his death. He spoke quietly, trying to humour the mad boy.

" You're wrong. We aren't mutineers. We want to obey orders. We want you to come and give us orders. Come down, now, won't you? "

He moved forward a pace or two, and Higgins screamed, " Stop there! Don't come any nearer. I know you; you'd like to get your hands on me; you'd like to kill me. But I'll beat you yet. "

Padgett said, " Nobody wants to kill you. You know we couldn't get on without you." And he moved another pace forward.

Higgins laughed sneeringly. " Of course you can't get on without me. You'd run the ship on the rocks. "

" Well, then," said Padgett, easing a little nearer, " why don't you come down? Why don't you come with me up to the bridge? Come and talk things over. "

He was within a few feet of Higgins now; another step, and he would be able to grasp him. The others watched, not daring to move; and from the Bofors platform Vernon and Warby looked down in bewilderment, wondering what was going on.

Then suddenly the ship's siren tore a hole in the silence, rending the tension to shreds and setting every one's nerves quivering. It had an immediate effect on Higgins: he shuddered, swung round on the taffrail so that he faced the sea, and released his hold upon the stanchion. At the same moment Padgett leaped forward, grasped him by the belt, and pulled him back to safety.

It took four men to hold him down on the deck and two more to tie him up, and he screamed and spat at them, mouthing obscenities. Then, quite suddenly, he began to weep, and his body went limp under their hands. He seemed to have come to his right senses, and instead of the wild look in his eyes there was now only fear. He was no longer a dangerous maniac, but a frightened child, caught up in forces he could neither understand nor control, a child scared because of what had happened to him.

They carried him down to the cabin, and he made no protest. And when the mate brought a strait-jacket from the ship's store, he allowed them to put it on him without offering any resistance. He even seemed eager to help, as though in propitiation for the trouble he had caused. He avoided looking at Petty Officer Donker, and when they laid him on his bunk he lay there quietly, with his pinched features seeming more thin and pale than ever, and his straw-like hair scattered untidily over his forehead. He knew that he had strayed briefly into some strange, terrible hell, and the fear was on him that he might wander that way again.

Two hours later the look-out sighted land.

That evening Andrews sat down to write a letter.

DARLING JACKIE,

I have been on a long journey, but it is nearly over. When you get this letter you will know that I'm not far away. You

can bet I'll follow it just as fast as I can, because I want to see
you again so much. Jackie darling, it seems years since I kissed
you good-bye. Has it seemed like that to you? I hope so. I
hope you've missed me too. Jackie, I've been dreaming about
you. Yes, straight up, I have. That's been the best part. I
keep your photo in my pocket always, but I don't need that to
remind me of you. I only have to close my eyes, and I can
see you clear as clear. . . .

He could, too. Jackie! Jacqueline Cooper! Before his
last leave he had not even known her; she had been no more
than a name on a card pinned to a Balaclava helmet—a
knitted 'comfort' issued to him in Liverpool. He had
unpinned the card, read it, and put it away in his wallet.

The card read: "Knitted by Miss J. Cooper, High Street,
Benford, Essex. Please write."

He did not write. He put the card away and forgot about it.
He did think that perhaps some day he might send a letter of
thanks to Miss Cooper; he even wondered for a moment what
she was like. He knew some fellows wrote to women who had
knitted comforts for them; sometimes they received letters
back; sometimes a regular correspondence sprang up, with
photographs exchanged and so on. He had often thought
about doing the same himself, for he had had many knitted
comforts since he had been at sea. But always he put off the
task of writing, and in the end he always forgot.

Just as he forgot to write to Miss Cooper of High Street,
Benford, Essex.

It was six months before he returned to England. Then he
was given fourteen days' leave. His home was in Cambridge-
shire, in a village in the Fen country. Half-way through the
first week of leave he was bored. Really, there was nothing
to do; the friends he had known before the War were either
in the Forces or away all day working; there was no excitement; even the beer was poor. He began to feel that it would
be a relief to be back at sea again.

Then, looking through his wallet, he came upon the card.
On an impulse he decided to go to Benford. Even if nothing

came of it it would be something to do; it would break the monotony.

His mother was surprised, but she knew better than to try to keep him from going. After all, it was his leave; he was entitled to spend it as he wished. Still, she did hope he would not be gone long; she and his father saw so little of him these days—and he was their only child.

Andrews told her he did not expect to be away more than one night; quite possibly he would be back again the same day. It depended on how things worked out.

He arrived at Benford a little before noon, and found it a small country town—in fact, scarcely more than a large village. High Street was easy to find, for it ran through the centre of the town. There were a few shops, four or five inns, a post-office, and a telephone kiosk. At one point a pond seemed to have thrust the houses back from the street in a rough semi-circle. Seated on the railings surrounding the pond were two small boys, dangling fishing-lines in the water with patience and perseverance deserving of better results. They looked up as Andrews approached, gazing at him with blank, expressionless faces.

Andrews said, " Can you tell me where Miss Cooper lives —Miss J. Cooper? "

The older boy answered him. " You mean Cooper's—the shop? "

" I've only got the address—Miss Cooper, High Street," Andrews said. " This is High Street, isn't it? "

The boy pointed across the street. " What's that there? "

Andrews followed the direction of the pointing finger, and saw on the opposite side of the street a small grocery shop. Over the door was a board, on which in faded paint were the words " J. Cooper. General Stores." He was surprised that he had not noticed it sooner.

He tossed sixpence to the boys, and walked across the road. Leaving their fishing-lines dangling in the water, they followed him, exhibiting that open and unabashed curiosity which is one of the characteristics of extreme youth.

Andrews was beginning to regret having made the journey to Benford. Seeing the faded name above the shop, the thought suddenly came to him that Miss Cooper was an ageing spinster. Until then, almost unconsciously, he had thought of her as young and, he had hoped, attractive. But he saw now that this was unlikely. Things did not work out that way.

He halted outside the shop, indecision taking hold of him. Should he give up the whole idea and go home again? He was a fool to have come. Scarcely knowing that he was doing so, he began reading the labels on the tins in the window—oxtail soup, baked beans, dried milk, baking-powder, iodized salt, ground pepper. Then he discovered two pairs of wide-open, childish eyes staring up at him inquiringly. He pushed open the door of the shop and walked in.

The odour of provisions met him like a gentle wave, reminding him of the village store where he used to go shopping for his mother. It was a conglomerate odour of dried fruit, ham, cheese, oranges, tobacco, vinegar, coffee, and tea, with a background of paraffin and methylated spirits. It was sickly-sweet, yet with a trace of bitterness, and was in the very character of the shop.

The counter was immediately opposite the door, and, but for an open space in the middle, was piled high with groceries. Behind the counter stood a girl wearing a white overall. There was no one else in the shop. Andrews stood with his back to the door, feeling foolish and not knowing what to say.

The girl asked, " Can I help you? "

She had brown hair and a rather wide, placid face. Her voice was tranquil.

Andrews moved forward a pace and said, " I was looking for Miss Cooper—Miss J. Cooper."

The girl appeared rather surprised. " I am Miss Cooper."

Andrews took the card from his pocket and dropped it on the counter. " It's about this. I ought to have written; but you know how it is. So, as I was this way, I thought I'd call and thank you."

The girl had glanced at the card, and a trace of colour had crept into her pale face. She seemed uncertain of herself, a shade nervous.

"What was it you had? I've knitted so many things."

"A Balaclava. It was real good. I've worn it a lot, and it's been right handy."

"I'm glad. Knitting isn't much; but I'm glad it helps."

"It does that—helps a lot."

A customer came into the shop, and Andrews stood on one side while Miss Cooper served her. He felt awkward, in the way; and again he doubted whether he had been wise in coming. When the customer had gone he said, "Well, I just wanted to thank you. Now I'd better be going."

The girl asked, "Do you have to go at once? I'm sure Mum would like to see you."

"Well, there's no real hurry," he admitted.

The girl lifted the flap in the counter and came through into the front of the shop. She locked the shop door and drew a blind down over the glass.

"This is early-closing day," she explained. "We've finished for to-day. Won't you come into the back? Mum would love to see you."

Andrews followed her past the flap in the counter and through into a small, rather dark room, filled to overflowing with furniture. Another door led from this room to what was obviously the kitchen, for a smell of cooking came from that region. "Mum!" the girl called. "Mum, we've got a visitor."

In answer to her call a dumpy woman with untidy hair and a bewildered expression came from the kitchen, wiping her hands on the apron she wore over a dress of some stiff black material. She looked from Andrews to her daughter questioningly, and with a hint of alarm in her eyes, as though she were in the habit of fearing anything that was not usual.

The girl reassured her. "He had one of the Balaclavas I knitted and came to thank me." She turned to Andrews. "You didn't tell me your name."

"Andrews—George Andrews."

Mrs Cooper gave her right hand an extra-hard rub with the apron and held it out in timid greeting. "Pleased to meet you, I'm sure. You live hereabouts, I expect."

"Not exactly. About fifty miles from here."

"As far as that! You didn't come special."

Andrews hesitated; then he grinned sheepishly. "Oh, well, I was on leave, and there wasn't much to do."

The girl broke in: "So you did come all that way specially. Oh, you shouldn't have. Did you come by train?"

"Yes."

"It was nice of you. There's not everybody would do that. Most of them don't even write."

"I didn't," said Andrews.

"No, but you've come yourself; that's better. You'll stay to dinner, of course. He must stay, mustn't he, Mum?"

Mrs Cooper looked doubtful. "If Mr Andrews doesn't mind stew? It's all we've got. But I'm sure he's welcome if he doesn't mind."

"Of course I don't mind," Andrews said. "But I don't want to eat your rations. I can get a meal somewhere."

"Not in Benford," said the girl. "No, I don't think so—not in Benford."

"There's plenty," said Mrs Cooper. "You needn't worry about that. There's plenty if you don't mind stew."

"I love it," Andrews said.

After that events had just taken their course, as though it were all inevitable. In the afternoon he and Jacqueline had gone for a walk, wandering along twisting woodland paths, and feeling that the War was very far away. He had missed his train back, and then, of course, he had allowed himself to be persuaded to stay the night.

Somehow then he had just stayed on—helping in the shop —walking out with Jacqueline in the evenings. Soon they had persuaded themselves that they were in love. It had been easy enough, for both were at the age when love comes easily, and both were a little lonely.

It was amazing how love had awakened the placid girl, lending a sparkle to her eyes and animation to her smile. Andrews wondered how it was that at first he had thought her plain. She was beautiful.

When Andrews left Benford there was only one day of his leave remaining. He had felt guilty; but his mother had understood.

"It was only to be expected," she had said. "I do hope she's the right girl for you."

"She is, Mother. Wait till you see her."

Andrews's pen scratched and spluttered over the cheap, ruled notepaper. He sat with his head bent down close to the pad, and as he wrote his tongue thrust itself out between his lips. The *Golden Ray* was steaming smoothly over a calm sea, and the cabin swayed hardly at all.

> Jackie darling, it's all over bar the shouting. We're pretty well out of danger while I write this. We've had some tough going, but I'll tell you about that when I see you. . . .

At daybreak the coast of Scotland was visible on the port side, and in two columns the ships steamed southward, heading for Loch Ewe, where they would anchor for the night, before being directed to their different ports.

The sea was still calm; the sun was pleasantly warm; and it did really seem, as Andrews had written in his letter, "all over bar the shouting."

Sergeant Willis was walking towards the forecastle when it happened. He wanted some paint to touch up the gun, and he was looking for the bosun. His errand brought him close to the explosion, for it was the bows which took the full force of the mine.

The noise deafened Willis; it seemed to thrust his eardrums in. The deck leaped under his feet, and he felt a searing pain across the eyes, as though some one had lashed them with a barbed whip. Instinctively he put up his hand and felt the warm wetness of blood. He dropped his hand and looked down at it, but he could see nothing. There was nothing in front of his eyes but an immense black void.

"God!" he muttered. "Oh, dear God Almighty! I'm blind!"

The deck was dropping under him, sloping at an acute angle. He fell forward upon his knees, groping for a hand-hold and finding none. In another moment he was on all fours, and cold water was creeping up his arms and legs. He tried to stand, but his feet slipped from under him, and he could no longer feel anything solid beneath them.

He wondered why he did not sink, why his head remained dry; and then he realized that he was wearing his life-jacket, and this was buoying him up. But the blackness pressed in around him, and he was alone. In all his life he had never felt so terribly alone.

Randall was walking along the after deck when the explosion occurred. The shock flung him against one of the hatches, and he fell with his arms stretched out on the canvas and his legs dangling over the coaming.

For a moment he lay there, dazed. Then, recovering his senses, he climbed on to the hatch and stood up, steadying himself with one hand upon a derrick-boom. The hatch was already sloping forward, and he could see that the ship was going down by the head. He felt immensely calm—even relieved. He felt like a man from whose shoulders a heavy burden of decision has been lifted.

The engines had stopped. That would be the engineers' immediate job—to stop the engines. Steam was spouting from the funnel in a great white cloud, and the whistle was sounding, its high-pitched wail going on and on like the last, despairing cry of some mortally stricken monster. Randall could see men running to the lifeboats on the port side. It was useless going to the starboard ones, since they had been smashed by the storm. The task of launching was made difficult by the slope of the deck, and he could see that they were having trouble with number two boat. He watched them detachedly as they worked feverishly at the ropes, and it was like a dumb show, because the rushing voice of the steam-whistle drowned all other sound.

As Randall stood there, hanging on the derrick-boom and watching the launching of the boats, three naval ratings who had been working on the four-inch gun ran past. Randall had leisure to notice the expressions of alarm on their faces as they padded by, and he thought suddenly of animals flee-ing from a prairie fire. One of the sailors shouted to him.

"Hi! Randie! Come along!"

But Randall smiled and let them go. It gave him a feeling of superiority to be so calm and detached while all the others were rushing wildly about. It was a feeling almost of power.

He saw that some of the men had got into number two lifeboat and that it was being lowered. It moved jerkily, dropping a little way, stopping, and then dropping again. Then something went wrong: one of the falls seemed to stick and the other suddenly ran out. In a moment the lifeboat was hanging in a vertical position, bows uppermost, spilling its human cargo into the sea.

One man only did not fall out of the boat. Somehow his foot had become caught, so that he hung head downward—helpless. Then the boat swung slowly round like the pendu-lum of a 365-day clock, and the man's head, swinging with it, was caught between the boat and the ship's side. When the boat swung back again the man still hung by one leg, but he had ceased to be interested in saving his life: he no longer had a life to save.

The other boat had reached the water safely, and men were slipping down the escape ropes. In a few moments the boat was full and could take no more. Randall watched the men handling the oars, thrusting the boat away from the ship's side. Then they began pulling away, striking raggedly, but opening a gap between ship and boat.

The slope of the deck had become more pronounced now as the ship's head sank lower. Half the midships upperworks was under water, and water was creeping up the after deck, creeping towards the poop. Randall steadied himself on wide-parted legs and began to take off his life-jacket. Having done that, he jumped down from the hatch, floundered across the deck, and climbed on to the bulwark. Standing there for a moment with one hand upon the rigging, he took a last look at what was still visible of the *Golden Ray*.

She was going down fast. Even as he stood there she gave a shudder like the nervous twitch of a dying animal, and bubbles came rippling up from some interior region to burst one by one upon the surface. The propeller was high out of the water now, and the Bofors pedestal was sloping at an angle of forty-five degrees. The Bofors barrel had swung round until it had come up against the safety-stop and was pointing futilely at the rising tide of water. Some of the smoke-floats on the poop had broken adrift from their stands and had rolled forward until brought to a halt by the rail. Randall noticed that one of the rafts had gone from the after rigging, and there were at least two rafts in the sea with men clinging to them.

Well, he thought, this is the end, Sid boy. This is it.

He released his hold on the rigging and let himself drop.

Bombardier Padgett was in the gunners' cabin when the mine exploded. Cowdrey and Payne were there also, and three of the naval ratings. The first leap and shudder of the vessel seemed to petrify them all, so that for a moment they just stood or sat where they were, looking at one another with a sudden fearful question in their eyes.

Then, as the cabin began to tilt, the idea swiftly came to each one of them that the ship was sinking, and they were spurred to action. Snatching up their life-jackets, they ran to the companion ladder and began climbing towards the deck. But when the first of them reached the top of the ladder he found that the iron door of the companion hatch—a door which was always kept open—had somehow been swung shut by the shock of the explosion, and now was jammed so tightly that they could not open it.

Crowded on the iron platform at the top of the ladder— a platform that was already sloping so acutely it was difficult to keep their footing on it—they tried desperately to force open the door. But, though they managed to push it a few inches, as soon as they released their pressure it closed fast again.

"Something's fallen against it outside," Padgett gasped; "a chest or something heavy like that. Give another heave, lads —altogether."

They heaved; the door opened an inch or two and then closed again. They tried again—again with the same result. And all the time they could feel the ship tilting farther as she settled by the head.

"It's no use," said Padgett. "We'll never make it. Is there any other way out?"

"How about the porthole?" Cowdrey suggested.

They grasped at this straw and clattered down the ladder and into the cabin. Padgett loosened the thumbscrews and swung the plate-glass cover inward. But they knew it was no use; they knew that no man could squeeze through a hole that size. They could see out, but they could not get out—and in a few minutes it would be too late.

Then the electric light went out, and at the same moment water began to pour in through the porthole. Padgett slammed it shut and fastened the screws.

"Get back to the ladder," he ordered.

His harsh voice of command killed the germ of panic that had started to grow in the others. They obeyed him in silence, groping through the darkness, splashing through the water that had flowed in, and feeling for the ladder. It was no easy task to climb it, for it leaned drunkenly to one side; but they clambered up—Padgett last of all.

"Try the door again, lads," he ordered. "Give a good heave."

But even as he gave the order the door swung open, and they could see Vernon and Warby standing in the opening, and behind them the steel locker that had jammed the door.

"Come on," said Vernon. "Time to leave."

Like men reprieved from the gallows, they streamed out into the good air.

Padgett was following when a thought halted him: Higgins!

They had forgotten Higgins. Higgins was still lying on his bunk, encased in a strait-jacket, unable to move.

For a moment Padgett hesitated—but only for a moment. Then he turned and raced down the ladder into the dark pit below.

The water in the wash-place was deeper than it had been; it was up to his knees. Padgett fought down a sudden wave of claustrophobia and groped his way towards the door of the naval gunners' quarters. His brain kept saying: " Hurry, hurry, hurry! " But it was difficult to hurry with water swilling round his legs, the deck sloping steeply, and everything in almost complete darkness.

Strange noises came to his ears—the rattlings and groanings made by the vessel in its death-throes. From somewhere came the sullen clang of metal upon metal, and, joining in, the sinister whisper of the rising tide.

He found the door at last, strangely tilted, and stepped down into the cabin beyond. Here the water was considerably deeper—waist-high—and it was more difficult to move. He paused for a moment, trying to find his bearings, and felt the deck shudder under his feet.

He shouted, " Higgins! Higgins! Where are you? "

His voice echoed hollowly in the half-submerged cabin, and he heard a cry that was half a sob. He floundered towards it. In a moment his questing hands fell upon the young sailor, and he could hear Higgins's terrified whimpering.

" All right," he said. " You're all right now, kid."

There was no hope of releasing the boy; there was no time to fumble with buckles that he could not see. Padgett put his arms around Higgins, lifted him from the bunk, and made for the faint glimmer of light that told him where the door was. The water was rising rapidly; it was almost up to his chest as he struggled through the doorway, and he realized that the ship could not last much longer.

In the wash-place he was on a higher level again, and the water dropped to his waist, but, hurrying towards the companion ladder, he stumbled and fell. Higgins screamed as the water closed over him, but in a moment Padgett had struggled to his feet and had lifted his burden out of the water.

But now they were not alone in the wash-place—not by any means alone. Everywhere he looked Padgett could see the glitter of eyes in the darkness, and he could hear fearful squeakings.

The water was alive with rats.

They had been flooded out from some nesting-place and were now trying madly to escape. Some of them climbed on to Padgett's shoulders and up to his head. He tried to shake them off, but they clung persistently, their fear of drowning driving away their fear of man. Padgett held Higgins with one hand, and with the other swept the rats from his head and shoulders. Then he began to climb the ladder—painfully— slow step by step—hauling himself upward to the light showing above.

The rats came with him, clawing at his trousers and getting under his feet.

He had almost reached the top of the ladder when water began to flow down from the companion hatch—at first a trickle, but rapidly increasing to a torrent. Padgett could scarcely breathe. His muscles were cracking under the strain of carrying Higgins and climbing up the sloping ladder. He could have dropped the boy and saved himself; that was the only sensible thing to do; if he did not it would simply mean two lives lost instead of one. Where was the sense in hanging on to a poor, crack-brained fellow who, if he lived, would probably spend half his time in an asylum? It would be much better to let him go; it would soon be over for him.

But Padgett did not let go. There was a streak of obstinacy in his nature, and, having gone down into the cabin to pull Higgins back to life, he was damned if he would now let death have the victory. To Padgett's mind the struggle became a personal one with death—and Higgins was the prize. Padgett summoned up all his great strength, cleared the last step, and burst through the deluge out on to the open deck.

At the same moment the *Golden Ray* gave up the struggle and slid silently down into the sea.

When Randall jumped into the sea he found that it was not so easy to commit suicide after all. He found that the instinct to preserve one's life is strong, even though that life may appear to have been ruined. Randall was a powerful swimmer: he had played water-polo before the War, and was almost as much at home in the waves as a seal. He had thought before leaping from the bulwark that he would simply let himself go down, making no resistance; it had seemed an easy thing to do. When he came to it he found that, far from being easy, it was very hard. For him, in fact, it was impossible.

His head broke surface, and he began to tread water. He knew that he could keep afloat for hours, that if he so wished he could swim ashore without difficulty; and he knew that he had left things too late; he ought to have gone overboard in the storm, when there would have been no possibility of survival. Now it was too late.

Paradoxically, having come to this conclusion, he felt a wave of relief sweep over him, and, turning on his breast, he began to swim away from the sinking ship.

He had jumped over on the starboard side, and all the activity was on the port. He seemed to be alone in the water —quite alone. But no, not quite alone! There was one other man on the starboard side; a man in a life-jacket; a man crying out for help; a man in agony.

Randall swam towards the man, and saw that it was Sergeant Willis. He saw, too, that something had happened to Willis's eyes, and that blood was running down his face. It shocked him to see Willis so helpless.

He shouted, " All right, sarge. It's me—Randall."

Willis cried, " My eyes! My eyes! I can't see. I'm blind. Something's bust my eyes."

" You'll be all right," said Randall. " Don't struggle now. Don't talk. Just leave everything to me."

He felt strong and capable. He was at home in the water, and he knew that he could save Willis. It was a job to do—something useful. For the first time in months he felt almost happy.

He slipped his hands under Willis's arm-pits and began to swim on his back, heading for a raft that he had seen floating about thirty yards away. He had to struggle hard to drag Willis on to the raft, but he succeeded.

From the raft they were picked up by a corvette.

As he felt the ship sinking Bombardier Padgett locked his arms round Higgins and drew in a deep breath of air. Then the water closed over his head, and he went down and down.

He kept his eyes open, and he could see light filtering down through the water and bubbles floating upward, passing him in a never ending stream. There seemed to be layer after layer of water, and it was cold, icily cold.

And still Padgett went down, caught by the suction of the ship. His chest seemed to be on fire; there was a drumming, throbbing sensation in his head, and he wondered how much longer it would be before something burst inside him. He knew that he could not endure much more of the pressure. Was the ship going to drag him to the bottom of the sea? He might as well have remained caught in the cabin if this were to be the end after all.

But he did not release his grip on Higgins, and when a sudden upward rush of water caught him and flung him out into the blessed air he still had Higgins locked to him, as though his arms had grown round the boy. Looking back on it afterwards, he could only think that he had been saved by a blast of air or steam bursting out from the boilers like an exhalation of breath and carrying him up with it.

He had never realized that air, good, clean air, could taste so sweet as when his head broke the surface and he was able to suck it into his lungs in great, gasping breaths. So for a time he floated—unmoving—letting his life-jacket support the two of them, while he gasped and panted, feeling life flow back into his body.

It seemed a very long while, but in fact was probably no more than a few minutes. Then he heard a shout, and, looking up, saw a corvette looming above him, with a net hanging from a boom thrust out over her side. Then hands were reaching down to haul him in, and other hands were lifting Higgins, and in a moment he was on board with warm blankets wrapped about him and hot cocoa pouring down his throat.

But all the time he was concerned for Higgins. In a way, he felt now that Higgins was more important than himself.

"Is the boy all right?" he kept asking. "Is the kid safe?"

When they told him that Higgins was dead he burst into tears. It surprised them. They had not expected such weakness in a man who looked so tough. They turned away, embarrassed by his tears. They turned away and left him to the bitterness of his grief.

CHAPTER FIFTEEN

Survivors' Leave

A WEEK had passed since the *Golden Ray* had blown her whistle for the last time, and Willis's gun-team was scattered. As a team it would never come together again. That was the way of things. For a few weeks, a few months, a year, perhaps, a little group of men slept and ate, toiled and played, grumbled and laughed, were happy and sad, within the narrow confines of a ship. They had less privacy, one from another, than a man has from his wife. They grew to love and to hate one another. Soon it was as though they had been together from the beginning of time; they were compact, a unit, an indivisible whole. It was unthinkable that they should ever again be split up, that they should ever forget.

But the bond of their unity was as nothing before the blind, unfeeling forces of war, which tore them apart and flung them hither and thither. And soon the memory of former comrades blurred. There were so many of them—a long line stretching back into the past; and some were dead; it was impossible to remember all of them. Each man found new comrades among those around him and forgot the past. It was more bearable that way.

A week had passed, and Vernon was saying, " Then will he strip his sleeve and show his scars—— " He held up his mangled thumb. " Though, really, it could hardly be called a battle wound. It was jammed under the lid of an ammo-box. Still, it's something."

Mr Tennyson smiled. It was typical of Vernon to make light of things in that way; but the experience must have been unpleasant. How cold it must have been—the ice and the snow and the winds. Mr Tennyson shivered at the thought, and put another log of wood on his study fire.

" Were any men lost when your ship sank? Those two— ahem!—shellbacks, as you call them—what happened to them? "

" Donker and Agnew? They were all right; it would take an earthquake to ruffle those lads. They stepped calmly on to a raft and waited for the corvette to pick them up."

" And the—er—Old Man? "

" Waited till the last and had to swim for it. He was all right, though—a tough old boy—in a blazing rage at losing his ship—so close to home, too. Some of the engine-room crew were trapped. They went down with the ship."

Mr Tennyson was silent for a while. Then he said, " Let us hope it will soon be over. It is difficult for me also—very difficult. I was lucky to obtain this house—a manor, you know—Elizabethan—capacious but archaic. Much needs doing to it; but in these times, how? How? Still, it is something to be able to keep the school going at all. Staff is the great problem. You have seen Forster? "

Vernon nodded.

"Fossilized—completely fossilized! But that's the sort we have to put up with now. It throws a great burden on me—too much. I am not as young as I was; I feel it."

Vernon lay back in the headmaster's armchair, smoking one of the headmaster's cigarettes, and thought that there was some truth in what he was saying. He looked much older than he had done only a few years ago. Well, he was no longer a young man. Sixty? Sixty-five? Possibly more. The school was probably a worry to him; there were so many added complications in wartime.

Mr Tennyson said, "I want to keep the school from disintegrating. I want to keep things going until peace comes. What I should wish then would be to take a partner—a younger man whom I could trust and respect—a man I should feel safe in handing the school on to when I am no longer able to continue. . . ."

Mr Tennyson got to his feet and walked to the window, turning his back on Vernon. With his curved shoulders and rather shiny black jacket, he looked from the rear like an immense beetle.

"Have you thought," he asked, "what you will do when you leave the Army?"

"No."

"It is not too early to begin thinking about such matters," said Mr Tennyson. "There will be a lot of jockeying for position when the War ends. It might be well to have something in view. . . ."

He opened the window suddenly and shouted, "Not on the grass, Temple! Not on the grass!"

Closing it again, he observed, "Boys are so unoriginal; generation after generation play the same pranks, break the same rules; and all feel that they are doing something that has never been thought of before."

He pulled the lobe of his left ear, stretching it downward, as though it were made of rubber.

"A school," he said, "is something worth working for. There is satisfaction in a school. Also—and this is a point not to be ignored—it pays tolerably well; yes, I think I may say tolerably well."

He turned and looked at Vernon from under his bushy white eyebrows.

"Think it over," he said. "Think it over. You have plenty of time."

Seated at the headmaster's table at lunch with the prefects on either side, Vernon felt almost as though he had never been away. It was a different room, of course, but, apart from that, everything was just as it had been before the War. There were six long tables flanked by boys of varying ages. At the head of one table sat the fossilized Mr Forster, at the head of another the matron; three other masters sat at the three other tables. There was a clink of knives and forks, a buzz of conversation, a surreptitious glancing at Vernon—the centre of interest. How unchanged it all was!

And how like, Vernon thought, was one generation of boys to another! The straight-haired, the curly-haired, the freckled, the snub-nosed, the spectacled, the podgy, the weedy—crop after crop they came, superficially indistinguishable. Sometimes you wondered whether these broken-voiced, pimply creatures would ever develop into normal human beings; then, suddenly, the pimples were gone; the voice had healed, and they were men. But always there was the influx of raw material at the bottom, growing, expanding, feeling its way upward, groping for knowledge and liberty.

"I suppose, sir, it's hard at first—the Army, I mean, sir—the training."

Vernon focused his attention on the boy who had spoken, trying mentally to remove three years from his age and recall his name. With an effort he succeeded.

"It's not a holiday, Meadows; but one gets through it. Which service do you intend to join when the time comes?"

Lord, he thought, the boy will be going soon, and he is little more than a child.

Meadows said, " Well, sir, I should prefer the R.A.F. After all, it is *the* Service to-day, isn't it, sir? "

Vernon smiled. " That, of course, is a matter of opinion. Some of us are old-fashioned enough to suppose that the Army and Navy still have their uses."

He looked along the table at the young, eager faces—the boys who were almost men and soon must go into the fighting. He supposed many of them were thrilled with the idea of fly-ing, of performing wonderful feats of single combat in Spit-fires. Well, let them have their dreams; they would find out soon enough that there was precious little joy in battle, whether on sea or land or in the air, precious little joy and plenty of terror and discomfort. If he were to tell them about Miller and Higgins and Willis and Panton-Smith, would they be so eager then? Yes, he supposed they would. You never imagined things like that would happen to you—to the other fellow, perhaps, but not to you.

" So you are intent on returning to London this afternoon," said Mr Tennyson. " You know you are welcome to stay here for the night if you wish."

" Thank you," said Vernon. " You are very kind, but I must get back."

Payne had picked the girl up in the street. She had blonde hair shading off into a darker colour near the roots. She had a pale, rather shapeless face with a bright red gash of a mouth. When she smoked Payne's cigarettes she left a red smear stain-ing the butt-ends.

Payne and the girl sat at a small marble-topped table in the corner of a crowded saloon bar. Payne was drinking mild and bitter from a pint mug; the girl drank port and lemon, lifting the glass daintily to her lips and sipping in a ladylike manner, over-emphasized.

Payne was saying: " You don't know what cold is till you bin up there. The wind cuts through you like a knife. You can't keep warm—not nohow. The spray comes over and freezes where it lights. Everything's icy—everything. And then there's subs and Jerry planes—a proper hell's kitchen, and no mistake."

The girl said, " Fancy! " and lit another cigarette from the stump of the old.

Payne went on talking. " We shot some planes down—two certain, two other possibles. We had a time getting through. Jerry sent everything at us. And then there was the storm. I've seen some storms, but never one like that. You'd have bin scared, I bet. But we got through, got nearly home, so near we could see the coast of Scotland. Then—*whoosh!*— a bloody mine gets us."

The girl said, " Well, I never! " She was wondering how much money Payne had—how much of it she could coax out of him. He looked big and soft; it ought not to be too difficult.

Payne was half-drunk, and his face was flushed. He leaned forward, resting his elbows on the table and breathing beer over the girl.

" Want another drink? "

She nodded, and he got to his feet, a little unsteadily, feeling his head swim slightly. He picked up the empty glasses and elbowed his way to the bar. When he returned the girl was repairing the ravages of time with more lipstick.

" Coo! You bin quick. I d'know 'ow you get through that crush."

" Trust me; trust old Ted."

She said archly, " I don't know as I should."

He let his hand fall on her knee.

" Now! " she said. " Naughty, naughty! " But she did not draw away.

" You got to make the most of leave," Payne said. " You don't get too much of it. So you got to make the most of it when it comes round."

" That's right enough. How long you bin 'ome? "

" Two days—not two yet—one and a bit, really."

The girl was thinking: If 'e's only 'ad two days as yet 'e won't 'ave spent 'is pay; there'll be a good bit left. Specially if 'e's bin at sea all that time like 'e said. There'd be back-pay to draw. That's if 'e wasn't just shooting a line.

"Yes," she said, "you got to make the most of your leave. Don't want to spend it on your Jack, do you? You want somebody to keep you company—to make things jolly."

Payne drank some more beer and felt suddenly ill.

He said, "I must go outside a minute."

The girl looked up at him. He looked properly sick, almost green.

"I think you'd better. But don't forget to come back."

He was only just in time. The beer and the fish and chips he had eaten earlier in the evening came surging up. He felt as though he were vomiting up the walls of his stomach, and the taste was bitter in his mouth. His head reeled, and the light hurt his eyes. He felt very ill indeed, and he wanted to lie down somewhere—anywhere. He wanted to go to bed and sleep. He leaned his forehead against the cold, damp bricks of the lavatory and groaned.

"You got to make the most of leave!"

Tommy Hewitt ran his hands over Padgett's muscles and shook his head.

"Too much flesh, Dick boy. You've put it on since you joined the Army. Too much flesh—far too much. It's fat, you know—no good to you—no good at all."

"I know," said Padgett. "I've got soft. I know."

He was stripped to the waist, looking like an advertisement for some physical-culture course as he tensed and slackened his muscles. He had wide shoulders and a strong, thick neck, a deep chest tapering down to a surprisingly slim waist. When he breathed in deeply his ribs lifted like an expanding cage, and his stomach receded. To the ordinary eye there did not appear to be much wrong with him.

But Tommy Hewitt's was no ordinary eye; it was the eye of an expert. Tommy was P.T. instructor at the young men's club to which Padgett had belonged before the War. Together they had built up Padgett's body. In a way, neither of them looked upon it simply as a human body; it was something made up of biceps and triceps, of flexors and tensors, a thing of bone and sinew and muscle, a thing of beauty, not so much by reason of its appearance, but because of its measurements, its proportions, its ability to lift weights, to extend springs, and to bend bars.

Tommy was like an artist who, himself withered and old, yet produces a work of beauty, youth, and vigour. For Tommy was grizzled, stringy, and toothless, a man from whom all the juice seemed to have dried out, so that the dirty white sweater and baggy flannel trousers hung as it were on the very husk of a man. The way his hands moved over Padgett's body, feeling this muscle, testing that, might have put an onlooker, had there been one, in mind of a sculptor. There was the same sensitive touch, the same delicate assessment, and the same dissatisfaction with something not perfect, something that might so easily have been better.

" They aren't getting enough exercise, Dick. You aren't working them enough."

" I know; I know," Padgett said. " But how can I on board ship? It's not so easy, I can tell you. I do my best; I do exercises; but I go soft."

" You have your springs, your chest-expanders? "

" I had them; they went down with the ship. But it's not that so much; it's the road work I miss—that and the punch-bag."

" What about skipping? "

" Have you tried skipping in a ship when she's rolling and pitching like nobody's business? "

" Well, there's only one thing; we shall have to see what we can do while you're on leave. How long have you got? "

" Fourteen days."

" Two weeks. We can get a lot of that flesh off in two weeks if we really go at it. You want to, don't you? "

" Why, of course, Tommy; of course."

" O.K., then. Here's the routine. . . . "

" Well, now," said Mrs Cowdrey, " and what is his lordship thinking of doing this evening? "

" His lordship," said Ben, " thought of going down to the local. Might meet a few of the boys. How about you? Will you come? "

" Of course I will. I wouldn't trust you else. Might get off with some flighty piece—an At or a Waaf. Wouldn't put it past you."

Ben Cowdrey's eyes twinkled. " How do you know I don't when I'm away? You can't keep your eye on me then."

" Oh, go away with you! Making out to be a Don Juan at your age! What girl would look twice at you, may I ask? "

" Oh, lots. I've got polish; that's what it takes—polish."

Mrs Cowdrey snorted. " Well, Mister Casanova, if you've got so much polish you can go and polish my shoes. Get a move on, or we shan't be down there before the place is full."

When the Cowdreys used to go to the ' local ' before the War it had been a quiet little pub with a handful of regular customers and only an occasional outsider. Now all that was changed; now it seemed to be bursting at the seams with customers; beer flowed like water, and, so said the older ones, was almost indistinguishable from it. And the price! Oh, dear, dear! It was sinful.

Ben was glad to see that Lucy was still serving behind the bar; the War had not taken her away yet. She was almost rushed off her feet, but she had time for a word with an old customer.

"Evening, Mr Cowdrey. 'Aven't sin you for quite a time. Bin fighting the War, I s'pose."

" A bit of it, Lucy—just a bit."

" Some 'as to; but some manages to stay at 'ome feathering their nests—mentioning no names. Beats me 'ow they do it, some of 'em. Well, what's it to be? "

"The usual, Lucy. Don't say you've forgotten."

" No bitter, I'm afraid, Mr Cowdrey; no more bitter till the end of the week. Will you 'ave mild? "

" As there's no choice, I shall have to. No bitter! Dear

me! Things are getting bad. I hope you've got a nice port for the missus. Never hear the last of it if I don't get that."

When Lucy brought the drinks Ben said, " Guess where I've been."

" You tell me."

" Russia."

" Russia," Lucy said. " Fancy that!"

Ben was disappointed with the reception of his revelation. If he had told her that he had spent his last holiday at Margate he felt that she would have used precisely the same tone of polite but very meagre surprise. " Margate. Fancy that!" " Russia. Fancy that!" Really, he thought, Russia ought to have been worth a little more astonishment, a shade more interest.

But Lucy was away serving another customer, and there was nothing for Ben to do but pocket his change and take the drinks.

" What a crowd!" said Mrs Cowdrey. " You can't hardly move."

" Like it everywhere now," Ben said. " It's the War."

He was looking for a familiar face—for some one he knew. He spotted old Bunty Caggs on the other side of the room, and pushed his way over to him. Bunty put an arm round Ben's shoulders and his face close to Ben's.

" Well, if it ain't old Bennie! Where'd you spring from? "

" I'm just back from Russia," Ben said.

" Russia, hey? " Bunty had had just a little too much to drink; it made him garrulous. He closed one eye and laid a finger along his nose.

" I hear the Russian women are pretty hot stuff. I bet you had a time up there. They play the ballyliker, don't they? I bet you had a time."

" A hell of a time," said Ben.

" Yes, I bet you did. You have the times, you soldiers. Us civvies has to take it back here. We don't grumble, though. But you have the times, you warriors." He laughed and dug Ben in the ribs with a dirty finger. " Warriors, hey!"

Ben said, " Our ship was blown up by a mine. We had to take to the boats."

" You did? " Bunty was silent for a moment, digesting this information. Then he said, " Did you hear what happened down our street last week? "

" No," said Ben, " no, I didn't."

" I says to the old woman, ' That's a Jerry plane,' I says. I can always tell Jerries by the engines, see. ' What's more,' I says, ' he's bang over the top of our house. You'd better get under the table,' I says. So that's what she done; and lucky, too, as it turned out."

" Look," said Ben, " you'll have to excuse me. I've got the missus. Excuse me."

" In some ways, old girl," Ben said, " I shall be glad to get to sea again—straight I shall."

Warby tilted his stool forward and rested his forehead on the cow's soft hide. His fingers worked automatically. He did not have to think about what he was doing. He had learnt this drill years ago when his legs were scarcely long enough to reach the ground from the milking-stool. His father had taught him to do this job, just as he had taught him to do the thousand and one other jobs that there are on a farm, just as he had taught Warby's elder brothers, Harry and Walter.

Warby's had always been a family farm. Before the boys grew up there had been old Grandfather Warby, doing a full day's work seven days of the week, and one hired labourer. Then, as the brothers became old enough to leave school and work on the farm, the hired man had gone. Then Grandfather Warby died, and Walter had married and gone off on his own.

So Warby, Harry, and their father had worked the farm until the outbreak of war. Then Warby had joined up. He supposed he might have avoided it if he had tried; but somehow he felt that one of the family at least ought to go and fight. It did not seem right to him that all of them should stay safely at home working in the fields—necessary though that work undoubtedly was. So he had gone, not because he wanted to, not because he had any false ideas of glory, but because, in his slow undemonstrative way, he had felt that it was his duty.

Now Harry and his father did the work that three of them had done before. There was not much rest for them; but they were strong—both of them; they never grumbled about hard work, only about the weather and forms and Government inspectors wasting their time. And when Warby had a bit of leave he lent a hand.

Warby listened to the *squirt, squirt, squirt* of milk spattering into the pail, a cock crowing in the distance, and the sudden squeal of a pig. He was half asleep, his eyes closing and opening as he gazed at the warm white froth on the milk. Then overhead he heard the drone of aircraft engines, and suddenly the milky froth was the wind-beaten foam of tumbling, icy waves, and he was back in the Arctic with the bitter lash of the gale and the *drum, drum, drum* of depth-charges. He had stopped milking; he was listening to the planes, his body rigid and tense.

Then the cow moved, swishing her tail impatiently, and Warby relaxed. In a moment the milk was again hissing into the pail.

Jacqueline Cooper had not received the letter which George Andrews, at so much pains, had written in the cabin of the *Golden Ray*. The letter had gone down with the ship. And because she was not his next-of-kin she had not heard what had happened to him. It was to be a long and weary time before the news leaked through to her, chilling her heart. Even then she would not hear the full details. George's father and mother would never hear them. Sometimes official messages are merciful in their brevity. Lost at sea—that was all any of them would ever know. It was enough.

It was well that Jacqueline could never know how futile, how unnecessary, that " lost at sea " had been; how easily it might have been avoided. For if George Andrews had not had such a burning desire to live he might not have died. It was his desire for life that had made him run to the lifeboat, his desire for life that had urged him to get into the boat while it was still hanging from the davits. Then the boat had shot stern first towards the sea, tipping out the men who were in it. And Andrews had found himself hanging head downward, caught by the foot, had found himself struggling, screaming, and weeping, while the boat swung from one twisted fall. And in a moment it was over.

It was Randall, watching calmly from the flooding deck, Randall, casting away his life-jacket, Randall, wanting to die; it was he who had lived. It was Andrews, leaping to the lifeboat, Andrews, with all the hot, ardent desire of youth for life, Andrews, with love waiting for him; it was he who died.

It was well that Jacqueline would never know the details.

There had been no need for Randall to go back to Yarmouth. It was a senseless thing to do. And yet he had felt that he must go, that he must see for himself.

Not that there was much to see when he got there: a few heaps of rubble, some charred timber, blackened and rain-sodden plaster, a strip or two of wallpaper still miraculously clinging—little else.

Mrs Hawkins's house had gone too. It had been a direct hit with a heavy bomb. You had to go four houses along the street to find a habitable dwelling.

Randall had heard about it as soon as he had landed; but it had happened weeks before that. Two bodies had been recovered from the debris; both had been unrecognizable. It had been assumed that they were the bodies of Mrs Randall and Mrs Hawkins.

Randall stood on the pavement and gazed at the rubble-heap, trying to figure out the bearings. It was all unfamiliar; none of it made sense; even the backyard did not look the same now that he could see right into it from the street. He wondered idly what had happened to the dust-bin and the tin bath that used to hang on the outhouse wall. He tried to work out exactly where the cupboard had been where he had hidden Lily's body; but there was nothing to work on, nothing but rubble and charred wood and plaster.

He started when the man's hand fell on his arm. The man was red-faced, cheerful-looking. He smelt of fish.

"Not much of it left, eh, soldier? Did you know the house? "

"I lived in it," Randall said.

The man shook his head sympathetically. "Too bad!" He appeared to hesitate, not quite knowing how to word the question. "Anybody—— "

Randall said, "My wife was killed in that house."

The man gripped his arm more tightly. "I'm sorry, mate. I am reelly." He looked at the bricks and the mortar and the sad remnants of wallpaper.

"Bloody swine!" he said. "Filthy rotten bastards!"

His face was even redder than it had been. Suddenly he said, "What you need, mate, is a drink. Come and have one on me."

Randall went with him. A drink was exactly what he did need—a strong one.

Sergeant Willis lay on his back enveloped by the darkness that had closed over him when the *Golden Ray* was blown up. There was a bandage over his eyes, and little flickering currents of pain still shot now and then up into his brain. But he was not unhappy; he knew that it might have been a great deal worse; he might have lost his sight for ever. As it was, he had been assured that he would be blind only in one eye. After a time, after the wound had healed, his left eye would be as good as new. That was something to be happy about.

Willis felt warm and comfortable; the mattress was soft beneath him, and the sheets smooth and clean; the bed did not leap and tilt, and he was able to lie, gently dozing, in the certain knowledge that he would not suddenly be lashed to action by the urgent ringing of an alarm-bell. For the first time in months he felt free from care and worry and responsibility. Nothing now depended on him; he had no orders to give, no equipment to maintain, no watches to set. All he had to do was to sleep and eat, to eat and sleep, while others waited on him, washed him, saw to his every want.

Lying there, he tried to calculate what effect the loss of an eye would have upon his life. Perhaps it was the end of sea-going for him. Perhaps when he was well again he would be given a staff job, even become one of the chairborne brigade he had always despised. 'They,' the omnipotent 'they,' who ordered such things, might make him an instructor, training recruits in the intricacies of gun-drill. The thought did not greatly please him; he was a man who had always preferred active service, liking the men in forward positions better than those at base. Yet, what had to be must be; he would have no cause to grumble. Better that than St. Dunstan's; better ten thousand times.

He felt the nurse smoothing out the sheets of his bed, raising his head and puffing up his pillow. Her hands were cool and capable. He tried to guess which nurse it was by the feel of her hands, trying to connect the hands to a voice; for it was as voices that he knew the nurses.

" Are you comfortable? Is there anything you want? "

He was boyishly pleased to find that he had guessed correctly. He had decided that he was in love with this nurse —in love with a voice.

" Yes," he said, " I want to see you."

" You will," she said, " when your eye is well. You've just got to be patient."

Her voice said she was young. Willis's imagination added that she was beautiful.

" When my eye is all right," he said, " I'm going to take you to the pictures, then supper afterwards."

" That will be nice."

" It's a date, then? "

" It's a date. Now you'd better go to sleep."

She moved away, and he followed her movement with his unseeing eyes. But the picture of her in his mind was slim, graceful, infinitely attractive. In that picture she was the girl he wanted her to be.

"It's a date," he whispered. "It's a date."

After a while he drifted off into sleep. When he awoke tea was being served. After tea he dozed again. It was the new pattern of his life.

Miller was dead—dead and buried. Fathoms deep he lay, where the waves no longer had any power to rock his stunted body, where no wind could flay and no bullet rend.

Soon the flesh would be off his bones; soon he would be nothing but a whitened skeleton. Mud would filter through the bars of his hollow chest, slimy growths stop up the sockets where once his eyes had been, and submarine creatures slither over his grinning jaws. And there he would lie amid the wasted iron and the wasted dead, the red hulks of ships and the white hulks of men, the metal and the bones.

Other convoys would pass over his head, fighting their way to Russia, and he would hear nothing of them. Bomb, torpedo, shell—they could hurt him no more. Communism, Fascism, Democracy—they were all one to him now. He had passed into oblivion or clearest light; now he knew all or nothing.

The ships would pass above him over the cold sea-miles, and blood would be the price of passage, as it had always been—a costly dye to sprinkle so uselessly upon the vast tapestry of waves, a dye lost immediately and for ever in the infinity of tumbled waters.

But Miller would sleep on in the long sleep from which there is no awakening. And his name would go down upon the roll of honour with those of better men and of worse. And the years would pass and the centuries, and the roll of honour would crumble into dust. Then Miller as an individual would vanish from the minds of men, to become just one of a great and nameless army, an army numberless as the stars, an army of Tartar and of Turk, of Goth and Mongol, Prussian and Spaniard, Saxon and Dane—an army without end.